AUGMENTED

THE TRANSCENDED BOOK 1

ANTHONY JAMES

THE GRAVEYARD

The sixth planet in the Hiol system was alight, its cold, rocky surface hidden beneath a conflagration of intense whites, oranges and reds.

High above this doomed world, the human and Estral fleets exchanged missile and particle beam fire. Incendiaries blossomed across a million kilometres of space, their detonations enough to destroy a number of the smaller ships outright and deplete the energy shields of the larger ones.

The Hadron battleship *Precept-2* launched wave upon wave of sublight missiles and its tactical computer kept track of a hundred thousand others already in flight. Gauss slugs from the Estral Vule cannons and the human Bulwarks streaked through space, thinning the salvos of inbound missiles.

The *Precept-2*'s battle computer recorded the impacts of its third wave of Lambda missiles against one of the Estral capital ships. The enemy craft was lost for a moment in a wave of thunderous explosions, and then it burst free from the inferno, its energy shield trailing plasma fire a thousand kilometres behind.

The battle continued for what seemed like an age, with each side unable to land the killing blow. In space combat, no stalemate could last forever. A group of Galactic class heavy cruisers broke away from the main human fleet and attempted to smash through a cluster of Estral vessels which acted as a soak for the enemy battleships.

For a moment, it looked as if the daring attack would be successful. Then, the *Precept-2* detected the deployment of an Obsidiar bomb. The battleship was too far away to be caught in the midst of the blast, but the heavy cruisers and the sixth planet were not. The Galactics vanished from the tactical screen and fifty percent of the planet disintegrated, leaving its molten core visible like a beacon.

Precept-2:: War protocol breached. Deploy Enlightenment.

The Hadron's sensors recorded the retaliatory deployment of a second Obsidiar bomb and this detonation was far larger than the first. Many Estral spaceships were completely obliterated, their energy shields incapable of withstanding the force of the explosion. The battle continued.

The soft bleeping of an alarm roused Lieutenant Becky Keller and she cut off her interface with the *Precept-2*, returning her consciousness to the cockpit of the shuttle which hovered high above the Graveyard on planet Eriol.

"You are not permitted to interface with these ships, Lieutenant," the shuttle's AI node, Exar chided her.

"You won't tell, will you?" she asked teasingly, not caring one way or another.

"If I had lips, they would be sealed, ma'am."

Keller lifted one arm and pointed a finger at the sensor screen. The feed was aimed directly at the left-most of the Hadrons. The battleship was a hulking wedge-shape, broad and menacing. Its six-thousand-metre hull was extensively cratered and burned, with hardly any of its armour plating intact.

"It's lost none of its pride. Exar, when was the *Precept-2* decommissioned?"

"The *Precept-2* was decommissioned 118 years ago, ma'am. It was one of the final Hadrons to leave service. Its duty lasted to the end of the third Estral war before it was classified as obsolete."

"Shame. It feels like a betrayal to abandon all of these ships. To leave them here like we never needed them."

There were hundreds of open receptors in the Graveyard and Keller reached out again to the *Precept-2*'s ancient processing cluster. The battleship's cores were painfully slow and incapable of preventing her gentle interrogation of its databanks. There was a yearning there, like an entity denied full access to the consciousness it was capable of. Keller pulled away, trying to convince herself she only imagined the spaceship's disappointment at her withdrawal.

Keller had seen enough. Darkness was creeping across the horizon and she suddenly wanted to be away from this place.

"Priority 1 message from Admiral Cody," said Exar.

"What is the message?"

"You will return to the base immediately. Please acknowledge."

"Of course I damn well acknowledge! What does he want?"

"I have no further information for you, ma'am."

"Can't he speak with me here?"

"I have no further information for you, ma'am."

Keller used her Faor augmentation to link with the transport's flight computer and ordered it to fly to the Fortress-3 base at top speed. The journey didn't take long, but Keller had ample time to interrogate the Space Corps databanks, where she discovered something entirely unexpected.

"Well, well," she said under her breath. "There's a name I haven't heard in a long time."

With a feeling of nervousness and anticipation, Lieutenant Becky Keller brought the shuttle in to land.

CHAPTER ONE

ADMIRAL SCOTT CODY was a broad man of advancing years and with the same short-cropped grey hair worn by seemingly every male admiral in the Space Corps, as well as some of the females. Cody paced the length of his office, making no effort to disguise his agitation. He stopped exactly two paces before one blue-painted wall, spun, walked and repeated the process at the opposite wall. Every so often, he cursed under his breath.

Admiral Cody was not renowned for his patience and today he looked properly pissed off.

Lieutenant <CovOps> Joe Nation shifted, unable to get comfortable in a chair which probably cost ten thousand fedbucks. The room smelled of coffee and leather, and he could hear a high-pitched background squeal of electronics.

Nation flexed his right arm and felt the faintest sensation of movement from the Istoliar motors which powered his body. There were some parts of him which were almost original, but he was damned if he could remember where in his body they were. He'd given up his flesh and here he was – a pile of augmentations clad in artificial skin, with his consciousness fed into a data array designed to withstand a direct hit from an Estral sledgehammer. He suppressed a shiver. Istoliar leaked cold and he could never seem to get warm since the surgeons finished with him.

Another five uneasy minutes passed before Nation heard the office door hiss open. He turned in his seat to see a very familiar woman enter – she was in her late twenties, with a slim, athletic build, dark hair tied up and the most piercing green eyes. She wore a tight-fitting black cloth uniform without adornment.

"Lieutenant Becky Keller," said Cody with a nod. His voice was deep, like he'd taken lessons in how to project it. "Take a seat."

Keller sat.

"This is Lieutenant Joe Nation," Cody went on. "He's another one from the labs. Covert Ops."

Nation nodded acknowledgement. "We've met before, sir."

"Once or twice," said Keller dryly.

"Well that's good," said Cody. "It means we don't have to waste time on how-do-you-dos." He began another trip towards the wall, thought better of it and sat opposite the two of them. His desk was clear apart from a communicator and a couple of screens. Without moving his eyes, Cody leaned forward and switched the communicator to silent. "Folks, there's some shit going on," he said.

Nation knew when it was time to stay quiet and Keller had the same instinct. They waited.

"We've got ourselves a problem over on Isob-2."

Nation scratched his head and took the bait. "That's an Estral facility, sir."

"Quite right, Lieutenant. It's one of their six Obsidiar-Teronium refinement bases. You know the ones – where they perform *civilian* research." He drummed his thick fingers on the desktop. "There's been an incident."

"What kind of incident?" asked Keller.

"It's one of those *everyone's dead* kind of incidents. Under the terms of our treaty, we sent a team out two days ago. Their attempts to find out what happened aren't going to plan."

Humans and Estral had been involved in on-off wars for decades and it was only recently the Confederation had gained enough of an upper hand to begin dictating conditions at the end of what was a long, drawn-out conflict. One of those conditions imposed strict controls on the Estral's ability to refine Obsidiar-Teronium into its much more potent form Istoliar, and, more specifically, to put it to military uses.

"Two days is plenty of time for a preliminary evaluation. What's the hold up?" asked Keller.

"The Estral don't want us there." Cody's face twisted angrily. "They're clearing up the evidence even while our team tries to find out what's going on."

"They signed an agreement to limit their refinement to just stabilised Obsidiar-Teronium. Why don't we clear the facility of Estral and get on with the job?" said Nation.

"Isob-2 is deep inside Estral territory, Lieutenant. It's all very well talking about *imposing* our wishes, it's another thing entirely when it comes to doing so. I think if we'd given our friends another few hours to get their act together, they'd have turned away our investigation team."

"And risk another war?"

"You know what they're like. Proud bastards. Like every other race is a piece of crap stuck to the sole of their shoes. The Confederation Council have made their wishes clear – this isn't worth a resumption of hostilities."

"The Estral take everything to the edge, sir. Every time we blink first, they become bolder."

Cody sighed. "You're not telling me anything new, Lieu-tenant Nation. If it were my choice, I'd turn up at Isob-2 with fifty warships and see what these alien bastards have to say about it. We can't piss around when it comes to Istoliar – it's the only thing keeping us ahead."

"Which is why they crave it so much," said Keller.

"We can't trust them with it. We know what the results will be."

The Estral were ruthless when they had an advantage. There was no way the Confederation was going to slacken the rules on the refinement of Obsidiar-Teronium. Humanity had teetered on the brink of extinction on more than one occasion and now the determination to survive was ingrained. Whatever it took.

"What information do we have about Isob-2, sir?" asked Nation. "Surely our team found something?"

"The Estral are playing their cards close to their chests. Our monitoring hardware picked up traces of certain contaminants within the facility. Granol-42, for instance."

"You said no survivors?"

"I said that to get your attention. We have no real evidence to say every Estral was killed - we're relying on a degree of assumption." Cody's expression told exactly what he thought about *assumption.*

"What killed them?"

"The Estral won't say or they don't know. We don't know either."

"Have we been given access to the bodies?"

"That's one of the main sticking points at the moment. They've locked the base down and the lower levels are off limits, ostensibly to allow the level of contaminants to subside."

"Smells fishy."

"You don't say?"

There was an elephant in the room and Nation felt obliged to mention it. "They're up to something at Isob-2 which breaks the treaty."

"More than likely."

"And they're shit scared we'll find the proof."

"I see all that training hasn't gone to waste, Lieutenant Nation."

Nation used his comm augmentation to tap into the Space Corps records and dozens of files streamed into his databanks. It took him a few nanoseconds to pick out the salient details. "We've been covertly monitoring Isob-2 for months."

"They've brought in several disguised shipments recently – in shielded containers, or mixed up with other materials which can produce false positives on our sensors."

"What's the best guess from the strategy guys?"

"Obsidiar-Teronium refinement gone wrong."

Nation watched Keller from the corner of his eye. "If it's so cut-and-dried, what do you need us for?" he asked.

"Proof. We can't act without it."

"And if we find proof?" asked Keller. "Is this the beginning of a new war?"

Cody didn't look entirely pleased with the question. "Quite the opposite. We see it as a method of stopping a war."

"What happens next?"

"You're going to join our existing team, except you aren't going to be playing it by the book. You're two of the Space Corps' most accomplished officers and you know how to get results."

"I take it we'll be catching a spaceship to Isob-2 and having a poke around the facility?"

"That's about it. The evidence we have suggests this is the tip of an iceberg that could be big enough to cause some real crap in our immediate future if we run into it."

"Or if it runs into us."

"A turn of phrase, Lieutenant Keller," said Cody testily.

"Does this mean we have clearance to take risks?"

"You know the answer to that."

Nation almost laughed. "Find out everything there is to be found out and don't get caught. One day I might get a mission with a different brief."

"Who else is on our team?" asked Keller.

"We've got some men and women already out there. Rapid Response Team Alpha from the SC *Givens*."

"So, when we pitch up uninvited, what exactly are we going to tell the Estral?"

"The story is, you're part of RRT Alpha. That makes you military scientists."

"I'm no scientist," said Nation. "And Lieutenant Keller is in Psi. What are we supposed to do when they start asking technical questions?"

"Use those core clusters the Space Corps implanted in your heads at vast expense. That's what they're there for. Try and sound convincing."

Nation shrugged. As far as briefings went, this was neither the longest nor the shortest he'd ever sat through. "I can do that."

"I saw the SC *Gundar* on the landing strip," said Keller.

Cody gave a half-smile. "We couldn't send you in a beat-up piece of crap. The Space Corps likes to look good when we're trying to strongarm a mob of warlike aliens into letting us into one of their prize facilities."

"A Class 1 Retaliator. I'm impressed," said Nation.

"One of thirty in the fleet. Four hundred metres from nose to tail." Admiral Cody was far too young to have flown one of the older-style warships, some of which exceeded five thousand metres in length, but the curl of his lip suggested he longed for the days he'd never experienced. "And we've had to remove some of its external armaments in case the Estral take offense." Cody's lip curled even further. "Damned tip-toeing around like we're the bad guys."

Nation kept his expression neutral. "Have we got clearance to fly or are we putting in a surprise appearance?"

"The Estral are expecting to see you on the far side of the Primol-1 wormhole within four hours. The urgency saves you from spending the next two weeks with one of my briefing teams. The Estral aren't happy about it, so don't expect handshakes and party hats." Cody stared for a long moment and then clapped his hands with a single, loud crack. "Why are you still in my office? Get moving and bring me back some good news!"

Keller and Nation exchanged glances. Whatever the outcome of this mission, it was unlikely to be anything which could be classified as good.

"Yes, sir. Good news it is." Nation stood easily and his chair creaked in relief.

Keller remained seated. "One more thing. Who is in charge?"

"You're a team, Lieutenant Keller. I trust there'll be no issues?"

"No, sir, I was referring to the guys on RRT Alpha. Do they know who we are?"

"We've sent them an encrypted comms message, telling them to give you whatever help you require." Cody smiled grimly. "And to pretend they know who you are."

"That's reassuring."

"And remember – both of you - the Estral don't need to know about your augmentations, so don't do anything that gives the game away."

It was the same message Nation had heard before. "I don't need reminding. It's all I seem to hear since they finished stitching me together."

Keller stood. "This is damned important, isn't it?"

"More important than you know. Things are strained - don't screw this one up."

The two of them left the room and Cody watched the automatic door shut behind them. With a stab of his finger, he took his desktop communicator out of silent mode and impassively waited for the inevitable rush.

CHAPTER TWO

THE FORTRESS-3 BASE was a place of sweeping architectural achievement. It covered an area of twenty-five square kilometres, and, while many of its structures were blocky and utilitarian. In places it possessed sweeping curves and unusual shapes designed to astound the eye. Most of the buildings were constructed from stone-clad alloy and painted white or green or blue. Wide, tree-lined streets played host to smart gravity cars, which danced gracefully through the traffic, whilst hundreds of shuttles sped through the air.

A row of well-polished pool cars gleamed in front of the command and control building. The closest one was all straight lines, with clear windows and metallic white paint. It hovered a few inches from the ground, waiting obediently. Keller pulled the door open and sat on the faux leather front passenger bench, while Nation climbed in the other side.

"The landing strip," Keller ordered. "*SC Gundar.*"

"Certainly, ma'am," replied the car. The onboard computer possessed an irritatingly cheerful voice which became grating after about thirty seconds of its inane patter.

The vehicle pulled out into the slow-moving traffic and the two passengers watched the bustle of the Fortress-3 base without much interest.

"It's been a long time," said Nation eventually.

"Yup."

"What did you think of that speech Cody gave us?"

"The same as you. He was worried, and if he's worried that means every other admiral is feeling it too."

"That's what I reckon. It was like someone had crapped in his favourite boots."

The gravity car hummed along one of the main thoroughfares, its navigational computer guiding it easily through the variety of other vehicles. Even during peacetime, the base was busy. Cars, lorries and light crawlers crowded the wide roads, along with a trio of light tanks heading towards one of the shuttle pads.

"This must be your first assignment in a while," said Nation.

Keller peered at him suspiciously, trying to decide if he was fishing for a reaction. "They tell me I'm too valuable to risk."

"Not this time, though."

"Evidently someone believes they had no choice."

"They don't want the Estral to clear up the site before we get there."

"That's my take on it."

"Our allies need to learn when to accept the hand of friendship."

"Maybe they don't have it in them. We have a peace treaty – there's nothing in it which says humans and Estral need to be drinking buddies."

Nation gave a snort of laughter. "I guess peace is always better than war."

"You don't sound like you believe it."

"Course I do. Are you getting any feel for what's happening?"

"Not yet. Perhaps I'll get a sense of the probabilities when we get there. It usually works better when I'm in proximity."

"The infinite model, huh?"

"It's still a thing."

Keller tilted her head back and closed her eyes. Few people understood how the members of the Psi team did what they did, but Lieutenant Nation knew better than most.

At the extremes of humanity's normal distribution curve, existed individuals with the ability to predict the outcome of any event with a far greater degree of accuracy than chance alone dictated. For these people, the universe existed as a probability model in which every possible event might happen. Occasionally, such a person was offered a glimpse of the model and therefore a hint of the future.

Lieutenant Becky Keller had all of that and much more.

Nation studied her carefully. "They invested a lot in you when they decided to fit you with a Faor augmentation."

She shrugged and tapped the side of her head with a finger. "The Faor implant constructs a simulation based on what I tell it. Sometimes it comes up with the goods, other times, nothing."

"And it makes you into one hell of a pilot. In an age where we bow down to the prowess of the battle computers, there's hardly anyone left who can outperform an AI."

"So they tell me. A great pilot. Not such a good killer, though."

She spoke with her eyes still closed and the hint of a smile played at one corner of her mouth.

"It doesn't sound like there'll be anything to kill on this mission."

"Since we'll be amongst *friends*." She opened her eyes. Nation was gone.

"You know I'm a covert op and not an assassin." His voice came from nowhere, but when Keller stuck out a hand it connected with a solid object which she guessed was his arm.

"Turn off your stealth modules when you're talking to me."

The air blurred for a split second and then Nation was visible once more. "It's going to be hard getting lost in the crowd when there're only two of us."

"Two or a hundred, the Estral won't watch us any less carefully."

"It's like we're talking about the enemy."

"They may as well be."

He looked at Keller sharply, wondering if she'd divined some probability of the future and wasn't letting on. There was no change in her face – at least, nothing he could read.

The gravity car continued its journey, through the main warehouse district of the base. It was a muggy, grey day on Eriol and the vehicle's air conditioning struggled to keep things cool. Nation turned one of the control knobs and it came off in his hand. He dropped it into the footwell in disgust.

"I thought you couldn't feel the heat?" said Keller.

"I can't. Not really." He pinched a flap of skin on the back of his hand. "I get signals telling me if it's hot or cold."

"What happens when it gets to three hundred degrees outside?"

"Unimportant stimuli get shut down, so they're no longer a distraction."

"You can shut them down at any time."

"I don't want to. There's not much left of Joe Nation, so I'll hold on tightly to what I can."

"Whatever they did to fix you up, you're still Joe Nation. You definitely look like Joe Nation." She prodded him in the arm. "Feels like skin as well."

"I'm not complaining. It's better to be like this than dead. Way better."

"I think I prefer the old Joe Nation." Keller was gently teasing, something she was good at.

"So what have you been up to?"

"This and that. Hush-hush."

"Let's find out."

Nation linked in with the Corps network and checked through Keller's files to see what she'd been up to in the last few years. There weren't many personnel in the Psi team – so few people in the Confederation possessed the gift, those the Space Corps managed to bring within the military fold were handled with exceptional care. The Psi team members were in the military, yet without being subject to the same discipline and it allowed them to retain far more of their individuality than many other Corps personnel. It wasn't much different for those in Covert Ops and rank wasn't always an accurate reflection of seniority.

Without warning, Nation found himself ejected from the records. His Istoliar processing cluster dragged a copy of the files into his databanks where, to his astonishment, they were force-deleted.

"Has anyone ever told you it's rude to pry?" asked Keller.

"Don't you ever do that again!" he said furiously. "Do you hear me?"

"I apologise, I was trying to make a point. Badly. I'm sorry. You can stop clenching your fists now."

"Don't do that again," he repeated. After a few deep breaths, he felt calm again. Keller was one of those people it was hard to stay mad at. "How did you do that?"

"The Faor is like nothing you ever guessed."

"Can I block you?"

She didn't answer directly. "That was the last time. I promise." Keller sat upright and peered through the glass windscreen. "We're coming onto the landing strip. The *Gundar* is the third ship parked up."

"There it is," said Nation. "It's a beauty."

"A weapon capable of incredible destruction."

The SC *Gundar* was V-shaped, covered in silver-grey alloy plates, and it rested on several dozen thick landing legs. The front of the ship narrowed to a squared-off point, while the main body of the craft was a tapered cylinder which housed the Istoliar power source. Two thick wings protruded a hundred metres from each side – they weren't to provide lift, instead, they housed the stasis emitters which could shut down enemy craft. The top-rear section contained the housing for the particle beam repeater weapon, this being the spaceship's main armament.

Compared to an old Hadron battleship from years gone by, the *Gundar* could generate a thousand times the power from a fraction of the volume.

"Deadly like a scalpel," said Keller.

From her eyes, Nation could tell Keller was lost in the memory of something and he didn't ask. The gravity car veered into a gap between a pile of metal crates and a maintenance crane, before coming alongside the first of the other craft parked up. This spaceship was a Class 3 Destroyer – similar in appearance to the *Gundar*, except with an old-style stabilised Obsidiar-Teronium drive and a hundred metres greater in length. The craft was so new its name was still visible on the side. SC *Hoplite*.

The gravity car went by a second Destroyer, this time with its name eroded by flight through grit and other atmospheric particles. The vehicle came to a halt.

"The *Gundar*," said Keller. She pushed open the door and climbed out. Nation got out of the opposite door and walked around to join her. He was a head taller and guessed his augmentations made him 250 pounds heavier. They were on the same team, but their methods of achieving mission goals were radically different.

"One of the fastest and deadliest ships in the fleet," said Nation.

"It makes a good statement of intent. The Estral won't dare tell us to piss off, unless they have plenty of backup."

The spaceship's front boarding ramp was lowered and a group of soldiers were standing guard at the bottom, accompanied by an evil-looking mobile repeater turret, with deflective front shields and a dense, angular main body. The device's nine-barrel gun rotated slowly. Keller did her best to ignore it and she approached the group.

A man in a plain, dark blue uniform approached with his rifle slung across his back and his sidearm within easy reach. He held a tablet in one hand and studied it as he walked.

"Lieutenants Keller and Nation." He snapped a salute. "I'm Corporal Hancock."

"The officer in charge."

"That's right. The *Gundar* is happy to have you onboard. It's a sweetheart."

"I'm sure it is, Corporal."

Hancock stepped aside and made an exaggerated flourish with one hand to indicate they could board whenever they wanted.

"Going somewhere special?"

"Very special," agreed Nation.

Hancock tried to hide his disappointment at being so easily rebuffed.

"Well then, have a nice trip."

"Thank you."

The soldiers – a full squad of twenty – watched Keller and Nation go by. In truth, stealing a Corps warship wasn't straightforward – it simply wouldn't take off if you didn't have clearance.

If anyone was somehow clever or stupid enough to sneak onboard, they would discover an impressive array of automated miniguns concealed throughout the interior.

The main airlock at the top of the boarding ramp was a plain walled space, cramped and bathed in red. The exit passage cut through ten metres of solid alloy and was protected by a pair of doors which vanished into ceiling recesses. Keller paused.

"Hello?"

"Hello, Lieutenant Keller," came the reply. There was perhaps more female than male to the tones.

"What's your name?"

"I am Teal. Welcome aboard."

Keller led the way from the airlock. The *Gundar* was mostly engines, with a little extra taken up by weapons and life support. Far down the priority list came the human occupants, and the warship's internal corridors were narrow, freezing cold and claustrophobic. Ships like the *Gundar* weren't designed to carry passengers – the fleet had other vessel types dedicated to the task of moving large numbers of armed personnel. A Retaliator was purely meant for offensive duties. In times of war, it could be equipped with a wide variety of weapons, some of which had the destructive power to annihilate a star.

The cockpit was a tiny, rectangular room, lit in a blue-white colour and with three front-facing seats. The front bulkhead was dominated by a huge display, designed to look like a car windscreen. At the moment, it showed the area of the Fortress-3 base which was visible to the warship's front sensor array. Nation peered through.

Keller sat in the middle seat, which was infinitely adjustable, covered in supple brown leather and surrounded by smaller screens and instrument panels. There was a complicated harness, which she ignored. In these days of sophisticated life support systems, if you needed to rely on something so basic as a harness for anything, it was likely you were already dead.

There was a second door in the rear bulkhead wall and Nation checked it out. It led onto a tiny corridor, with a row of low, narrow doors. He yanked one of them open. Inside was a stark white room about four feet wide, eight long and furnished with a single bed, a viewscreen and a tiny bedside table.

"No surprises here," he shouted. "Same as pretty much every other warship - six sleep pods, one replicator and a place to take a crap."

"Great. We should get moving."

Nation ducked back through the doorway and got into the left-hand seat. "I'll let you handle the AI. Flying isn't my thing."

Keller cleared her throat. It was a couple of years since she'd been onboard a Retaliator. "Teal, are we cleared to take off?"

"I thought you would never ask. We have priority clearance to depart," said the ship's AI. "I have the details of your destination and my databanks are up-to-date with your mission priorities."

"Is there anything new?" asked Nation.

"There is a 972-page mission briefing file if you would care to take a look, Lieutenant? I can download it directly into your databanks if you wish."

"I wouldn't bother," said Keller. "I just read it."

Nation was at that moment digesting the last few pages of the same document. It was crammed with cobbled-together pieces of speculation, guesswork and three hundred probability tables. The roundup pages may as well have been blank for all the insight they contained. "Full of crap," he muttered. "No one has a damn clue."

"I have just received a query from a source with Admiral Cody's signature," said Teal. "He wonders why I am still, and I quote, *sitting on the goddamn landing strip.*"

"Close up the ramp and send a message to Corporal Hancock telling him its time to be on his way," said Keller. "At the double."

"I completed both of those tasks before you arrived on the bridge, Lieutenant."

"An AI that takes pride in its work. Let's get on with this," said Nation.

"Initiating take-off routine," said Teal. "Hold onto your hats."

The *Gundar*'s Istoliar drive came online with a grumbling roar from its detonators. The hull shook for a moment, before the main engine settled into a smooth, background whine. The ship's AI scanned the surrounding area, checked in for a final time with the Fortress-3 Exar mainframe and decided there was no risk of harming any nearby ground crew.

The whining of the engine climbed steadily and the SC *Gundar* took off. It rose vertically from its berth into the grey skies of Eriol. Through the front viewscreen, the two crewmembers watched the distant horizon. Far away, on a huge, levelled area of ground to the north of Fortress-3, ancient spaceships were lined up in neat rows. Their scarred armour plates were unreflective, as though these proud, indomitable craft defied even the light of the sun.

"There's the Graveyard," said Keller. "Three hundred and twenty decommissioned warships from a hundred years ago. It gives me the shivers every time I go there. So many records and so much death."

"I try not to think about it too hard."

The *Gundar*'s ascent was rapid and it soon entered the clouds. Mist clouded the viewscreen, hiding the Graveyard from sight.

"Clear the screen," ordered Keller. "I don't want any of this crap obscuring the view."

Instantly, the image sharpened and the warship's sensors pierced directly through the cloud cover, filtering them out as if they didn't exist. The Graveyard was already lost below and now they could see the cusp of Eriol as a line dividing the drab greens and blues from the pure blackness of space.

"The beauty of the infinite," said Teal wistfully.

"You're not one of those fruitcake AIs are you?" asked Keller.

"The word is *unique*, Lieutenant Keller."

"I prefer *nuts*."

The AI wasn't programmed to take offense and it didn't respond. The SC *Gundar* climbed much faster now that it was outside the planet's atmosphere. The Istoliar drive's whine was in perfect harmony with the rest of the ship.

"Six thousand klicks per second," said Keller. "And only using 0.0003% of our available power."

"Target set: Primol-1. Arrival time: eighteen minutes," said Teal. "Activating lightspeed drive."

The SC *Gundar* rumbled again and its engines took on a howling note, which gave hints at how much it had in reserve. The warship opened a passage into high lightspeed and raced towards its destination.

CHAPTER THREE

THE *SC GUNDAR* exited lightspeed and the hum from its Istoliar drive dropped away into the background.

"Primol-1," announced Teal.

Under the terms of the Human-Estral peace accord, no spaceship from either side was permitted to simply enter the territory of the other. All traffic was required to traverse one of the small number of wormholes which linked the two parts of the universe. The Estral didn't encourage trade and therefore not many transits took place.

Nation glanced at one of the screens next to his chair. "Two hundred thousand klicks out. Bang on the nose."

"I aim to please, Lieutenant," said Teal. "The McKinney station acknowledges our presence and the warships *Eagle*, *Linster*, *Canyon* and *Pincer* say hello."

"Return the greeting," said Keller. "Ask them if the weather has been good."

The four Class 2 Invokes kept their stealth modules active, though it didn't stop the *Gundar*'s tactical screen identifying them and displaying their position. A warship on the Space

Corps network was normally visible to any other on the same network.

"Only four. I guess there are more running silent?" asked Nation out of curiosity.

Keller gave him a nod. "Undoubtedly."

The main screen showed an image of the McKinney station. It was a vast, hulking construction of dark alloys, six thousand metres in length and two thousand in height and depth. The station was equipped with dozens of beam repeaters and an energy shield with enough power to repel an attack from a hundred or more enemy spaceships. It was also rumoured to be equipped with an Istoliar bomb, which, if detonated, would destroy everything within eighty billion kilometres, including the wormhole.

Keller wasn't meant to know, since the files were highly classified, but the rumours were true.

"Show me Primol-1," she said.

Instantly, the main screen switched to high zoom, focused straight on the wormhole. The portal itself wasn't much to look at, being nothing more than a circle of darkness a few hundred kilometres across. Without the ship's sensors to adjust the colours, Primol-1 would have been undistinguishable from the background.

The wormhole wasn't a natural phenomenon. Arranged about it was a series of immense, dark-grey spheres, each with a diameter of two thousand metres. These spheres crackled and spat blue shards of energy into the vacuum. Power flowed from them in a torrent and, in tandem, they kept the wormhole from collapsing into nothingness. Given how few spaceships travelled through, it was a tremendous waste of resources, especially since a warship such as the SC *Gundar* could use its lightspeed catapult to create its own temporary wormhole in order to cross vast distances in a short space of time.

"Anything to report before I give the order?" asked Keller.

"I am checking with McKinney station," said Teal. "Apparently we're the first spaceship to go through since the SC *Givens* carrying the Response Team. Before that, you have to go back five weeks."

"Five weeks?" Nation had enough clout to learn a few things when he wanted to and he knew this was far longer than usual. "Why so long?"

Keller didn't need to interrogate the Space Corps network to guess. "Simmering tensions."

"Another degeneration towards war," spat Nation. "This visit is going to be fun."

"Handshakes and party hats," said Keller, repeating Admiral Cody's words from earlier.

"This was bad enough without additional complications."

Nation wasn't happy and he tightened his fists, feeling the strength in his alloy fingers as they dug into his toughened flesh.

Keller smiled. "I thought Covert Ops lived for this."

"I prefer to arrive unexpected."

The *Gundar* had clearance for the transit and there was no reason for delay.

"The sooner we get there, the sooner we find out." Keller itched to interface with the ship and throw it into the wormhole. It wasn't part of the mission and she left it to Teal. "Let's do this."

"I have informed the McKinney station about our imminent departure. Energy shield online, Istoliar drive warming up for a sublight run," said the AI.

The *Gundar* accelerated towards the wormhole and passed within a few hundred kilometres of the closest nullification sphere. Keller manually adjusted the sensor feed so they could see it clearly. The spheres were an excellent example of stolen alien tech put to more benign use by the human Confederation. They housed such colossal reserves, they were able to counter the crushing gravity of the wormhole. In theory, a soldier in a space-suit could drift happily through without ill-effects.

Keller switched to the main front sensor array. Primol-1 came closer, until it filled the screen. The main indicator of its presence was the way it blocked out the stars from the background. The *Gundar*'s acceleration stopped, leaving the warship travelling at a shade over twenty thousand kilometres per second.

"Here we go."

Without fuss, the SC *Gundar* went through the wormhole. In a time too short for its sophisticated monitoring tools to register, it travelled a distance which would take a ship without a lightspeed catapult five or more years to complete. There was no sensation of movement and no suggestion that anything monumental had occurred.

"We have arrived," announced Teal. "Shields remain active. The local star chart is populating."

On a screen to her right, Keller saw the warship's core clusters updating the tactical and navigational systems with details from the sensors. "Where's our welcoming party?"

There were spaceships, but they didn't look especially welcoming.

"I am reading signs of twenty-three Estral ships in the vicinity, nine of which are running stealth modules," said Teal. "There are eight target locks on our hull. As per Space Corps protocol, I am diverting power to our beam repeater and stasis emitters in preparation for retaliation."

"There'll be no shooting," snapped Keller. "Contact the Estral and instruct them to de-target. Message our base and let them know what we've found."

A comms message to base would take an hour to travel from out here, but it made sense to send a record of events.

"Message sent. I am awaiting a response from the Estral."

Once more, Keller fought the urge to take control of the

Gundar. The warship's battle computer wouldn't do anything stupid, she knew that.

"A couple of new types amongst them," said Nation.

The local Estral fleet was made from a mixture of large, older-style vessels, some of them between two and three thousand metres long. These older craft were elaborately designed, with struts and beams protruding from their elongated hulls. They looked delicate and, in fact, they were somewhat less robust than an equivalent Space Corps model.

The newer spaceships were far smaller and vaguely similar in design to the *Gundar*, though they were flatter and looked less cutting-edge. The Estral had only recently figured out how to refine Obsidiar-Teronium into pure Istoliar, but they weren't meant to be using it on their spaceships. The existing peace treaty only permitted them to create limited quantities of Istoliar and then only for civilian uses.

"Plenty of beam weapons and plasma incendiaries," said Keller, reading through the raw sensor data. "Missiles and lots of high explosives on the older ones."

"Shield busters?" asked Nation.

"Of course."

The SC *Gundar* was equipped with a phase-changing shield. Any weapons which relied on phase-shifting to bypass an energy shield – such as an overcharge particle beam or a shield buster missile – would simply fail to penetrate. The Estral were known to be working hard on the same line of tech, though the Space Corps intel was limited on how much progress the aliens had made.

A tense few moments went by and the Estral maintained their weapons lock. The SC *Gundar* was an exceptionally capable ship, but it was highly doubtful if it could withstand a sustained barrage from all twenty-three. Not that an exchange of fire was an option.

One-by-one, the Estral ships disengaged their locks. Nation blew out a pent-up breath.

"I thought you'd be used to the uncertainty," said Keller.

"The unknown is *your* field, not mine. I prefer control."

Teal cut across the exchange. "Comms request from Tarjos Gial-Eld on the Estral vessel *Axiniar*. He will not speak to an AI."

"Bring him in," said Keller. "I'll handle this."

The Estral spoke a harsh tongue, which grated and scraped. The Space Corps' language modules automatically interpreted the words and added a humanness to them. The alien's voice retained a level of roughness, which even 150 years of development on the language modules couldn't smooth away. Keller wondered if the language guys had simply stopped trying and left the tech as it was in order to add a layer of authenticity, to remind people that they were speaking to an alien species, with every pitfall and potential for misunderstanding that entailed.

"You are late," said Tarjos Gial-Eld.

Keller rolled her eyes at the pettiness of it. "Good day, Tarjos. We are part of Rapid Response Team Alpha, and, under the terms of the Human-Estral peace accord, we are here to investigate the issue on Isob-2."

"Why were you not onboard the *SC Givens* like the others?"

"We were on shore leave. Shore leave which has been rescinded."

Keller wasn't expecting her lie to produce any sympathy, and she wasn't disappointed.

"There is no issue, human. We do not need assistance."

"Nevertheless, we will join with the others of our team."

"There is nothing to be found on Isob-2. You are wasting your time and our time."

Keller raised an eyebrow. The Estral were known to be poor liars and terrible when it came to subterfuge. If they couldn't answer a question directly without compromising themselves, they would either answer a similar question or simply not answer at all. The Space Corps put its officers through a simulator to teach them how to handle the Estral. Therefore, Keller wasn't surprised by Gial-Eld's evasiveness.

She muted the comms. "The usual crap."

"I agree," said Nation. "Let's get to our destination and see what's up. This Tarjos might not even know."

With a poke of her forefinger, Keller opened the channel again. "Will you take us to Isob-2 or are we free to make the journey ourselves?"

"You will have an escort. I will transmit synchronisation codes."

"We await your codes. Over." She closed the channel. "Teal, when the codes come through, please confirm the target is Isob-2, rather than anywhere unexpected like the middle of a star."

A few seconds later, they received the *Axiniar*'s transmission.

"Synchronisation codes accepted and the target is confirmed as Isob-2," said Teal. "They are bringing eight of their warships along for the ride."

"Admiral Cody wasn't wrong when he called them untrusting bastards," laughed Nation. "You'd think they were doing us a favour."

"I thought we'd find our problems once we arrived at the Isob-2 facility," said Keller. "It seems like the Estral fleet is going to be a thorn in our sides as well."

"Preparing Istoliar drive," said Teal.

The warship's engine reached a muted howl and held there for a few seconds while the Estral ships caught up with the light-speed calculations.

Nation made a play of checking his watch. "What's keeping them?"

Keller's eyes flicked across the *Gundar*'s numerous status

displays. "Every journey is conducted at the speed of the slowest member. Either that or they're trying their damnedest to make us think their processing clusters aren't capable of rapid lightspeed calculations."

"Which we know to be false."

After a wait of ten seconds, the SC *Gundar* entered lightspeed, along with the eight Estral warships. A ten second warmup was so pitifully long, Keller was convinced the Estral had introduced a delay. The aliens weren't known for subtlety, so she wondered what they were up to.

"Teal, how long until we reach Isob-2?"

"Eighteen hours, Lieutenant."

"How long would it take the *Gundar* at top speed?"

"Seventy-three minutes."

Nation stretched. It was only out of habit, since he didn't have any of his original muscle tissue left to relieve. "Maybe one of those old clockwork models from Primol-1 has tagged along for the ride."

"Or maybe they just need some extra time to finish a clean-up operation."

"We're safe at lightspeed, so I'm going to have a lie-down in one of those pod rooms."

Neither of them required sleep, but it was good to have the opportunity for downtime.

"Sure. I'm going to stay here and do some thinking."

Keller turned and watched Nation as he disappeared through the door leading to the cramped personnel living area. He was tall and broad, but not unusually so, and his blond hair was cropped short in the style of many Rank 1 Troopers. There was no external indication he was anything other than a normal human being. He fitted in, exactly like he was meant to.

The hours rolled by and the only time Keller moved was to pull on a spacesuit from the bridge locker. There was a stack of visors on a shelf underneath and she dragged one out and put it to one side in case she needed it in a hurry.

Lightspeed travel was boring once you got over the novelty of travelling far quicker than nature ever intended and Keller had done countless transits. She interfaced gently with the *Gundar*'s Istoliar core cluster and felt the warship's inner life wash over her. It wasn't alive, of course, but in some senses, it bore striking similarities.

She detached herself without Teal even detecting her presence. With her eyes closed, she tried to will herself to experience a premonition. As usual, they came when they chose and not before. She was starting to believe the Faor augmentation had interfered with what they called her *gift*. It had been nearly a month since her last insight and that was unusual. Perhaps they'd come in a bunch later.

The rest of the trip went by as they all did. Keller tried a couple of options from the food replicator, without much appetite. She knew most people couldn't tell the difference between the copy and the real thing, but to her, it had always been obvious.

Lieutenant Nation returned from his solitude and sat in his chair, where the dull glow from the bridge display screens lit up his smooth skin.

"We will arrive in Isob-2 in ten minutes," said Teal.

"You should put a suit on," said Keller. "Otherwise, you'll look obvious."

"True." Nation went to the locker and chose one. It took practise to put a spacesuit on in less than two minutes and he managed it in ninety seconds. He dropped back into his seat, clutching his own visor.

They looked at each other, trying to gauge the mood. The Confederation had been at peace for a few years and neither of them was particularly keen for a change.

"Let's hope this is an in-and-out job," Nation said. "An accident. A toxic leak."

Keller gave a noncommittal noise. "With no sign whatsoever of a military purpose. Perhaps there will be pretty flowers and butterflies."

"Cynic," he laughed.

"Whatever comes from this..." She tailed off, not sure what else to say.

At precisely its expected time, the SC *Gundar* emerged from lightspeed, sixty thousand kilometres from the planet Isob-2. A few seconds later, the first Estral ship did likewise, shortly followed by the other seven.

"Energy shield active," said Teal. "Commencing local area scan. I have located the SC *Givens* in high, stationary orbit, as well as several Estral vessels in addition to those which accompanied us from Primol-1."

"Let me see the *Givens*."

Teal updated the sensor feed, to show the Class 2 rapid response craft SC *Givens*. At three thousand metres in length, it was far larger than the *Gundar* and most of its interior was taken up by a shielded cargo hold designed to contain unstable or volatile substances, such as might be produced during a failed attempt to refine Obsidiar-Teronium.

"Looks like a massive, grey cigar," said Nation.

"It can lift ten billion tonnes using its gravity winches."

"I know. It still looks like a cigar."

"Local area scan complete," announced Teal. "There were twelve Estral vessels in the vicinity of Isob-2 before our arrival, with a chance of others remaining undetected."

"That's a lot of resources to commit to a single installation," said Nation. "What the hell are they up to?"

"And look at this," said Keller, adjusting the sensors until they were focused on a spaceship, which, from its size and shape, conformed to the standard Estral design for a transport vessel.

Nation stared long and hard at the image. "Maybe it makes sense to someone."

"Yeah, maybe. Let's see what's going on below."

The front viewscreen changed to show the planet Isob-2. It was a sphere of cold, grey rock, with a quarter of its surface scoured from an incendiary attack during one of the many wars the Estral had started before the Vraxar brought their expansion to a halt. It was mountainous and inhospitable, with sporadic, violent storms of dust.

"Low oxygen atmosphere, nothing toxic, certainly not breathable," said Keller.

The planet's attributes were all in the records. The only place able to sustain life on Isob-2 was the refinement facility, deep beneath the surface, and that hadn't been enough to stop whatever killed the Estral.

"Are we on the blindside?" asked Nation.

"Nope, here's the upper level of the plant."

Keller tweaked the sensors until they were aimed directly at the Estral base. The above-ground section was little more than a featureless grey structure of alloy, extending for twelve hundred metres on each side and with a height of six hundred.

"Tarjos Gial-Eld is on the comms," said Teal.

"What took him so long? Bring him through."

The Estral was as blunt as the previous occasion. "You will land and speak with Koltar-Reon. You will do this immediately."

"We will leave the SC *Gundar* in orbit with the SC *Givens*," said Keller, with equal bluntness. "We will descend to the surface in our shuttle and meet with the rest of our team."

"Very well. My warships will remain in escort."

With that, Gial-Eld was gone.

Keller sighed. "Teal, make contact with the *Givens* and find out who they've got in the facility. After that, speak with the surface team and tell them we've arrived."

The response didn't take long. "Lieutenant Hattie Mack is expecting you," said Teal.

"That's it?"

"She did not elaborate."

"When we're gone, stay close to the *Givens*. We may lose comms contact if we're required to visit the deeper parts of the facility. Don't do anything rash."

The AI didn't respond with a wisecrack. "Acknowledged."

"Do we have landing clearance?"

"I have programmed the shuttle accordingly."

"Let's go," said Nation.

"Suddenly keen?"

"Yeah, that's me."

"Safe journey," said Teal, surprising them both.

They made their way from the bridge until they located the airlock door leading to one of the *Gundar*'s two shuttles. There was a tight corridor to squeeze through which put Nation in mind of a convict's escape tunnel out of a prison, except this one was taking them back beneath the walls rather than away from them. He sidled along it until he reached what appeared to be a dead-end wall. The wall slid open to reveal the brooding green light of the six-seater shuttle's interior. He stepped inside, keeping a wary eye on the low ceiling.

There were two rows of three seats, with a narrow aisle on either side. Only the front two seats had a good view of the main viewscreen and were intended for the pilots should the unthinkable happen and the shuttle's navigational system suffer some kind of catastrophic failure.

Nation dropped into the left seat. The shuttle wasn't designed for long journeys but it was comfortable enough. He ignored the control panel in front of him and waited for Keller.

"You going to fly this one?"

"Tempting, but no. Let's sit back and let the autopilot do its thing."

Keller interfaced with the autopilot and triggered the shuttle's release. They felt the sensation of high acceleration and the transport dropped through an underside hatch on the *Gundar*. The front viewscreen updated to show darkness speckled with stars.

Then, the shuttle's tiny stabilised Obsidiar-Teronium engine fired up and the transport sped towards the Isob-2 facility, sixty thousand kilometres away.

CHAPTER FOUR

VIEWED from a height of one thousand metres, the Isob-2 facility was rather more impressive in appearance than it was when seen from high orbit. It had a solid, industrial design that was unusual amongst the Estral and its thick walls looked like they could withstand a sustained aerial bombardment, even without the protection of the energy shield which was currently holding up the progress of the *Gundar*'s shuttle.

"What's keeping them?" muttered Nation.

"Why would they be in a hurry? They don't want us here."

"I know, I'm just letting my mouth go."

A green light appeared on the shuttle's central panel.

"There's the clearance."

The energy shield wasn't visible to the naked eye, but the shuttle's sensors showed it as a shimmering blue-tinged sphere covering the entire facility. The transport descended rapidly through a temporary opening in the shield, whilst two wide doors in the facility roof opened. There was a red light within, illuminating a cavernous airlock space which kept the facility hangar bay from depressurizing every time something landed.

Once the shuttle was inside the airlock, the outer doors closed and the inner space repressurized. It was a crude, unsafe system which would never have got past the approval stage in the Space Corps. The airlock's second set of doors opened, revealing the hangar.

Nation pointed a finger at the screen. "There's one of the shuttles from the *Givens*."

"And a further twelve Estral transports. Pretty big ones."

"Enough to carry a few thousand personnel from the looks of it."

"Five thousand in each if you accepted standing room only."

"They're identical. They've come from the same spaceship, or the same class of spaceship."

The Estral shuttles were lined up in three rows and, even at two hundred metres in length and forty wide, they didn't come close to filling the hangar bay. They were completely functional in appearance and equipped with front and rear low-yield plasma missile launchers, designed to take out lightly-armoured opponents and nothing more.

"What are they all doing down here?" asked Nation. "Evac?"

"Not a chance."

"Hunch?"

"It just doesn't look right. What do you reckon?"

"It stinks. I'm keeping an open mind for the moment."

"Well, we're here to find out what happened." Keller pointed at a few areas of the bay floor. There were groups of grey figures, wearing full protective spacesuits. "These aren't maintenance crew."

"Not with those guns, they aren't."

"Something tells me this place is even more screwed up than we've been led to believe."

"Maybe the new personnel are all on the lower levels, fixing stuff up."

"Right."

The shuttle's engine was near-inaudible during the short period of time it took the autopilot to manoeuvre the craft into position offset from the overhead doors. It settled on the far side of the bay from the Estral transports and with hardly a bump. A red light stayed on the control panel for several long seconds.

"Still not breathable," said Nation.

"The readings suggest the repressurization is nearly done."

Nation switched between sensor feeds. The bay was several hundred metres across and situated a few hundred below the planet's surface. Its alloy walls were reinforced with massive vertical beams, which, to Nation's eye were overkill if the engineers simply wanted to support the walls. Above, the outer bay doors were badly scraped and dented. They were powered by a pair of immense gravity motors anchored to the support beams, which gave off an unhealthy, high-pitched buzzing sound.

"I count six banks of airlifts," he said. "These ones over here are for the heavy cargo."

"Still no sign of anyone coming to greet us."

"Anything on the comms?"

"Here we are – there's an automated message from the base mainframe letting us know we're free to disembark."

The red light on the door changed to a steady green.

Nation turned his gaze to towards the shuttle exit. "Where are we meant to go? I don't want to get shot up by an Estral soldier who thinks we're wandering off-limits. Maybe we should wait."

The momentary indecision was cleared up.

"One of the airlifts on the eastern wall has just opened," said Keller.

The airlifts were larger than they appeared and the one which opened was wide enough to allow three Estral to walk out abreast, with more coming behind.

"More guns," said Nation.

"They're probably jumpy."

"As long as they aren't trigger-happy as well as jumpy. Let's get out and say hello."

Keller leaned over and pressed the release panel for the shuttle's side door. It vanished into its side recess and a draught of icy cold air rushed in, bringing with it the kind of oily smell which only seemed to exist in hangar bays. She took her visor and climbed out through the opening and stepped onto the alloy floor. The plate must have been fifty metres thick and it sucked the sound from her footsteps. She walked around the wedge nose of the transport and leaned against the housing for the front chaingun. Nation stopped nearby and used his optical augmentation to zoom in on the approaching Estral.

"Six in total, two with repeaters, all wearing armoured vests and no sign of Lieutenant Mack."

The Estral were huge, with the majority of the males growing to a height of between seven and eight feet. They were broad and strong, and only slightly less agile than a human. Their skin was grey, along with their eyes. Most of them had thick, black hair. When up close, Nation knew they had an unsettling humanness about them, particularly in some of the expressions and gestures. These ones were dressed in military spacesuits made from a flexible, rubbery grey material and with dark alloy helmets. Impassive eyes stared out through the flat, clear visors.

Two legs, two arms and a head. The universe knows a good design when it sees one.

"Let's go speak with them," Nation said, setting off.

Keller kept pace. Neither of them was armed, though she wasn't expecting a confrontation. It wouldn't go well for the aliens if they were stupid enough to break the peace treaty.

It took a minute for the two parties to meet. Nation chose the largest Estral and kept his eyes locked directly onto its face. This one carried a long, tube-shaped gauss rifle with a bore the size of an eyeball, and the weapon could no doubt punch a hole through a line of ten human soldiers if aimed properly. The two groups stopped a short distance apart.

"You know why we're here," Nation said, his eyes still on the same Estral. He'd dealt with the aliens on many occasions and had yet to find one who either possessed, or cared about, politeness or good manners. "Take us to our team."

He'd guessed the leader right. "I am Koltar-Reon," said the largest Estral through the tiny language module stitched to his shoulder. "I command this base. Come, I will take you to your team. You are aware you're not welcome."

"That is not important. We are here."

Koltar-Reon didn't offer any more conversation. All six of the Estral wheeled about and strode off without looking back. The aliens wore solid-looking grey boots and the metal soles clunked against the alloy floor.

Nation was mid-stride after them when he saw the expression on Keller's face. He recognized the look and made a comms link to her neural augmentation.

JN> What's wrong?

BK> Got a premonition. This base is screwed.

JN> How sure?

BK> Eighty percent minimum. I'm running it through the Faor.

JN> When? Where? What? Do we need to evac?

BK> Don't know.

JN> Nothing more?

BK> Nope.

JN> Do we need to abort?

BK> I don't think Admiral Cody would be too impressed. The model just came back at 81.7%.

JN> Sucks. We should inform RRT Alpha.

BK> Yep. Let's act fast and stay on our toes.

Nation terminated the link. The conversation had taken less than a hundredth of a second - far too little time for the Estral to notice.

The airlift was still open and the Estral filed into it. Nation and Keller came last and waited for Koltar-Reon to activate the lift. The Estral swiped his fingers across the control panel in a complicated gesture and the doors closed. The lift started its descent with a noticeable lurch.

"What happened here?" asked Nation.

"Research carries danger," replied Koltar-Reon. It was classic evasion.

"We saw soldiers in the hangar bay."

"They are here to assist."

"Did any personnel survive the incident?"

"We had a crew in the upper hangar. They survived."

"Where are they?"

"They were taken elsewhere."

"For their safety?"

"No."

"Why did you take them off Isob-2?"

The lift stopped, this time with a hollow bang which suggested the presence of a fault in its gravity winch.

"We have arrived," said Koltar-Reon.

The display panel on the airlift showed the words *Personnel Quarters*. The doors opened, to reveal a large room hewn out of the solid rock and reinforced with alloy beams. The room was empty except for a row of four monitoring screens on the opposite wall, with only one of them switched on. It was dimly lit in blue and the temperature was even lower than it was in the hangar above. Keller's breath steamed in the air.

They didn't wait for an invitation and stepped out. The floor was dense stone and gave no echo. The Estral had always been skilled when it came to shaping stone, and the surfaces were smooth, with a faint sheen.

The opposite passage vanished into the gloom, as did those to the left and right. Nation used his optical augmentation to see through the darkness. The corridors went on and on, with doors at regular intervals in both walls.

JN> What a shitty place to get posted.

BK> Maybe this is great if you're an Estral.

JN> Not a chance. I think the power is failing.

BK> Yep. What do you reckon keeps this place going? Obsidiar main and Gallenium backup?

JN> Yeah, almost certainly. It seems funny for both to fail. You can do some digging once we get somewhere a bit less overlooked.

BK> It'll be my pleasure. I am intrigued.

JN> Me too.

Koltar-Reon strode past and the other five Estral filed carefully around the two humans. For all their bluntness, the aliens had plenty of respect for personal space.

"Your team is this way."

"Just tell us the number on the door and we'll find them."

"You will be accompanied."

The Estral led them along the opposite passage until it reached a T-junction. They passed four pairs of doors which led to quarters for the base scientists. Nation looked at each door carefully – they were all closed and the panels were not only locked, but disabled, presumably by the Isob-2 control mainframe.

BK> They don't want anyone poking around.

JN> Nope.

Koltar-Reon turned right at the T-junction and led them along a near-identical corridor. Nation saw what he thought were steps at the far end and a sign hung from the ceiling. *Up: Personnel. Down: Laboratory Area 1.*

Their destination was closer. Koltar-Reon brought the group to a halt outside a door which looked exactly like all the others – a grey metal slab without markings, except this one had a group of eight armed Estral waiting outside. The soldiers stepped aside to give space.

The door's control panel was active and it glowed with blue symbols. Koltar-Reon paused, with one hand halfway towards the panel.

"Most of your team is in here."

"Only most?"

"They are free to move around the upper levels of Isob-2." Koltar-Reon smiled, without sign of genuine humour. "As per the terms of our peace treaty."

The Estral repeated the gesture to open the door. There was a short passage beyond, cut through the grey rock and with thick beams of alloy overhead. At the end of the passage was a large room, which had been set up as a makeshift lab.

Nation and Keller walked through. The room was furnished with Estral-sized metal tables and chairs. There were Space Corps diagnostic tablets scattered here and there, along with a cylindrical number cruncher bot and a gravity-engined analyser, more commonly referred to as a sniffer. The place was as cold and dimly-lit as everywhere else in the facility and gloom clung to the air like a miasma, which not even the glow from the sniffer's bright guidelights could dispel.

Ten members of Rapid Response Team Alpha worked here and they talked amongst themselves in low voices. Most of them looked up at the sound of the new arrivals. The men and women looked drawn and tired, as if this was the end of a double-shift.

The entrance door closed and Keller glanced behind to make

sure no Estral had followed into the room. The passage was empty.

"Lieutenant Mack," said Nation, identifying the lead member of the team from the file images. He spoke the name confidently, like he'd worked with her for ten years. It was probable the Estral were monitoring the room.

Mack came over, carrying her diagnostic tablet. She was dressed in a silvery, flexible spacesuit which covered her entire body and most of her head. Mack was blonde-haired and middle-aged. Her blue eyes were hard, suggesting she'd been in some bad places before. Whatever confidence she once possessed had been unmistakeably eroded by her short time in the Isob-2 facility, and she was clearly relieved at the arrival of these two *specialists*.

"Lieutenants Keller, Nation," she greeted them. "Welcome to a shitstorm in the making."

CHAPTER FIVE

KELLER USED her augmentation to link with Mack's diagnostic tablet, and switched out of its existing program into a text editor. Bright red letters appeared on screen and the tablet started beeping softly.

ARE WE BEING WATCHED?

Mack was surprised but she hid it well. "They have basic monitoring facilities in this room, which they aren't currently using to snoop on us," she said. "The sniffer can do a whole lot more than detect traces of Istoliar and it's watching the link to this room. The Space Corps wants us to do our job free from interference and they gave us the tools to do it."

"What about elsewhere?"

"I'm sure the lower levels are closely monitored. We haven't been allowed to look."

Nation thumbed over his shoulder. "What's down those stairs at the end of this corridor?"

"A room, a sealed door and a bunch of Estral guards. We're on level Subterranean-5, which is as deep as the Estral will let us go."

"They aren't supposed to impede an RRT."

"No they aren't, Lieutenant Keller. Yet that's exactly what they're doing." Mack sighed. "A few of us saw real, genuine action in the Eighth War, but we're still scientists and we're not planning to shoot our way to victory, whatever that might be. If the Estral say *no,* there's not much we can do about it." Mack perched herself on the edge of one of the oversized chairs. Her feet dangled to the ground and she looked like a child with an adult face.

The rest of the response team were listening in and a woman spoke up – Research Lead Enny Hunter from the badge on her spacesuit. "We thought they'd send more. Y'know – like a gazillion ships or something."

The research team members had a high level of security clearance, so Nation wasn't too worried about giving away classified Space Corps information. Besides, opinions were allowed. "We don't want to start another war."

"Definitely not," said RL Matthew Griffin. "We just won the last one."

Another woman jabbed him playfully in the ribs. "Four years ago, Matt. Back when you were learning how to walk."

"Cut it out, Fletcher. This is serious crap here. You know what we've been talking about," Griffin looked furtive for a moment and then attempted an authoritative stare in the direction of Keller and Nation. "I guess they sent you here because you can get a job done?"

"That's the idea."

"Top secret, huh?"

"For the moment." Keller could see that Griffin was scared and she intended to find out what had left this team so spooked. "What's going on here, Lieutenant Mack?"

"The Estral are – were - using this place to refine Obsidiar-Teronium into Istoliar. I have no doubt about that. Isob-2 isn't permitted to produce any whatsoever, but it appears as though they've been giving it a go."

"You received a Granol-42 detection alert, didn't you?" asked Keller.

"That's what brought us here in the first place. We've got monitoring tools installed in each of the Estral refinement facilities and we got a Granol-42 warning from levels Sub-12 all the way through to Sub-62. Granol-42 is a known by-product of a near-miss," said Mack with a tight smile. "They tried and failed to make a chunk of Istoliar somewhere below us."

"Does that suggest this is their first attempt?" asked Nation.

"Not necessarily. It takes a few things working in tandem to make Istoliar. They could have been successfully producing it for some time without us knowing about it."

"Don't we have monitoring tools that can pick up Istoliar as well?"

"Of course, Lieutenant Keller. All the way down to level Sub-62."

Keller caught the unspoken words. "You think they've enlarged the facility?"

"I think there's an excellent chance of it."

"Yeah," said Hunter. "The Granol-42 concentration at Sub-62 is waaay higher than it should be. The main kit they have which could be used in a refinement process is on levels Sub-30 through Sub-45. That's where I'd expect to see the highest concentration of contaminants."

"Exposure to Granol-42 is invariably fatal, unless you're wearing a decent suit," said Keller. "No cure, no comeback."

Mack nodded. "That's why we're assuming everyone is dead."

JN> Admiral Cody must have known all this before he sent us.

BK> You'd think.

JN> What are we missing?

BK> Let's ask them and find out.

"It sounds like we've got enough proof to show the Confederation Council," said Nation. "Why haven't you been recalled?"

"Because we have only found *evidence*, Lieutenant Nation. Not proof."

"So this Granol-42 could have come from another source?"

"In certain circumstances, unstable Obsidiar-Teronium can produce a quantity of it, along with Istilin and Polysempe, both of which are similarly toxic."

"The sniffer can read those ones through two klicks of solid stone," drawled Hunter. "And it's picking up traces right now."

"One thing's for certain, Lieutenant," Mack resumed. "There has been some extensive pissing about on Isob-2 and it's definitely not within the spirit of the Eighth War Peace Treaty Agreement."

"Have you managed to get anything from Koltar-Reon or any of the Estral? It's a long shot, but they have been known to slip up."

"Oh, they're up to something. Mark my words," said Hunter. "This is the shadiest bunch of Estral I ever did see, and I've seen some good ones."

"We can't send a fleet out here on the basis they've been acting a bit strange," said Keller. "This is their facility after all and they don't like us being here."

"Have you got any idea if the Estral are planning to clean the place up?" asked Nation. "I assume they won't need to abandon everything here?"

"I was coming to that," said Mack, "And you aren't going to like what I'm about to tell you."

"Let's have it."

"You'll have no doubt noticed the presence of an Estral fleet in orbit above Isob-2. When we arrived with the SC *Givens*, several of those warships were in the process of deploying shuttles."

Keller nodded. "We saw them in the hangar bay – big ones. We were hoping to find out what they were doing here."

"We didn't exactly get a guided tour, but as far as we know, those shuttles were empty by the time we received clearance to come into the hangar bay," Mack continued. "So they either sent down empty shuttles to bring up the dead, with no one actually left on the base to haul up the bodies, or they sent shuttles filled with their own personnel."

"By which she means *soldiers*," said Hunter, butting in again.

"It would make sense for them to try and clean the place up," said Keller. "If they went deeper than Sub-5, they must have been gone for a couple of days now. The aftereffects of a major incident would take a lot longer than that to fix, right?"

"They've been down there a couple of days that we know of," said RL Hunter. "It could have been longer."

Mack's jaw tightened at the interruption. "A clean up might take months, Lieutenant Keller. I assume the Estral are far below here, doing everything possible to sweep away the evidence of their Obsidiar-Teronium refinement operation. Once they're done, they could throw open the doors to Sub-6, invite us down for a look, and try to convince us everything is as per the terms of the treaty." Mack dropped down from the chair and rubbed the back of her legs. "Except, we saw them send about three hundred troops into Sub-6 only a few hours ago."

"Heavily armed troops," said Griffin. "They must have just got here."

"And they tried their damnedest to keep us away from them," said Hunter. "Like we weren't going to notice that happening."

"It's not unusual to expect troops to be involved, given the scale of the problem," said Nation.

"It's not only the troops," said Hunter. "Tell them what the sniffer found, Lieutenant."

The flicker of irritation appeared again on Lieutenant Mack's face. "Ever since we got here, the sniffer's been picking up vibrations which it attributes to moderate-sized explosive blasts."

The implication was clear, but Nation had to be sure.

"Would they use charges to destroy their refinement hardware? Maybe they could use them to cut off access to some of the lower areas."

"All of these things are possible, Lieutenant Nation. I can't imagine the requirement for several hundred separate detonations."

"They're fighting," said Griffin helpfully. "We think maybe there's been a rebellion within the Estral and for some reason it's playing out on Isob-2."

"Terrorists, or something," added Hunter. "Stupid aliens," she added for good measure. It wasn't the kind of attitude personnel were meant to display, but after eight discrete wars it was a widely-held view.

"And here we are, stuck on level Sub-5, waiting to see how it all pans out," said R2 Lola Fletcher, another member of the team who'd been quiet up until now.

"If the terrorists win, they're going to come up here and murder us all," added Hunter with apparent relish.

"Have you told Admiral Jacks?" asked Nation. "Since he's in charge of your RRT, he should order a withdrawal."

"We've been told to stop acting jumpy and wait for support," said Lieutenant Mack. She pointed with two fingers at once. "And here you are."

RL Hunter gave a cackling laugh. "Like she said, welcome to the shitstorm, ladies and gentlemen."

BK> This isn't good.

JN> Tell me about it. We need to find proof or otherwise of a refinement operation. These poor bastards on RRT Alpha have been dumped on.

BK> We could order them back to the SC *Givens* and deal with any crap from Admiral Jacks later?

JN> Tempting. It'll make our job a lot harder if they leave. How's about we handle this fast and withdraw in a group?

BK> Sounds like a plan. What's your take on this terrorist thing?

JN> Not convinced. There's more going on than meets the eye.

BK> Agreed. That 81.7% chance is beginning to look realistic.

JN> Do you ever doubt yourself?

BK> A topic for later.

JN> This is going to require a certain amount of openness with the RRT. Think you can tap into the Estral security system and have a look into the lower levels without getting caught?

BK> I *never* get caught.

JN> Liar.

BK> I can't remote-link into the Estral systems the same way I can with the Space Corps gear. I'll need to be at a terminal and hard-linked.

JN> Fine. The alternative is that I take a look myself. Let's speak to Lieutenant Mack and see if she knows a secluded spot where you can do your work.

Keller ended the link. "Lieutenant Mack, I require uninterrupted access to an Estral terminal in order to access their security systems and remote monitoring tools."

"That's easier said than done. They allow us to roam the upper levels, Lieutenant Keller, except there're always shadows behind us."

"Big, grey shadows. With guns," said Griffin.

"And definitely no sense of humour," added Fletcher.

"I can deal with the shadows. How closely do they watch this room? Will they notice if you're down on numbers?"

Mack shrugged. "As long as we stay here, they don't seem too interested. As soon as we leave this room, that's when they start paying attention."

"That's what I hoped you'd say. Where's the closest terminal?"

"There are plenty on this level." Mack pointed towards the wall next to the door. There was a viewscreen fixed to the surface, along with a speaker unit and a flat, silvery rectangle a few inches square, which was the remote interface receptor.

Keller had already spotted the panel. "I can't plug into that one." She eyed it up again. "I need something bigger – with a wide-bore interface."

Mack rubbed her finger along her lower lip. "I can't think of anything like that here on Sub-5. I mean, there are a couple of stations not far from the eastern airlifts, but from memory they're just bigger versions of this wall unit." She raised her voice so that everyone else in RRT Alpha could hear. "Where's the closest terminal with an interface socket?"

"There's definitely a load of them in Sub-2 where they monitor the bay doors," said R2 Otto Spinks.

"Along with a dozen Estral in attendance at all time," said Mack. "Anywhere else?"

"Sub-3 secondary comms room," said Hunter. "I've only been in once. There were a couple of Estral, but it looked automated, so there may not be a round-the-clock shift. You'll find what you need in there."

Keller nodded. "Sounds good. Is it hard to find?"

Hunter waved an arm towards the ceiling. "Up there and along."

"Fine." Keller looked towards Nation. "We should both go. Just in case."

Lieutenant Mack screwed up her face in surprise. "You want to go now?"

"This situation isn't going away."

"Point taken. They have a permanent guard on us. If you're hoping to sneak out, it won't be easy."

"We saw them already." Nation gestured towards the anxious-looking members of RRT. "Someone needs to go out ahead of us. I don't care what excuse you have to make."

"I'll go," said Griffin. He picked up a tablet from the table and pulled some kind of cylindrical micro-sniffer from his pocket. "Give me a chance to finish dressing." His eyes searched for where he'd left his suit visor. Hunter held one out for him, which he took.

"Thanks." Griffin put the visor on top of his head, snapped it into the fastenings on the suit and pulled it down over his face. It was reflective and hid everything that was going on behind. "Just say the word. I'll tell them I need to check out Sub-3 for contaminants."

"That's perfect," said Keller. "We'll follow you to the comms room."

Mack suddenly understood. "You have stealth modules fitted," she said in awe.

"Not me," said Keller, tapping the side of her head. "Psi. They won't see a thing."

"Whoa a real Psi!" said Hunter. From the look on her face, she was preparing to spew out a dozen banal questions, with the most common one being *can you read my mind?*

Keller was familiar with the expression and raised her hand. "Don't."

Hunter closed her mouth.

Griffin took it in his stride. "Do I need to do something specific to help?"

Nation shook his head. "Act normal. The rest of you in here

will need to come up with something convincing if the Estral start asking questions about us."

"And if they don't believe what we tell them?"

"Refer them to the terms of the peace treaty. We're allowed to be here."

Lieutenant Mack wasn't reassured, but her face hardened. "They've been taking the piss out of my team ever since we arrived. Screw the Estral."

It was the right attitude and Nation gave her a single nod of approval. "If the Estral threaten you, then they've escalated it beyond your remit. If that happens, return to the SC *Givens* and let Admiral Jacks deal with it."

"If they let us leave."

It was a genuine concern and Nation didn't treat them like fools by pretending otherwise. If you joined the Space Corps, there was a decent chance you'd find yourself in a bad situation. RRT Alpha might not like it, but they were trained to deal with it.

"RL Griffin, please lead on," said Keller, indicating the door through which they'd entered. She put on her own visor and tapped into the RRT Alpha local comms network. There was no one in the channel at the moment apart from RL Griffin and the signal probably wouldn't penetrate very far through the walls of the Isob-2 facility if they got separated.

Nation dropped his visor onto a table and activated his stealth modules. He felt the Istoliar power cores in his chest thrum faintly and he disappeared from sight. There were only a handful of operatives in the Space Corps equipped with stealth augmentations and it was doubtful anyone in RRT Alpha had ever seen one in action. Their faces said everything.

They had a similar lack of experience when it came to the Psi team.

"Uh, I can still see you, ma'am," said Griffin, staring directly at Keller.

"You can, they can't."

"I'll take your word for it."

"Go."

Griffin went. He swiped at the door panel. It took him two attempts to trigger it and he laughed nervously through the speaker on his visor. "Second time lucky," he said when the door opened.

BK> Here we go.

JN> Hell, yeah.

They followed RL Griffin into the passage outside.

CHAPTER SIX

THE PASSAGE WAS EVEN GLOOMIER than Nation remembered and a thickness to the air made everything indistinct. He ran a substance check and found nothing unexpected. His environmental augmentation unit was far more sensitive than that in a spacesuit visor, but he wasn't convinced by the all-clear.

The guards outside were quickly alert to the opening of the door. Two of them approached, blocking the corridor. A few metres away, the other Estral soldiers watched with unconcealed contempt.

"Where are you going?" asked the taller of the two aliens.

Griffin spoke with confidence. He was unarmed and dealing with semi-hostile aliens which were two feet taller and far stronger than he was, but his voice didn't waver. "We have detected possible contaminants on Sub-3. I am going to look."

"You will stay in this room until you have clearance."

"No. As per the terms of our peace treaty, I will go now."

The Estral were intimidating and they stared at Griffin as though he was an insect they would prefer to crush. For a moment, it looked as if they'd push the matter.

"You will move," said Griffin.

The Estral stepped aside to allow him past. "We will accompany you."

Griffin was evidently jumpy and finding it hard not to look over his shoulder. "Yeah, whatever," he said, and walked between the soldiers. They fell in behind him, their gauss cannons held menacingly, like they'd been told to make the lives of RRT Alpha as stressful as possible.

Nation followed afterwards, his stealth modules completely masking the sight and sound of his passing. Keller was two paces behind. Not once did the Estral turn in her direction – it was as though she wasn't there.

JN> Any problems?

BK> They must have posted a few more guards after they brought us here. Not enough to make it too hard for me to fool them. How's your power cell?

JN> Power cells plural. Got plenty of juice.

RL Griffin headed towards the airlifts, occasionally checking his diagnostic tablet and muttering under his breath. The Estral stayed with him, a few metres back and not speaking.

Level Sub-5 was quiet. Keller listened carefully for sound and heard nothing whatsoever beyond that made by the Estral and RL Griffin. It was eerie – as though the entire facility was utterly deserted. There were signs of condensation on the grey walls which she couldn't remember from the first time she'd come along here.

BK> See this?

JN> Yeah. Life support on the blink.

BK> Not a good sign.

JN> An incredibly bad sign.

Griffin activated the airlift on the first attempt. One of the cars was on level Sub-5 and it opened immediately. He stepped inside and the Estral strode past him to stand against the rear wall. There was plenty of room for Nation and Keller to enter without having to come into physical contact with the aliens. As she walked past Griffin, Keller gave him a wide grin. His expression was hidden behind the suit visor, but his hands fidgeted with his diagnostic tablet.

JN> Stop teasing him.

BK> Whatever do you mean?

JN> He's nervous enough as it is.

Griffin reached for the lift panel and took three attempts to get it going. The Estral made no effort to intervene.

"You're doing well," said Keller through the RRT Alpha comms channel. The aliens wouldn't be able to hear any conversation conducted through the suit comms.

"Thanks." Griffin's voice was more or less steady.

Nation didn't have a visor and didn't need one to access the suit comms. He chose his words and sent them into the channel, where they were converted to speech. "Hold it together," he said. "How far to the comms station?"

"Two or three hundred metres."

"Once we're there, you don't need to stick around."

"Okay."

The lift stopped and something screeched far below. Nation pressed his hand to the wall and detected vibration, though he had no idea where it was coming from. The door opened halfway, stopped, and then slid fully aside.

"Your whole damn place is falling to pieces," said Griffin aloud.

The Estral didn't respond or even acknowledge he'd spoken. Nation studied the parts of their faces he could see through their suit helmets and the aliens were giving nothing away. There was clearly something wrong and Nation doubted it was confined to the airlifts.

There were no surprises outside the lift. The doors opened to reveal a large room, with bare metal floors, smooth walls and a ceiling supported by thick beams. Nation idly noted fractures in the stone around one of the beams, as well as signs of the metal bowing under the immense strain. The Estral were renowned experts when it came to tunnelling through rock, so it was odd to see signs of failure. There again, the Isob-2 facility likely had many untold tales.

This room was empty of personnel. In terms of equipment, a row of four status screens was fixed to the left-hand wall. Two of the screens were blank, a third flickered wildly and the fourth showed a series of temperature alerts for level Sub-3. Five passages led deeper into the complex, only one of which had a sign above it.

Communication Centre – Secondary Routing Hub

RL Griffin made directly for this passage and his escort followed. There was a compact gravity car at an angle across the way, with no driver and a large metal crate on its flat bed. The corridor was wide, allowing plenty of room to walk past the vehicle. There was no obvious reason it had been abandoned here.

"Explosives," said Nation, spotting the Estral symbols on top of the crate.

"That wasn't here last time I came this way," said Griffin.

"They're trying hard to keep something hidden from us," said Keller. "And they want to get it done so quickly it's making them careless."

Griffin's curiosity overcame his nervousness. "How are you doing that, ma'am? I mean, I can see you and the Estral can't. Stealth augmentations are something I can understand, but this?"

"I just tell their minds that I'm not here, Lieutenant. The more of them there are, the harder it becomes to fool them. It works on any sentient being. Now please, no more questions." She didn't speak the last words unkindly, it just wasn't a good time to be talking about her psi capabilities.

They entered a second large room, with several exits. There were four console stations in the middle of the floor and Nation saw Keller studying them carefully. They were ten-screen models, probably used by comms technicians to keep an eye on the main array. The seats were empty and most of the screens were switched off or tied in to a failed system.

BK> I can hard connect to this closest one.

JN> It's quite open here. You might have to break off if someone comes by.

BK> No sign of anyone.

JN> Let's keep it in mind if the comms station doesn't work out.

BK> Agreed. I'm beginning to doubt if there's any hardware in Isob-2 that's working well enough for me to tap into it with confidence.

JN> It's that bad?

BK> We'll see.

At that moment, Nation sensed something coming along one of the side passages. Visibility was exceptionally poor in that direction – the cold blue lighting was low and it appeared to be completely out further into the distance. He was forced to use his sensor augmentation to get a clear image.

"Soldiers," he said. "Lots of them and coming straight this way. RL Griffin, pick up the pace."

"Coming for us?" he gulped.

"I doubt it. Move."

Griffin increased the length of his stride without trying to be subtle about it. He led them into one of the other passages and kept going. They reached a T-junction and Griffin turned left.

"Hold," said Keller.

"What?" said Griffin, startled.

"Take a reading or something."

While Griffin fumbled with his portable sniffer, Keller and

Nation watched the Estral soldiers file past in the room behind. The aliens carried a full loadout of gauss cannons and repeaters, and a few lugged shoulder launchers. In addition, they wore thick plates of alloy armour which were fixed to the front of their spacesuits. They crossed the room, heading for the airlifts. On and on they came, hundreds and hundreds, marching three abreast. In the centre of their line was an evil-looking selection of Gallenium-powered artillery guns. Nation counted two brutal plasma repeaters and a heavy-duty guided plasma rocket launcher which was so large it was a wonder they'd got it down here.

BK> Sixty seconds earlier and I'd have had a job on my hands trying to keep hidden.

JN> What the hell are they doing? That launcher could flatten a town. There's no way they can think it's a good idea to fire it down here.

BK> And why aren't they using the cargo lift?

"What's wrong?" asked Griffin nervously. Further along the passage, he waved the sniffer around and scrutinised his diagnostic tablet as if he'd discovered the most lethal cocktail of toxins in the entire universe. The Estral watched him closely, as if they suspected foul play.

"Troops," said Keller. "They're not even trying to hide."

"I've seen enough," said Nation. He checked his Istoliar power cells. The stealth modules were draining them, but nothing to be concerned about. "Let's go."

Griffin didn't need to be asked twice. He pocketed the sniffer and set off again. Doors punctuated the walls at regular intervals and the alien script etched into their metal surfaces indicated the rooms beyond were for storage or other mundane uses. Their access panels were locked down and disabled in the way they had been on Sub-5. The Estral didn't want anyone getting inside.

Keller remembered something. "When Koltar-Reon first took us to the room on Sub-5, he told us that *most* of RRT Alpha was down there."

"That's right. We've got R2 Rich Bonner and R2 Kelly Sasso trying to find anything that might be useful on Sub-4."

"Is there something there?"

"No, ma'am. All the answers are on Sub-6 or lower. We've got to do something, though, so we try to make a nuisance of ourselves. We figure the Estral might make a mistake at some point and we could learn something."

"Doesn't seem as if it's working out too well for you."

"Between you and me, this is the worst assignment I can remember. In spite of what my colleagues would have you believe, I served a couple of years moving between Estral facilities like this one at the end of the Eighth War. Things were a lot easier back then – the Estral were just as rude and stubborn as they are now, but our teams had backup. Out here? It feels like we've been abandoned."

"If it's any consolation, I think the Space Corps' hands are tied by the Confederation Council's fears of upsetting the Estral without having absolute certainty of a treaty breach," said Keller. "Once they have proof of whatever there is to prove, they'll send that backup."

Once she'd spoken the words, Keller realised she didn't believe them herself. Admiral Cody had been well aware of the ramifications, but didn't once commit to sending more spaceships.

Griffin was equally sceptical. "You sound sure, ma'am. I don't share your confidence. The Estral are getting harder to handle – each time I come to a new facility to do an inspection with one of our teams, we face more and more obstacles. We write up our reports and nothing ever happens. It's like the Estral know we don't want to start another war, so they've decided to do what they damn well please."

"We have far more Istoliar than they do," said Nation. "The SC *Gundar* alone could knock out a dozen of their spaceships."

"Maybe the advantage isn't as great as you think," said Griffin with a bitter laugh. "They've been refining Obsidiar-Teronium under our noses for years and shipping it out. Do you really think they're installing it in their hospitals and power stations?"

"Our Estral friends are manoeuvring for war again."

"Same as it always was, Lieutenant Nation. Same as it always was."

They crossed another open space, this one with a high, domed ceiling supported by a thick central pillar of metal. A console surrounded the pillar, with none of its screens working properly. Occasionally, sparks of white jumped from screen to screen, or from operator pad to control joystick. There was an unpleasant hum in the room and the acrid stench of burning ozone.

"Was it like this when you got here?" asked Keller.

"No, ma'am. This whole place is going to fail if they don't get a handle on whatever's happening below Sub-5."

"They must have abandoned most of the maintenance areas like this one. That means it's either not safe to work or there's something stopping them getting it operational again."

"I've not seen any evidence the Estral care about a few accidents," said Griffin.

They exited the room, into another passage similar to the others. There was so much dampness on the walls here, it dripped to the floor and formed pools. The temperature was hardly above freezing point and falling slowly. The light remained poor and the ceiling orbs created blue halos in the air. It was oppressive and reminded Nation of an old mineworks, rather than an advanced research and processing facility.

"Your door is coming up on the right," said Griffin. "You're sure you can get inside?"

"One way or another," Nation replied grimly. "The door will need brute force; the terminal inside will require finesse."

The entrance to the secondary comms room was hard to miss. Midway along a corridor, a sign saying *Communications Room* hung from the ceiling and the adjacent door was much wider than the others, suggesting a lot of personnel came through. Keller and Nation hung back and watched Griffin heading away with his escort in tow.

"I'm going back. Good luck," Griffin said. "Remember, the suit comms won't easily reach between the levels of the facility. If you need to speak to anyone, you'll have to drop down to Sub-5. Even then, the thickness of the walls means it's hit and miss."

"We'll work with it. Thanks for the guided tour."

"No problem."

Keller and Nation checked out what they faced. Each of the sliding doors had a warning etched into the surface of the metal, advising it was a restricted area. To the side, an access panel waited for the right input. The panel was active, but the orange colour of the text indicated it was inaccessible to anyone without the highest level of clearance.

BK> What do you reckon?

JN> Hmmm.

BK> What does *hmmm* mean?

JN> It means I'm thinking.

BK> RL Griffin and his pals just disappeared around that corner. Stop thinking and start doing.

There was no way to hard link into an Estral door panel. They were sealed units designed to open doors or deny access to people without clearance, and they had no ports. One of Nation's many augmentations was a development of the old Internal Security Override Packs, generally called an ISOP or a number cruncher. He stood close to the door panel and activated his ISOP.

The ISOP connected remotely. Immediately, the door panel changed rapidly between its *access denied* and *no entry* notifications as the number cruncher bombarded its security software with octillions of permutations per second. Nation checked the utilisation on his processing cluster. It peaked at its fifty percent permitted maximum and remained there.

The use of the number cruncher on top of the stealth modules increased the power usage across his internal systems and his power cells drained at an increased rate. They recharged naturally over time, but it wasn't a good idea to let them fall too low.

"They must have improved their encryption algorithms since last time," he grunted. Chill from his Istoliar processing cores radiated through his skull and he gritted his teeth.

Keller stepped away from the wall and looked both ways. She turned her head, to give the visor sensor a better chance of picking up noise. "I've got no idea if there's anything coming. Sound doesn't carry too well down here. How long till the ISOP finishes?"

"It doesn't give me a progress report."

"It's going to bring every Estral running this way once they realise there's someone pissing about with their door."

"I don't need reminding."

Nation was on the brink of overriding the fifty percent core cap to see if he could speed things up, when the door panel abruptly changed from orange to blue.

"Bingo."

The doors slid open and Nation took a moment to reassure himself that the secondary comms hub wasn't filled with Estral soldiers. Anyone inside would have been ignorant of the break-in attempt, but they would probably be suspicious when the doors opened without reason.

"Looks empty," said Keller.

Nation gave a nod. "In."

Having to force the door open meant their time was already limited and there was plenty to do in the comms hub. Without any more delay, the two of them hurried inside.

CHAPTER SEVEN

THE SECONDARY COMMS hub was a square space, twenty-five metres to each side. The walls, floor and domed ceiling were undressed stone. There was nothing so crude as a support beam and the low thrum of a gravity field generator betrayed the method the Estral used to guard against collapse. A central post joined floor to ceiling. This post had a diameter of three metres and was pure black in colour. Cold spilled away from it and a thick layer of ice covered much of the floor.

The doors closed behind them and the script on the inner access panels stayed blue. At least they weren't going to be locked inside. The comms console which circled the secondary antenna was free of ice, but it was completely dead. Keller dashed over to it, swearing under her breath.

"You dare be broken."

Her boots crunched across the ice as she made her way around to the far side of the antenna.

"I'm going around here so the Estral won't see me straight away if any come through that door," she said.

Nation stood to one side of the lone entrance with his stealth augmentation activated. There was a waist-high metal bench nearby, with a couple of metal trays covered in some of the pastes the Estral replicators disgorged. The food looked frozen and completely unappetising.

"I'll keep watch from here." Nation had nonlethal methods of disabling an opponent, but it would be for the best if they simply got this over with before the Estral showed up.

"Remember, I can't hide myself while I'm interfaced."

"I know. Any life in the console?"

"Checking."

The comms console looked similarly advanced to something in a Space Corps hub, with touch indentations, screens, keypads and switches. Keller was fully trained in the use of alien tech, but the Space Corps didn't exactly receive a regular supply of the newest gear off the Estral production line. She tentatively tried to activate it.

"Dead," she muttered.

"Do we need to move on?" asked Nation.

"That'll waste too much time. I'm going to plug in – it's possible only the front-end has failed and it's still linked to the base mainframe."

She sat on one of the hard, cold seats and pressed the space-suit-covered tip of her index finger against one of the several open ports just below the bank of status screens. She called it *hard linking* when in reality there weren't any physical wires involved. All Keller required was touching distance to a wide-bore data port in order for her Faor augmentation to establish a connection.

As soon as she made contact, she *felt* every single nuance within the hardware. There were multiple hardware failures in this console – burnouts probably resulting from a huge unregulated power spike. She reached out further, the incredible processing power of the Faor able to slip amongst the Estral security walls with barely a hesitation.

"It *is* linked to the mainframe," she said, her voice taut with the effort of concentration.

Keller was hidden from the door, but when Nation leaned out, he could see from her pose the effort it took to harness the augmentation.

"This secondary antenna is linked to every sub-floor," she continued. "There's no traffic coming through it."

"Can you find their lower level monitoring sensors?"

"I'm in them now. There's Istilin, Granol-42 and Polysempe. A crapload of each. Other stuff too that I don't recognize."

"What else?"

"Traces of plasma on levels Sub-60 through to Sub-70."

"Except there's only meant to be a level Sub-62."

"Eight hidden levels. The lower level sensors are no longer gathering a live feed."

It was Nation's turn to swear. "We need *something,* damnit. Can you reactivate them?"

"Maybe not. I think they severed the link."

"They're really doing the business on this one."

Keller dug deeper into the Isob-2 system. The Faor cluster was so crushingly fast it could effectively bypass any security in nanoseconds and without triggering alarms, like a ghost seen so fleetingly it was impossible to believe it was there. It wasn't all straightforward and a few systems could slow things down – if she ran into enough Istoliar cores working in tandem, they could block the Faor for long enough that she risked setting off alerts. She reached the Isob-2 central mainframe, searching for a way to re-establish the sensor feed.

"Too risky," she said to herself. Then, louder, "They've got a new model processing cluster down on level 40. I can get inside, but they'll know about it."

"They must be aware we broke into this room already."

"That's low-level stuff. If I start poking around inside the mainframe, it might be programmed to shut itself down or wipe its data arrays."

"Well do something. We don't have long."

Keller had a flash of inspiration. "They might keep their recorded feeds elsewhere...checking."

At that moment, the entrance doors opened and a dozen or more Estral soldiers rushed in. They carried gauss cannons and it didn't take an expert in alien diplomacy to see they were agitated.

JN> Keller!

Nation fell back from the entrance, in case any of the soldiers stumbled into him. He was just in time to see Keller break contact with the comms console. She could make people unable to see her, but she couldn't make them forget they'd seen her.

BK> Damnit!

The Estral advanced rapidly across the room. One of them swung a leg and kicked a chair into the wall. Whatever they were saying, it was hidden behind their suit helmets.

BK> Made it.

JN> Close.

Keller trod carefully towards the back wall of the comms hub, putting distance between herself and the soldiers. Apart from the central antenna, there weren't many other places to hide in the hub. The soldiers checked behind the main console and circled the antenna. The tension faded visibly from them. One of the Estral gestured towards the door using the barrel of his gun and the soldiers filed from the room, leaving two behind to stand guard.

BK> Shit. I was *this* close to finding the feed recordings.

JN> Not close enough. Did you check out the upper level sensor feeds?

BK> What would I want to do that for?

JN> So they're working?

BK> Yep.

JN> I want to see how full that hangar bay is getting. That's where we go to get out of here.

BK> Fine, I'll check it out. What about these two?

JN> It's their lucky day. Timestop.

BK> That gives us what? A few seconds?

JN> Twelve.

BK> Great!!

JN> Ready?

BK> Always.

The two Estral evidently thought they'd been served up an easy job looking after an empty room. They leaned against the central console and watched the entrance. Nation targeted them and discharged his timestop augmentation. The name of the device wasn't wholly accurate – it didn't exactly stop time, so much as it created a limited, localised field in which time ran exceptionally slowly. As far as tools of the trade went, the stasis emitter was invaluable and only hampered by its very high power draw and long recharge.

The Estral soldiers were frozen in place.

JN> Go.

Keller sprang at the console and re-established the interface. This time, she knew exactly what she was looking for. Except that what she was looking for was no longer there.

BK> They deleted the recordings!

JN> That means they found out what you were doing?

BK> Yes.

JN> Do they know where you were doing it from?

BK> Maybe.

JN> That means there's going to be a whole lot more Estral inside this room shortly.

BK> You always look on the bad side of things, Nation.

JN> Get me that hangar feed.

BK> Already done – I've pulled out the last sixty minutes of every upper-level sensor recording. I've also squirted in some code which should allow our suit comms to piggyback up this antenna without the Estral knowing about it. *Grins* They aren't sending traffic through it so someone may as well get use out of it.

JN> I'm impressed. Now let's get out of here.

Nation waited impatiently while Keller picked her way over the ice. The time field collapsed and the Estral carried on as before, unaware anything was wrong.

BK> They'll get a shock when the door opens.

JN> We'll get more of a shock if it opens and a hundred more come through, looking for us.

With practised ease, Nation swiped his fingers over the entrance access panel. The doors slid open and the two of them hurried through before the Estral realised something wasn't right. The alien soldiers were in the process of walking to investigate when the doors closed automatically.

The corridor outside was empty.

"This way," said Nation over the suit comms. "Back to the airlifts."

Keller had something to say and she switched back to neural augmentation talk, where they weren't constrained by the speed of spoken language.

BK> I got you two lots of bad news.

JN> Only two?

BK> I checked out the hangar feed on ultra-high speed. Here.

Keller pushed a big data packet at Nation's neural receptor. He accepted it and the sensor feed from the upper hanger streamed into his data arrays. Without waiting for the entire file to arrive, he began playing it on ultra-high speed. What he saw wasn't a positive development. Another seven Estral shuttles had landed and alien troops flooded across the hangar floor, doubtless heading for the Isob-2 lower levels.

JN> Lots of troops. That *is* bad news.

BK> Oh, I wasn't counting the troops as bad news. That makes three lots of bad news. Have you seen the bomb yet?

The recorded stream continued until it showed the Estral unloading a huge, cuboid object from the rear doors of a shuttle. The device was thirty metres long, ten deep and ten high, with a grey shell and rounded edges.

JN> Holy crap, that's a damned planet buster!

BK> Yeah. Once you've seen one, you don't forget.

JN> We can't hang around on Isob-2.

BK> Neither can we leave. Do you remember Admiral Cody talking about that iceberg?

JN> Yeah.

BK> Well, we're balanced on top of it and we need to find out exactly what's below the water.

Keller was right and Nation didn't argue. It was one thing for the Estral to try and hide the evidence of a messed-up refinement operation underneath the noses of the Confederation's inspection team, it was another thing entirely for them to bring a planet buster into the equation.

JN> There is absolutely nothing I can think of which would require the use of a planet buster. Why not seal the place with small-scale explosives? It would be easy enough to bring this entire facility down and destroy the evidence.

BK> Which brings me to the third piece of bad news.

JN> We have to go below Sub-5 and find out what's down there?

BK> Exactly. I'm not sure it requires both of us.

JN> Agreed. First, we should speak to the inspection team and find out if any of them has a theory about what kind of refinement failure might require a whole damn planet buster to put right.

BK> They need to evac immediately. Even if it makes the Estral suspicious.

JN> Let's deal with that when we've spoken to Lieutenant Mack.

Nation checked the RRT Alpha open comms channel. The names of the personnel were listed and available.

"That was a good plan to hijack the Estral antenna."

"I have my uses."

Nation pushed open a connection to Lieutenant Mack. She was mid-conversation with someone else in RRT Alpha but took the interruption in her stride.

"Lieutenant Mack, you need to evacuate. That means the entire team. The Estral have brought in a planet buster."

"What the hell do they..."

"Let's keep the questions for later. Recall anyone you've got out there."

"Bonner and Sasso."

"Get them back at the double."

"Acknowledged. Are we expecting to waltz out of here without trouble?"

"Stay put. Lieutenant Keller and I will take care of that."

Nation closed the channel and he ran with Keller in the direction of the airlifts. The air was already three degrees cooler and it was just enough to cause the first signs of ice to appear on the walls. There were no more alien soldiers to avoid, though it was certain they were heading towards either the lower levels or the secondary comms hub room. The two of them kept a careful watch along the few side passages, with Nation using his advanced optics to search through the shadows. It was as if the Sub-3 level was suddenly empty and without apparent reason.

The room leading to the airlifts was deserted and Keller called the lift. The centre doors opened and they got into the car. This time, the lights were completely out and when the doors closed, the only illumination came from the symbols on the access panel.

BK> Shit, check this out.

Keller linked and pushed another file at Nation. When he accepted it, he could almost feel her cramming it through into his data arrays, as if she were desperate for him to see what it contained.

He played it on highest speed.

JN> Damn.

BK> R2s Bonner and Sasso?

JN> Got to be.

The two investigators were caught on one of the recordings, poking around in a room filled with crates. The label on the feed showed the location as Sub-9 Storage-8, so they'd somehow managed to get to one of the sealed-off levels. One of the two – R2 Kelly Sasso, judging by her build - held a portable sniffer close to one of the containers and then excitedly waved Bonner over. A group of Estral soldiers appeared on the feed, armed with gauss cannons. It wasn't clear if the two sides exchanged words, but after a few seconds, the Estral raised their weapons and shot the RRT Alpha investigators. Sasso and Bonner collapsed to the floor, their bodies a bloody mess, and they were simply left where they'd fallen.

BK> We've got to warn the others. Get them out of here.

The airlift banged and scraped, before it shuddered to a halt. The doors opened on level Sub-5. Nation looked out, shaking with anger and wondering if he'd be able to prevent himself from using lethal force against any Estral he found.

BK> Stay calm. Focus.

JN> Yes.

There were no Estral in the antechamber. Keller and Nation sprinted for the room where RRT Alpha were stationed.

CHAPTER EIGHT

IT ONLY TOOK a few seconds to reach their destination. Keller didn't need to open the door to the room to know something was amiss. The Estral guards were exactly where they'd left them and they had an air about them which suggested they were ready for violence.

Nation hit them with a focused blast from his shockwave augmentation. Ten Estral soldiers were punched from their feet, hurled into the walls or thrown onto the floor. One of them discharged his weapon aimlessly and a gauss projectile cracked off the ceiling, sending a shower of rock fragments to the floor. Once they were down, the soldiers didn't get back up.

The shockwave had a short cooldown. If any more Estral appeared in the next few seconds, it would require more direct action to finish them off. There was no sound of reinforcements.

Nation checked his power cells to find they'd fallen significantly from the weapon discharge. With inexorable steadiness, they began recharging.

BK> Dead?

JN> Yes.

BK> That's not going to go down too well in the next diplomatic meeting.

JN> Justifiable retaliation for murder. We have the evidence.

Nation sprinted towards the door, still alert for the sound of footsteps. One of the Estral had fallen nearby, losing its suit helmet in the process. Nation glanced at the alien's face. The soldier's eyes were open, but its expression was peaceful.

Nation reached out and activated the door panel. The members of RRT Alpha were inside, gathering their belongings. Across the room, R2 Otto Spinks was doing something to the sniffer.

"Sasso and Bonner are dead. Murdered. We're leaving. Now," Keller said loudly.

Keller's words got their attention. However, instead of working faster, the inspectors stopped packing their gear and stared at her, as if they suddenly had no idea what to say or do.

"We're leaving!" Keller repeated, her voice close to a shout. "There's no time to pack a suitcase!"

RL Enny Hunter caught sight of the bodies in the corridor outside. Keller was expecting her to ask a stupid question, but she kept her mouth closed.

"Come on, guys, get it together!" said Hunter. "The shit just hit the fan and it's blowing our way!"

"What about the sniffer and the number cruncher?" asked Lieutenant Mack. "Are we bringing them?"

The two robots were exceptionally valuable pieces of equipment and doubtless the Estral would gain something useful if they were given the opportunity to salvage them. Keller remote connected to each and activated their emergency shutdown routines, rendering the hardware useless until they were returned to a Space Corps repair facility.

"They'll slow us down. I've deactivated them."

"The data..."

"Too late. Now move, unless you want to end up like Sasso and Bonner!"

RRT Alpha had been caught unawares by this change in circumstances, but they were trained to respond in emergency situations. In moments, they were hurrying through the door after Keller.

"Oh, crap," said Griffin, when he saw the bodies.

JN> You can cover the whole group, right? To stop the Estral seeing them?

BK> One way or another. If we're lucky, we might get to the hangar bay before the Estral catch on.

JN> Let's get going.

BK> Taking a gun?

Nation stooped and picked up one of the Estral gauss cannons. It was comparatively lightweight for its size and it felt comfortable in his hand. With a five-foot barrel, it took some getting used to, but he'd fired one in the past.

JN> Gauss coils screw with the stealth modules.

BK> Only when you pull the trigger.

JN> It can't harm to bring one.

The group got moving in the direction of the airlifts. The members of RRT Alpha had come to the realisation that their lives were in the balance and they followed Keller. Nation was hidden by his stealth modules and he caught one or two of the investigators trying to see through the cloak. The older version of the tech had its flaws, however, the augmentations he was fitted with made him entirely invisible to human senses. There were other methods of detection which were harder to fool and he hoped he wouldn't run into any of those on Isob-2.

They reached the bank of airlifts and Lieutenant Mack called one. The group shifted nervously as they waited for it to arrive.

"Straight up to the hangar bay, walk to our shuttle and take off, right?" said Mack.

"Yes. Don't request clearance to depart until you're all inside."

"What about you?"

"I'll take the *Gundar*'s shuttle. Once you reach the SC *Givens*, I recommend you leave this place immediately. Head to Primol-1 and leave the fallout from this to Admiral Jacks."

Mack sounded as if she'd had enough. "I will. This is way beyond anything we're equipped for. It's like a damn war zone in here."

"What about the proof of what's happening on Isob-2?" asked Griffin. "If we leave, the Estral will be able to deny everything."

"I think that's what they were planning to do anyway," said Nation. "We're not leaving them to it. Once you're safely away, I'm going for a look around below."

"And I'll use the SC *Gundar* to keep the Estral guessing."

"Is it enough?" said R2 Fletcher doubtfully.

"Let me worry about that."

One of the two centre lifts banged against the inside of its chute and the doors opened. It was dark inside and Keller spotted shapes within. It was too late to hide the others and she swore at her oversight.

Estral soldiers stepped out of the lift, lowering their gauss cannons and pointing them at the members of RRT Alpha. Keller's quick count came to eight.

BK> Crap, crap, crap!

JN> I'll deal with them.

BK> Wait.

One of the Estral spoke in his harsh tongue. There was nothing marking him as the commanding officer of this squad, but the aliens didn't usually wear insignia. "You are not allowed here."

"Why not?" asked Keller.

"I was speaking to your Lieutenant Mack," said the Estral.

"Why aren't we allowed here?" asked Mack. "Our investigation is complete and we are returning to our shuttle."

The words took the alien by surprise and he furrowed his brow while he tried to think up a suitable response. "We will accompany you."

"Fine."

It wasn't easy to fit everyone in the lift, mostly because of the Estral's requirement for personal space. The aliens shuffled uncomfortably towards the rear of the lift car and pushed their backs against the wall. It would have been comical were the situation not critical. The members of RRT Alpha stood nearer the front and Nation found it difficult to get inside without making an obvious gap in the crowd. He managed it by crouching close to the door.

Eventually, the lift got moving towards the hangar bay. Lieutenant Mack turned on her visor torch and the stark light filled the space. The grey skins of the Estral looked eerie and pale through their helmet faceplates, like they were rotting corpses found at the bottom of an ocean.

BK> They're scared.

JN> Not of us.

BK> Nope. They don't want to go to the lower levels of Isob-2.

JN> Maybe they won't have to. Not if whoever is in charge plans to let that planet buster off any time soon.

BK> They're in the dark like we are. Not just the soldiers – all of the Estral.

JN> Was that a Psi premonition?

BK> Not a full one. Just a hint.

JN> That has me worried.

BK> It has me worried too.

The lift took an age to climb to the hangar level. Usually, an airlift could travel hundreds of metres in only a few seconds, so whatever was afflicting this one, it was serious. Nation guessed it was running on backup power, along with the rest of the facility. Not only that, he was sure the backup power was failing or at least partially malfunctioning. Eventually, the lifts and doors would stop working entirely, along with everything else tapping into the backup generators. He had an unwanted thought.

JN> What if they can't get the main hangar doors open?

BK> Let's pretend that hurdle doesn't exist until we reach it.

The lift stopped and for a few seconds, the doors didn't open. Lieutenant Mack swiped the panel twice before the doors finally slid halfway to the side.

"Out," said Mack.

Nation was able to get through the doors first and he emerged into the hangar bay. It was far more crowded than last time and he thought there might be another six or seven large shuttles. In addition, a fully-fledged, older-style light cruiser, pushing five hundred metres in length, was parked against the far wall. The spaceship's upper section loomed over the other, much smaller vessels.

"What the hell have they brought that here for?" asked RL Griffin.

JN> Ideas?

BK> Beats me.

There were hundreds of Estral soldiers moving amongst the shuttles, dressed in their battle suits and every one of them carried some kind of armament. Nation spotted a row of plasma repeater artillery guns, along with crates of ammunition stacked next to one wall.

The Estral came from the lift and the lead alien spoke. "You will wait here."

"We would prefer to find our shuttle and leave," said Mack coldly.

"You will wait here," repeated the alien. This time the threat was clear.

"What's happening?" said Hunter across the open channel.

"These soldiers don't have the authority to simply let us go. They are waiting for Koltar-Reon or someone else," said Keller. "Then they'll start asking questions."

"They can't do this!" said Spinks.

"Have you had your eyes closed for the last two days?" snapped Mack.

"They don't have the right," persisted Spinks.

"Be quiet," said Nation, the steadiness of his tones unable to disguise his simmering anger.

Spinks shut his mouth.

It was an uncomfortable wait. Ten minutes passed and then twenty. Enny Hunter and Lola Fletcher sat with their backs against the hangar wall, adjacent to the airlifts. Keller stood impassively, exuding a calm she didn't entirely feel. Using the base comms antenna, she checked in with the SC *Gundar*.

"Teal, how are things?"

"There are actually fewer Estral ships here than when we first arrived, ma'am. A group of nine performed a lightspeed transit not fifteen minutes ago. Those which remain are pretending the *Gundar* does not exist."

"Any news from base?"

"Only what you know, ma'am."

Keller frowned. "They haven't responded to your updates?"

"Not that I am aware."

"Someone in high command has their head buried in the sand."

"I am not permitted to offer a subjective opinion on the matter, ma'am."

"Of course not. Anyway, we're evacuating, assuming the Estral don't conjure up obstacles."

"I can open those hangar doors if you require."

"It might come to that."

While Keller talked, Nation took himself off to explore under the cover of his stealth cloak. He didn't want to go too far in case the Estral commanding officer showed up, but he had some checking to do. There were plenty of Estral and spacecraft, but the hangar bay was large enough that there was no danger one of the aliens might stumble into him.

He located the shuttles belonging to the SC *Gundar* and the SC *Givens*. They were both sealed and with no sign of tampering. Nation was trained to be suspicious and he ran a quick diagnostic check over the vessels in case the Estral had planted charges on the hulls. He turned up blank on all known explosive substances.

BK> I just realised something.

JN> Don't keep me in suspense.

BK> What are all these Estral doing?

Nation paused and watched a few different groups. It dawned on him.

JN> They aren't exactly getting ready to leave, but they aren't heading to the lower levels either.

BK> What do you think that means?

JN> They've either contained the threat, or they've given up on containing it and are waiting for something to happen.

BK> That's what I think.

JN> What about that group we saw near the comms hub? It looked like they were heading down, not up.

BK> Maybe the orders just came through.

JN> Conclusions?

BK> I was hoping you would have some.

JN> I'll let you know.

BK> There are some Estral heading our way. You'd better get back here.

Nation broke off the neural link, ducked under a nearby shuttle and ran towards the airlift. He reached RRT Alpha at the same time as a group of twenty Estral. The aliens spread out in a semi-circle around the humans. These ones carried plasma repeaters, which were shockingly effective weapons at close-to-medium range and which could bring down a small shuttle if given sufficient time.

The soldiers were led by another Estral, this one close to eight feet in height. His spacesuit was identical to the others, except for a green, rectangular badge on the shoulder. He carried no gun.

JN> An admiral, or the Estral equivalent.

BK> Koltar-Reon must have been muscled out.

JN> I'm not surprised.

BK> Let's hope this new one is not well-informed.

The lead Estral made a rumbling, growling sound, to suggest he would happily strangle everyone in RRT Alpha if he could get away with it. His hatred of humanity roiled out like a physical wave and he snarled. Nation clenched his fists tightly. It was Estral like this one who were responsible for war after war, death heaped upon more death.

Nation watched and waited to see what would happen.

CHAPTER NINE

THE CONVERSATION BEGAN PREDICTABLY ENOUGH.

"I am Redar-Finor and you are human shit."

Lieutenant Mack quailed at the outright hostility. Not so, Lieutenant Keller. She took a single step forward and kept her eyes fixed directly on Redar-Finor.

"Shut up and listen! We are leaving here and you will *not* impede us! We will return to our shuttles and you will order the hangar bay doors to open."

For a human, this would have been a challenge. With the Estral it was different and if you didn't stand up to them – within reason and following a set of nuanced rules – then you lost face.

"Treat me with respect or I will destroy your shuttles and your spaceships afterwards."

"Your threats are unimportant, but here is my promise; the SC *Gundar* will annihilate this facility if we are not permitted to leave. Your spaceships lack the capability to prevent it."

"One ship amongst many," growled Redar-Finor.

Keller recognized the concession underlying the words – the

early exchanges of the conversation were over and now they might be able to move on to the details of an agreement.

"Our inspection is complete, though not to our satisfaction."

"There is nothing here to find, human."

"That is for our superiors to decide. You will order the hangar doors open."

Keller saw Redar-Finor's eyes narrowing. "I was told to expect fourteen of you. I count eleven."

The Estral had been waiting for the right moment to drop that one in.

Keller thought quickly. "They will follow later with our number cruncher and sniffer. We will send the shuttle for them."

There was a collective holding of breath. It was possible Redar-Finor was unaware of the murder of Sasso and Bonner, or simply might not think it important. The Estral played by different rules and it wasn't always easy to guess what they were thinking, especially the more intelligent ones like this admiral. Keller allowed her psi powers to brush across the Estral's upper consciousness and she saw at once that he knew. Redar-Finor was fully aware of the murders and though he was curious about the third missing member of RRT Alpha, the Estral didn't especially care one way or another.

JN> What's up?

BK> I'm pretty sure Redar-Finor ordered the murders. The only thing stopping him killing us is the threat of the SC *Gundar* destroying the facility.

JN> I didn't know the Estral cared so much for their miserable skins.

BK> Something's worrying him.

In the split second it took for the neural exchange to take place, Redar-Finor reached a decision.

"Go, otherwise I will have you killed."

Keller addressed the others across the open channel. "Move,

before he changes his mind. Don't act grateful and whatever you do, don't offer thanks."

They strode past the Estral soldiers. One or two of the aliens made aggressive movements with their guns. Keller ignored them, but a couple of her companions flinched.

"Lieutenant Mack, do you know which way you're going?" she asked.

"Yes, our shuttle is over this way."

They passed two Estral shuttles and then the group split. It was clear most of RRT Alpha were finding it hard to stay calm and Keller kept her fingers crossed they'd keep it together until they reached the SC *Givens*.

BK> Watch them.

JN> On it.

Nation followed the group of investigators towards their boxy, lightly-armoured shuttle. The Estral didn't attempt to stop them and most of the alien soldiers acted like the group of humans didn't exist.

"Here goes," said Mack, activating the shuttle's side door. It dropped smoothly open to reveal the brightly-lit interior. The readings on Nation's sensor told him it was much warmer inside than it was in the bay.

"Take off and wait for Lieutenant Keller's word," he advised.

"I'll be so glad to get out of here," said Hunter.

The group climbed onboard and the door closed behind them. Nation turned at once and jogged to where the SC *Gundar*'s much smaller, sleeker shuttle was berthed. Keller was already inside and the craft lifted off vertically, with Nation still fifty metres away. The shuttle hung in the air, with the barrels of its massive chaingun aimed directly at the place where Redar-Finor and his group of soldiers stood watching.

Keller spun the barrels up, without firing.

JN> Nice touch.

BK> It's the kind of thing the Estral appreciate.

The second shuttle was still planted on the ground. Nation focused his sensor to try and pick up how warm the vessel's engines were. There was too much going on in the bay and he got a garbled reading. He linked to its comms.

"How long?"

"Not long," said Mack.

Keller joined the channel. "I'm waiting for confirmation from the base mainframe that it's going to open the doors."

The shuttle carrying RRT Alpha finished its brief warmup and it, too, rose into the air. It was an older model than the one from the *Gundar*, but there was nothing slow or ponderous about it and it could carry many more passengers. The only thing it lacked was design flair and a nose gun, not that they'd be shooting their way through the enormous bay doors.

Minutes passed and Nation became progressively more concerned that the Estral were about to change their minds. His mood wasn't helped by another development.

"That light cruiser just locked on with its missiles," said Keller.

"It's locked on to us as well," said Mack. Her voice was an octave higher than normal. She was out of her depth and struggling to stay afloat. "They won't fire at us in here, will they?"

It would get messy if the cruiser launched high-explosives in the hangar bay. Past experience suggested the Estral didn't mind a few friendly-fire kills and would probably do whatever they wanted.

"Don't worry," said Keller soothingly. "It's only for show."

Just when Nation was wondering if the bay doors had a manual element he should go and check out, a siren started. The noise was loud and piercing, and it filled the bay.

"Got clearance!" said Keller.

Lieutenant Mack wasn't ready to be reassured. "The cruiser is still locked on."

"Ignore it."

Slowly, and with a deep, uneven vibration, the hangar doors slid apart. Nation crouched at the nose of an Estral shuttle and craned his neck to watch. There was nothing smooth about the movement of the alloy slabs and at one point, he was sure they would grind to a halt.

Keller didn't wait for the doors to reach the end of their travel. Once the aperture was wide enough for the shuttle, she took the craft straight through the gap. Nation knew she had skill, but seeing how tight the margins were left him impressed.

Lieutenant Mack was a competent pilot and nothing more. She waited fifteen seconds longer and then guided the larger shuttle into the upper airlock.

"Those missiles are still locked," she said.

The inner hangar doors opened completely and the two shuttles remained suspended in the upper space. Keller positioned her own craft to cut out the cruiser's firing angle. In reality, it didn't matter – the Estral missiles travelled so fast that their guidance systems might not be able to make the turn, but the detonation of the warheads would be more than enough to reduce the shuttles to molten wreckage.

After a short delay, the hangar doors began closing with an equal lack of speed. Nation watched the aperture become progressively narrower until he could no longer see the shuttles. Soon, a faint seam was the only sign of a join between the two massive pieces of alloy.

"I'll get you out of there," said Keller on a private channel. "One way or another."

"Let's hope you don't have to come through the base energy shield to do it. Anyway, this is too important a mission to leave unfinished, whatever it takes."

"They're opening the outer doors. If we're lucky, the orbiting Estral fleet won't blow us to pieces on the way back to our ships."

"Will the *Gundar* respond?"

"I don't know. It might have received high-level instructions that we're unaware of, telling it to do something else." She gave a short laugh. "I'll have a little look when I get onboard."

"I wonder how divided the Confederation Council is on this."

"Something to wonder about later. I'm outside the facility and waiting at an altitude of ten klicks for Lieutenant Mack."

"I'll wait until you're docked, then I'll hit the lower levels and find out what the Estral are hiding."

"Here we go – I'm heading towards the *Gundar*."

"How long till you get there?"

"A few minutes. You may as well get on with it."

"Good idea. I'll see if I can find an empty lift."

Nation left his position beneath the Estral shuttle and jogged across the floor towards the nearest bank of airlifts. There was no change in the level of activity since the shuttles departed, not that he was expecting the Estral to suddenly reveal a bunch of secrets now that RRT Alpha was gone. He crouched near to the airlifts and waited for an opportunity.

For some reason, he didn't want to commit until he was sure the others were safe and he hesitated. The comms had been quiet for Keller's vague *few minutes* and he assumed something was keeping her distracted.

"Keller?"

"Just docking."

"What about RRT Alpha?"

"Same. Well, Lieutenant Nation, it appears as though we made it to safety."

The link went quiet again and Nation was gripped by an unshakeable conviction that he was about to hear something bad.

"Holy crap!" said Keller.

Somehow, Nation knew immediately what she was going to tell him.

"What?" he asked, in case he was wrong.

"Just had word from Teal. There's been an Estral attack on our Istoliar plant on Sindar. There aren't many details yet, but it looks like the bastards have started another war!"

Nation closed his eyes for a moment, searching deep inside to find anything which might resemble shock or even surprise. There was neither. The Estral considered themselves proud, strong and superior. To the Confederation, they were a treacherous species responsible for billions of deaths on both sides.

"How the hell did they find Sindar? I thought they only knew about a handful of our worlds."

"The Space Corps' deep space monitoring stations can detect a dog crap on the pavement of a city six galaxies away. I'm sure the Estral can pull off a similar trick."

"I'm sure you're right. They must have got lucky."

"Enough to embolden them to attack us."

Nation switched to the neural link to save time.

JN> If we'd got that news fifteen minutes ago, I could have been on the shuttle with you.

BK> Sucks, huh?

In spite of the situation, Nation laughed at the response.

JN> What now?

BK> Teal has put the *Gundar* into stealth and taken the ship to a quarter of a million klicks out. It has orders to return through Primol-1.

JN> Damn.

BK> I have put a block on those orders and sent a message to base, requesting confirmation that they are happy to abandon personnel in hostile territory. The comms message will require more than one hour to reach its destination and then a further hour to return.

JN> There were a lot of Estral ships up there.

BK> They're scanning for us. Nothing I can't evade, as long as I'm not required to discharge the *Gundar*'s weapons. They don't seem any more agitated than when we first got here.

JN> Perhaps they are unsure of their orders. Where is the SC *Givens*?

BK> It's just this second gone to lightspeed. The Estral didn't take hostile action.

JN> Their high command kept everything so secret, not every ship in their fleet was made aware.

BK> That's my guess. If it was anything else, they'd have destroyed our shuttles in flight and opened up on the *Gundar* and the *Givens*.

Nation's Istoliar-biological brain churned through the possibilities. The Confederation had its failings, but it didn't abandon its people. *Whatever it takes,* he thought, remembering the words from all the way back in his training days.

Keller was equally familiar with the saying.

BK> I can have the *Gundar* blow that facility wide open any time you choose. You'll need to steal your own shuttle. I can't do that bit for you.

JN> There are too many unknowns to just start blowing the crap out of stuff.

BK> You think the reports of the attack on Sindar could be wrong?

JN> I'm sure they're right.

BK> It might be best to wait a short time, in order to be certain.

JN> Two hours should give me an opportunity to see what we missed here on the facility.

BK> Don't go too far.

JN> An airlift down, an airlift up, steal a shuttle and away we go.

BK> As easy as that.

JN> Yep.

BK> The ISOP doesn't work on lifts, does it? Anything that isn't a simple choice between open and close results in failure.

JN> You got me. I'll have to use the stairs to reach Sub-6 and hope the lower lifts haven't been locked down.

BK> You'd best get moving, if you aren't already halfway there. I'll stay here until you're done, whatever it takes.

JN> It's good working with you again.

BK> You too. As long as the Estral don't flush out my code from the comms array, I'll be able to stay in touch.

JN> Okay. Got to go.

One of the airlifts opposite opened. A group of Estral soldiers came out and no more got in. Nation made a dash for it and got inside just as the doors closed. He made a brief check to see if the deeper levels were available on the lift panel. They were still inaccessible, so he chose Sub-5. With his gauss cannon in hand, Nation stood against the rear wall of the car. He had no idea what the hell was going on here in the Isob-2 facility and it might not even be relevant anymore.

Either way, he was going to find out.

CHAPTER TEN

THE LIFT STOPPED at level Sub-5 and Nation waited for the doors to open, half expecting to find a battalion of Estral soldiers waiting to get inside. His power cells had climbed above ninety percent after his earlier use of the shockwave, but the continuous use of the stealth augmentation was a constant drain, bringing the recharge to a crawl.

There were no Estral waiting and he dashed through the room, heading in the direction of the stairwell he'd noticed the first time Koltar-Reon had brought him and Keller this way. The Estral soldiers he'd killed earlier were exactly where they'd fallen. The shockwave blast had been a fairly high intensity and would have finished off a bigger group than this one.

JN> They haven't moved these dead soldiers.

BK> I can't believe no one noticed they were missing.

JN> They know. This place is in chaos and I reckon they just haven't organised a party to recover the bodies. If they even care.

Nation reached the stairwell opening, just as four Estral soldiers ran through it. He pressed himself to one side and the troops sprinted past, their gauss cannons clattering against the sides of their armoured chest plates. Nation watched them meet up with another group coming from the opposite direction.

JN> Things are getting hot in here. I nearly got pincered.

He glanced at the sign overhead.

JN> Down to Laboratory Area 1.

BK> Lieutenant Mack warned us about the guards.

JN> Screw them.

The stairwell opening led to a landing area. Wide steps with high risers went up and down. Ice clung to the walls and a single lighting orb flickered wildly. Nation went carefully, finding it took an effort to get into a rhythm. At the bottom of this flight, he reached another, smaller landing, and the steps switched back on themselves. There were eight more switchbacks and on the ninth, the steps ended at an opening. He descended quickly, listening carefully for the sound of movement.

At the bottom, Nation sprinted into the room, with stealth modules active, and his shockwave augmentation charged and ready to use against the Estral soldiers he expected to find. He pulled up short and looked around.

JN> Empty.

The neural link didn't convey emotion, yet somehow Keller picked up on the nuance in that single word.

BK> You sound disappointed. Are you still pissed about Bonner and Sasso?

JN> Yeah. I checked their records. They were young and now they're dead. I shouldn't let it get to me.

BK> Since we're at war again.

JN> And now anything goes.

There wasn't much to see in the room. A single, heavy-duty door blocked the way ahead, this being the only exit. There was a large viewscreen on the left-hand wall and an access panel to the right of the door.

Nation activated his number cruncher and aimed it at the panel. The utilisation on his core cluster jumped to fifty percent. He overrode it and allowed it to climb to eighty percent. The lab guys didn't like it when he came back from a mission with burned out Istoliar processors, but they didn't want to deny him the capability in case it made the difference between life and death.

His sensor picked up the sound of footsteps in the stairwell behind him and he swore softly.

JN> I've got incoming.

BK> How many?

JN> Lots.

BK> Can you handle them?

JN> Don't know.

The footsteps came closer. The Estral were descending at speed, as if they had advance warning someone was hacking their door. Nation thought he would have to abandon the number cruncher in order to deal with the approaching Estral. Instead, the ISOP finished with the door security and the slab of metal rose into the ceiling. There was a long, dark passage on the other side, with green light at the far end. Nation sprinted through and smashed his hand against the panel on the laboratory side of the door as he ran. The door dropped down with an air of finality, leaving him in darkness.

The walls and floor of the passage were slick with moisture, and it was treacherous enough that Nation was required to take extra care. His sensor augmentation kicked in automatically and it was able to cut through the darkness well enough for him to see what he needed to. The sensor processor did its best to add artificial colour to the feed, but it didn't entirely remove the green tint from the images streamed into his brain.

BK> How about you let me tap into your sensor augmentation? Otherwise I'm blind.

JN> You can do that? Silly question. Of course you can do that.

BK> I'm up here, skirting around the edges of a hostile Estral fleet, yet with nothing much to do other than watch. Until someone orders me to start shooting, that is.

The latest Space Corps stealth modules were incredible and the Estral had yet to find a way to reliably penetrate them. Unfortunately, these modules were so expensive to manufacture only a few warships were equipped with the newest kit, the SC *Gundar* being one of them. Nation's stealth augmentation was a triumph of miniaturisation, yet it was nothing like as effective as a full-sized model.

JN> You won't do anything other than view the feed?

BK> I promised, didn't I?

JN> Fine, go ahead. No pissing about.

BK> That's done – I'm linked. Everything you see, I can see as well.

There was no discernible change to his internal systems. Nation ran a diagnostic and it flagged up no anomalies. Keller was a pro, no doubt about it.

The sound of the Sub-6 door opening made Nation twist around. He saw a large group of Estral, framed in the dim light from the room at the bottom of the stairwell. They didn't hesitate and piled through into the passage.

JN> Damnit, they're coming.

BK> They can't know you're there.

JN> They can guess well enough.

He looked to the front – the source of light he'd noticed earlier was coming from a large room. There was no visible movement, but he didn't have enough of an angle to see everything. He paused at the entrance and looked inside.

BK> Guard station.

JN> Looks like. No turrets.

BK> And no guards.

There was only a single exit corridor, positioned on the far side of the room and behind a clear screen of toughened polymer. On the far side of the polymer wall, consoles shaped like rectangular desks were fixed to the floor, with their viewscreens facing away. Multi-lens sensor units, mounted in each of the far corners, aimed directly at the three openings in the clear screen.

JN> They watch everyone coming through.

BK> Must be a really secure area.

Nation looked at the sensor units. They had no power lights on them, but that didn't necessarily mean they weren't operational.

JN> Didn't you say the lower level feeds were switched off?

BK> Yep. Those sensors won't be recording. They might, however, still detect you passing and trigger an alarm.

JN> It doesn't matter one way or another. I've got to go through.

BK> The exit door might come down if the sensors detect anything unusual.

Nation grimaced. The access panel adjacent to the exit door no doubt had top-level security on it. If the door came down, he'd be stuck using the number cruncher with a squad of Estral soldiers bearing down on him. He turned his head to better pick up the sounds of approaching troops.

JN> Sounds like fifteen or twenty.

BK> No point in trying to take them on.

The weight of the gauss cannon in Nation's hand reminded him it was there. With the Estral bunched up, it would be a devastating weapon, able to punch through the front soldier and all the way through the back one, with or without body armour. The trouble was, it was slow-firing and he'd become briefly visible every time he pulled the trigger. There was always a chance one of the Estral carried a plasma launcher and he didn't want to get caught out by rocket splash. The aliens were still about sixty metres away and he couldn't tell for sure what armaments they had.

JN> Can you use the Isob-2 comms antenna to get into the base mainframe and shut those sensors off?

BK> If you want me to. Every time I access their systems, there's a chance they might discover what I'm doing.

JN> What's the worst that can happen?

BK> They perform a detailed audit, locate my code and disable our access to the comms antenna. Then where would you be? Hmm?

JN> Point taken.

Without waiting any longer, Nation chose the closest opening through the polymer wall. He charged through at full speed, his eyes on the exit doorway fifteen metres away.

Immediately, he crossed from one side of the room to the other, the green light on the access panel changed to orange.

JN> Shit.

He put his head down and kept going. Nation could run much faster than anyone who wasn't packed with the Space Corps' most advanced augmentation technology, but he couldn't run fast enough to beat a closing security door. His brain – capable of responding far quicker than his physical body - registered the event in slow motion. A plate of metal moved from a recess in the left side of the doorway and sped across towards the right.

JN> Not going to make it.

Without warning, the door stuttered once, slowed and then juddered to a halt, leaving a two-foot gap to the side. Nation threw himself through the gap without slowing, put a hand against the wall to keep himself upright and sprinted on.

JN> Thanks.

BK> Wasn't me.

JN> Then what?

BK> Power failure. Everything on the base is screwy.

Nation ground his teeth together.

JN> I hate relying on luck.

BK> You should embrace it.

The passage ended in another, even larger, open area. This space was cavernous – at least two hundred metres from one side to the other, and with a ceiling twenty metres above. There were pillars of solid alloy at regular intervals, which reached to the stone overhead. Horizontal beams joined the pillars, supporting the immense weight. In one glance, Nation spotted the network of cracks snaking across the ceiling, extending as far as he could see.

The floor was covered at irregular intervals in a mixture of consoles, metal work benches, cylindrical analytical robots, crates, cabinets and also a rock grinder, with a long conveyor belt powered by Gallenium. Ice covered everything and it glistened in the green light. Shadows stretched their tendrils into every corner, making it hard to clearly distinguish the function of each object in the room.

There were two exits from each of the walls, including what appeared to be a bank of airlifts on the far wall. The sounds of pursuit hadn't faded, so Nation hurried into the room, hoping to lose the Estral amongst the piles of their own crap.

BK> Are you going for the airlifts?

JN> Not yet. Got to lose these Estral first. Waiting for a lift isn't the best way to do that.

BK> Any signs of Granol-42?

JN> Traces only. The largest concentrations will be lower down.

BK> You're definitely okay with toxins?

JN> The few parts of me which are still organic are completely shielded.

Nation squeezed between two looming analytical devices which were covered in screens and gauges. There was no sign of life from them, as if they'd been switched off and forgotten long ago. He was certain they carried their own power units, so their inactive state struck him as odd.

When Nation was less than halfway across the room, he heard the Estral enter through the passageway. He checked over his shoulder. He caught hints of movement and sound as the aliens picked their way through the many obstacles on the floor. Even with his stealth modules, Nation was grateful for the additional cover.

He noticed a console on his left, which was semi-circular in shape. It was powered up, but not connected to anything and it hummed quietly. There was a dead Estral slumped on the floor behind it. This one was dressed in a civilian uniform, which provided no protection against toxins or the biting cold of a base in which the temperature was slowly falling to the ambient of Isob-2's surface. There were no obvious marks on the alien's body and its thick hair and eyebrows were covered in frost.

JN> Strange.

BK> Yeah.

It wasn't the best time to take an interest in a single, dead Estral, but something caught Nation's eye. He stooped next to the body and pulled its arm so he could get a better look at its hand. The skin was black and split like it had suffered some kind of infection. The affliction spread to its wrist and then vanished underneath its sleeve.

BK> Can you analyse that?

JN> Yes and the cause is unknown. I'm not stopping to take skin samples.

He stayed low and moved on. He could hear the Estral clattering on the far side of the room and coming closer. They had no realistic hope of finding him and he was surprised they hadn't given up by now. The fact they maintained pursuit suggested they were certain of his presence.

The airlifts were close and more brightly illuminated than the rest of the room. To the left, was another exit corridor, leading to somewhere he couldn't see. He would have preferred to use the lifts but it left him vulnerable to explosives. As soon as the Estral saw the lift doors open, there was a chance they'd open up with plasma rockets or repeaters.

BK> There's plenty of time. No hurry.

JN> Stop reading my mind. I'm going for the corridor.

BK> There should be several banks of airlifts on each level, even if not all the ones we saw in the hangar bay go right to the bottom.

JN> I don't want to use the main cargo lift or anything near it. Those lifts will be crawling with Estral.

BK> Uh-oh.

JN> ?

BK> The main surface hangar doors just opened and two shuttles came out.

JN> They must know the SC *Gundar* is still somewhere close by.

BK> Yet here they come.

JN> Keep an eye on it.

BK> You should consider aborting.

JN> I've considered it.

BK> Okay.

Nation swore under his breath. He'd anticipated having a couple of hours to gather intel on what the Estral were keeping under wraps here on Isob-2. If the departing shuttles meant the aliens were preparing for an evacuation, that implied they were finished with the facility. They'd brought in a planet buster and Nation was absolutely certain they hadn't done so without the intention of using it.

He hurried on towards the exit passage.

CHAPTER ELEVEN

IF A BASE-WIDE ORDER to evacuate was in force, the Estral in the lab area hadn't received it and they continued their advance. Nation took a second to find out where the nearest ones were located. He saw shapes moving between pieces of equipment, still fifty metres away. It was hard to be certain of the numbers, but Nation got a feeling they'd been reinforced from somewhere – no doubt through another of the passages.

Without warning, something detonated twenty metres to one side in a flash of white plasma. The blast sent chairs flying through the air and nearly tore one of the consoles from its moorings. Nation dropped to the floor next to a support pillar and crawled rapidly towards his escape route.

A second blast followed and then a third. Shards of metal pinged away from the pillar above Nation's head and he was buffeted by a wave of hot air which his sensor advised him was in excess of two hundred degrees.

He thought frantically. There was no way the Estral were able to see him with his stealth activated, so the only reason he could imagine for this behaviour was that they had, in fact, been ordered to evacuate and had decided to throw a few explosives randomly before they left, in the hope of flushing him out.

Then, he saw it, high above, built into one of the support posts and in exactly the same colour as the surrounding metal. An octagonal arrangement of wide-angle lenses peered into the lab area. He moved his head and saw another one on the next pillar.

JN> Crap.

BK> Damn – ceiling sensors.

JN> The stealth augmentation has never triggered them before.

BK> The Estral tech doesn't stand still. The same as ours doesn't.

An object shrieked through the air overhead and Nation's sensor registered it as a plasma rocket. He threw himself behind the support pillar just as the projectile struck the wall thirty metres ahead, adjacent to the airlifts. It expanded into a vast sphere of incredible heat, and flames licked at the exposed leg of Nation's spacesuit, turning the material black.

JN> They know I'm here, just not exactly where.

Other movement caught Nation's eye and he saw an Estral snap its arm in a throwing action. A cylindrical object left the alien's hand and spun through the air, with a tiny blue light flashing clearly on one end. It sailed over the top of a metal cabinet, bounced once off the surface of a workbench and then rolled. The grenade exploded next to the pillar where Nation had been hiding only three seconds earlier.

On the far side of the alloy post, Nation ran hard, trying to estimate how long it would take the plasma launcher to recharge for a second shot. *Not long enough.*

He sprinted along an aisle between two chest-high workbenches, keeping his head down in case of any shrapnel. Directly ahead, a wide metal cabinet would afford him some cover. After that came a ten-metre open space between the cabinet and the exit corridor. Another grenade exploded to his left and when the percussive thump faded, he heard the roar of an Estral plasma repeater. White-hot gauss slugs left streaks across his periphery as one of the Estral soldiers strafed an area a few metres away. Bullets clattered into the hollow cabinet, leaving fist-sized holes on their way through.

Nation dropped to all-fours and crawled. He was just in time and he sensed movement and light from repeater slugs tearing through the air a couple of feet above his head. At the end of the aisle, he turned parallel to the front of the cabinet, which was full of heat-edged holes.

At the edge of the cabinet, he paused and looked around towards his destination. The airlifts were close, but no way in hell he was going to attempt to use them. The passage remained his best bet and he prepared himself for a burst of speed to reach it. A split-second after he committed, he spotted a dark-coloured, trapezoidal object about five feet in height on the far side of the airlifts from his intended escape route – an object which had been hidden from view until now.

BK> Repeater turret!

The gun was facing the other way and the spinning barrels jutted outwards. The turret had been caught by the edge of the plasma rocket's blast and heat shimmered in the air above the gun. From experience, Nation knew the turrets weren't equipped with particularly sophisticated targeting systems – they were a distinctly spray-and-pray weapon. This one was receiving instructions from the base security system and it rotated in Nation's direction.

BK> Run!

JN> Too late.

The gun began firing early, spilling tens of thousands of rounds into the lab area. A tall console unit was smashed to pieces and the cabinet was shredded into chunks of razor-sharp metal. The noise was tremendous – the turrets were designed to shock as well as destroy.

Nation wasn't sure what made him look. He saw the figure of an Estral soldier standing to one side of a support post, little more than thirty metres away. The alien had a plasma launcher over one shoulder and the weapon was aimed at the ground slightly ahead of Nation's path to the exit corridor.

Before the alien could fire, it was spun around and its body chewed into bloody pieces by the repeater turret. The launcher was midway through its warmup and the rocket burst from the end of the tube. The projectile screamed away, flew through the remains of the cabinet and struck the repeater turret dead-on.

Nation dived for the passage, where he was buffeted violently by a blast of expanding, burning-hot air. He was too heavy and his control units were too advanced for him to be easily knocked over. Struggling with the icy ground, he scrambled onwards until he recovered his balance and set off again, running flat-out.

He found himself in another corridor, a joyless path through the stone like all the others in this facility. It was the sort of place he imagined the Estral lived, worked and died, without recognition or thanks. There were doors on both sides, their access panels keyed to certain personnel. Nation ignored them and continued for another forty metres until he reached a place where another corridor intersected this main one. A left-right check showed nothing of obvious interest along either way. He got himself around the left corner and paused to get his bearings.

His sensor was doing its best to construct a 3D map of level Sub-6 and also to pinpoint his location relative to the banks of airlifts in the hangar bay. Blank areas littered the map, but he was reasonably sure the left turn would bring him closer to the projected location of the airlifts. He checked for signs of pursuit and saw no movement. He wasn't greatly reassured and set off, increasing his distance from the laboratory area, his feet pounding along the corridor.

BK> So much for *Covert* Ops. Why don't you put in a request for your division name to be changed to simply *Ops*?

JN> You should be on stage.

The corridor branched and branched again. Each time, Nation took the option he hoped would lead him to a way down.

BK> I was expecting a few more bodies.

JN> They probably got most of the dead away before RRT Alpha arrived.

BK> Yeah, we can't trust a word the Estral say. Especially now they've attacked Sindar.

JN> Any new details?

BK> Bits and pieces. Nothing confirmed.

After two more turns, Nation was confident any pursuers would not easily find him. He kept an eye out for concealed monitoring sensors, and found no security covering these corridors. There were many doors, all closed and all with low-level security locks on their panels. It would likely only take a few seconds for his number cruncher to break through one and he was tempted to take a look. In the end, he didn't want to give away his position. He was hopeful the Estral already believed him dead and he didn't want to start setting off random alarms.

His chance came in one of the passages he believed led to the airlifts. The body of an Estral was sprawled face-down across the floor, half in and half out of a room. The door had descended, presumably at the start of the lockdown, but it was prevented from closing entirely by the presence of the corpse.

JN> I'm getting readings of Granol-42, Istilin and Polysempe in moderately large quantities.

BK> Ambient?

JN> Coming from the body.

BK> He must have been down there when the accident happened. Or whatever it was.

Nation crouched and did a quick check. He found more of the black decay, this time on the alien's face and neck. For some reason, its eyes were unaffected and they were pale grey and clear.

JN> There's nothing in the data files to suggest refinement toxins would cause this.

BK> Can you see under the door?

The door had fallen with sufficient force to crush the Estral's legs and the remaining gap was only a few inches high. Nation put down the gauss cannon, pressed the side of his head against the cold ground and peered through.

JN> Looks like an office.

BK> Get inside and take a look.

JN> There's not much to see.

BK> You need to go inside.

Nation had worked with Keller enough times to know when she was on to something. He rose from the ground and got as close to the door as he could manage. The smell from his damaged suit was sharp in his nostrils. There was plenty of room to get his hands into the gap and he got a good grip. If the door was still held by its gravity controller there was no way he was going to shift it.

He gave it a go, pushing with his legs and straining with his arms. The door was damned heavy, but the Istoliar motors powering his alloy skeleton were up to the task. With a judder, it rose upwards. He grunted and lifted it higher.

BK> Ooh! So strong!

JN> Don't you ever stop?

BK> Nope.

When the door was high enough, Nation ducked under it into the office and awkwardly tried to lower it again. The slab of metal dropped faster than he intended and landed with a sickening crunch on the damaged legs of the Estral. He turned away.

JN> Let's see. What have we got here?

The office was furnished in the standard Estral style, which was extremely spartan. The walls were bare rock, along with the ceiling. There was a square of grey-striped material on the floor which was perhaps intended as a rug. Other than that, there was a simple, two-screen console, which sat upon a metal desk, in front of a metal chair.

BK> The console is powered on.

JN> I thought I wasn't supposed to try connecting to any of the base systems?

BK> You aren't. Check for anything stored locally on the device itself.

Nation moved the seat to one side and pushed it clear. An empty metal cup perched on the edge of the desk, along with a plate of something pale green which may once have been almost edible. Faint traces of Granol-42 on the rim of the cup set off a warning on his sensor. He knocked the cup onto the floor, while his eyes scanned the two displays. They were both switched on, with a few lines of text on each.

JN> A couple of menus.

BK> Go into Option 2.

Nation touched the screen and a new list of options appeared.

JN> Come out of there and go into Option 6. Or maybe Option 4.

BK> You're guessing.

JN> I'm sure there's something significant here. Find it.

In the same manner as the Space Corps, the Estral military had a standardized front-end to control many of their major systems. The dead Estral's console was working within the science research area of the software. Nation was familiar with the setup and he was able to navigate fairly easily.

JN> If you were hoping to find a journal of events, there isn't one.

BK> Keep looking.

JN> There are some output graphs here. I think they were taken from a monitoring system on the lower levels.

BK> And there's an efficiency curve.

JN> I recognize this. It's the same sort of check the Space Corps runs on Obsidiar-Teronium to see if it's stable enough to go through the refinement process into Istoliar.

BK> Call up the next curve.

JN> Well damn!

BK> There's the same efficiency curve, this time derived from Istoliar. The test was run less than four days ago.

JN> We know there's a refining operation here on Isob-2, but this still isn't enough proof.

BK> Is there any evidence of their yields or the output of the facility? Each one of their warships fitted with an Istoliar drive is a significant opponent and if they have twice as many such ships as our intel guys believe...

JN> You don't need to spell it out.

Aware that time was passing Nation checked through the information on the console and streamed the recording from his sensor off through the Estral comms antenna, to the databanks on the SC *Gundar*.

BK> Same old shit from the Estral. They never give up.

JN> There's some other stuff here. They detected a massive spike in Granol-42, at the same time as they experienced a drop in output from their Istoliar refinement modules.

BK> Explosion?

JN> Nothing to indicate one. This dead Estral here sent a

series of shut-down commands to the kit he was in charge of. Whatever he tried, I don't think it worked.

BK> He must have known he was going to die at that point.

JN> Yeah. There's something else - the time stamps on each of these charts look off.

BK> How come?

JN> I don't know. It's like the measuring intervals become longer.

BK> I have no idea what that might indicate. Maybe it's not important.

JN> Well, this all looks like everyone expected. A broken peace treaty and a failed refinement process.

BK> I've got a feeling there's more to it. I can't shake it – like this is a pivotal moment.

JN> They just declared war. That's pivotal.

BK> I dunno. Maybe you should come back to the hangar bay and we'll work out how to get you out of there.

JN> And waste an opportunity like this? Why don't I take a look on one of the lower levels and then we talk about evac?

BK> I don't want to be wrong and have you get blown up by a planet buster.

JN> There's no reason for the planet buster to be here, or for armed troops with artillery units. RL Griffin already speculated that there's been some kind of terrorist incident here. Maybe the Estral aren't as united as we think. Anyway, we've been working on the assumption that a planet buster is an overkill solution. What if it isn't? What if the Estral believe the only way to resolve the problem on Isob-2 is to destroy the planet? You said there's an 81% chance the facility will be destroyed.

BK> In that case, you'd better get a move on.

Nation found himself worried by his own words. He left the console and returned to the door. With effort, he raised it far enough to get under and then let it drop behind him. The gauss cannon was where he'd left it and he picked it up. His feet carried him onwards, away from the office. After another two turns he located what he was searching for, within a few metres of where his 3D map predicted.

BK> Airlifts.

JN> Unguarded airlifts.

BK> What are you waiting for?

Keeping a wary eye out, Joe Nation entered the airlift room. The symbols on the access panel told him there were no restrictions on these ones. He readied his gauss cannon, reached out and called one of the lifts.

CHAPTER TWELVE

THE AIRLIFT CAR WAS EMPTY. Nation stepped inside and accessed the lift menu in order to pick a floor.

JN> This one only goes as low as Sub-62.

BK> Makes sense – I bet they tunnelled out the other levels later and gave them a different access shaft from Sub-62, just in case some of our inspectors managed to get down there and stumbled on a few secrets.

JN> Sub-62 is sure to be busy. It's tempting to go for Sub-61 and find some stairs. It's easier to avoid opponents on stairs than it is in a lift.

BK> Do what you think is best.

JN> Level Sub-62 it is.

He selected his destination and the doors closed jerkily. The airlift took an age to begin moving and the light on its access panel dimmed. After a few seconds, Nation detected the lurch of the lift starting downwards. His eyes roved around the interior, searching for an exit route if it failed between floors. There was a hatch in the ceiling, with no apparent means of opening it.

Once he felt confident the airlift wasn't going to give up,

Nation accessed the Space Corps databank files relating to the Isob-2 facility. He'd already checked them out on the way from Primol-1 and this second examination didn't provide any greater enlightenment.

JN> The Space Corps knows hardly anything about this place.

BK> Yup. The Estral classified it as a civilian research facility, which exempts it from certain rules under the peace treaty. Even though it has military-grade hardware and security inside.

JN> Taking us for fools again. I've met a couple of members from the Confederation Council and they were both exceptionally competent individuals.

BK> Yet we've been weak.

JN> And now we have to fight.

BK> What do you do against a species that will never accept us as equals?

JN> I don't spend time thinking about it.

BK> Just do your job, huh?

JN> I'm not that shallow.

The lift completed its journey. Nation stood close to the doors in case he was required to make a fast exit. Whatever lay on Sub-62, it was unknown except for supposition, and he fully expected it to be crawling with troops. The door opened and he found himself looking into a square, bare-walled room, with a squad of eight Estral soldiers waiting for the adjacent airlift. A draught of sub-zero air was sucked into the car, bringing with it high enough concentrations of Istilin, Granol-42 and Polysempe to kill an unprotected human in a few excruciating minutes.

The timing was perfect – the Estral were evidently expecting a lift to arrive and were therefore not alarmed to see the doors of this one open. Nation dashed out before the enemy troops could crowd into the car. The moment he got outside, something felt wrong, but he wasn't able to put his finger on exactly what it was.

He waited briefly next to the opposite wall and watched the Estral. One of them carried a plasma launcher tube that had a larger bore than the usual version. Nation's augmented sight was good enough for him to make out the tiny letters on the tube's magazine display.

JN> Empty.

BK> He's been shooting at something.

The lift door closed and the access panel display showed the aliens were heading all the way up to Sub-6. Nation didn't give them another thought and looked around. There were three corridors leading from this room and his 3D map predicted that the central corridor would lead towards the centre of Sub-62. There were no signs, or any other indication of this level's specific function.

Nation stared along the centre passage, his sensor on maximum zoom. The lights appeared to be fully operational, but the miasma he'd noticed on the upper levels was far more tangible. It was like something from a dream, where no amount of illumination would clear the gloom from the visions thrown up by a sleeping mind. It wasn't so bad that it prevented him from making out the presence of a vast space three hundred metres away. There were indistinct objects, and he watched a large squad of Estral walk in front of the corridor exit. They vanished from sight, rather than turning in his direction.

JN> Time to go.

The air was biting, but there was no moisture to freeze. Out of habit, Nation kept close to the wall and watched out for more of the concealed security sensors. Another squad of Estral came into sight, once again crossing the opening and then disappearing. Nation stopped for a moment and listened carefully. There were sounds, but nothing he considered worthy of alarm.

BK> The time stamp on your visual feed is no longer in perfect synch with the clock on the SC *Gundar*.

JN> Ahead or behind?

BK> Behind. It's only slight. Enough to mention.

JN> There's a strange feeling down here – like the air is thicker than it should be and it's interfering with the light.

BK> I wonder if the Estral have been experimenting with phase technology.

JN> Stasis stuff?

BK> This would be the logical place to do the research.

JN> You could be on to something. The time stamps on those output plots I found on Sub-6 weren't right either.

Phase tech was something the Space Corps stumbled upon over a century ago, but lacked the capabilities to explore until many decades later. The substance Istoliar possessed such incredible power it could not only cast a spaceship across incredible distances in the blinking of an eye, it also gave hints about how to manipulate time itself.

The Faor was a tier above Istoliar and the Space Corps' brightest minds believed there might be many tiers above Faor. It was already known that beings existed in the universe which were, for all intents and purposes, godlike in their power. The refinement of the base material Obsidiar into these progressively more incredible forms was seen by many as the first step on a path which might conceivably lead to anywhere or anything.

There were others amongst humanity who decried this endless pursuit of new forms of power. Some believed that each step along the road brought a greater chance that these *transcended* beings might notice the efforts of mankind and become interested. It had happened once before and few people in the Confederation were left with any realistic hope of encountering a benign species in the universe. Bitter, hard-won experience had taught its lessons. In this universe, it was dog eat dog.

Nation came to the end of the corridor and looked into what was perhaps the most expansive underground space he'd ever seen. In all his many covert missions into Estral facilities, he'd never seen anything like this before.

BK> Whoa.

JN> Yes whoa.

The ceiling of the cavern was lost in the gloom high overhead and Nation's sensor was unable to get an accurate ping off it, only providing an estimate range that it was between two and three thousand metres away. The walls were sheer and the far one was just about visible at twelve hundred metres distant. There were no supporting pillars; instead, a bone-deep vibration was enough to alert Nation to the presence of enormously powerful gravity fields, designed to keep this entire place from falling in on itself. It wasn't going to plan and the vibration from the field was sporadic. He knew the power was failing and he didn't want to be in here if it ever went completely offline.

The floor was highly-polished stone and the space was filled with a haphazard arrangement of differently-shaped structures made from spaceship grade alloy. Some of these structures were hundreds of metres tall, with bases two hundred metres wide. They had doorways and loading ports, designed to accept huge loads fed in by the dozens of bulky gravity cranes and crawlers, all of which were currently stationary.

Hundreds of Estral soldiers were visible and they marched a left-to-right path across the floor. With them came artillery repeaters and plasma launchers, one of which wasn't floating quite straight. Nation craned to see where they were heading. The enemy passed through one of two routes between the buildings and were lost from sight.

JN> My 3D map predicts the cargo lifts are in the direction they're going.

BK> In that case, they're leaving. I can't see many walking the opposite way.

JN> Yeah – they're getting out of here.

BK> As it happens, the surface hangar doors are just beginning to open again. Rats leaving a sinking ship.

JN> Why is it sinking? That's what has me bothered.

BK> I'm sure you'll find out once you get deeper into the facility.

JN> The temperature readings from the walls of those buildings suggest they contain a crapload of Obsidiar.

BK> Look to the left for me.

Nation turned his head.

BK> See that thing on the back of that crawler over there?

The crawler was little more than a Gallenium-powered flatbed, fifty metres long, twenty wide and with a cabin up front. It was carrying a thirty-metre cylindrical object, which was supported by alloy blocks at both ends. There were signs of damage – the furthest block was melted out of shape and the cylinder itself had a series of wide cracks across it. Toxins spilled away from its surface. When he focused, Nation could just about make out a series of control panels embedded into the closest end block.

JN> It can't be.

BK> It is. That's definitely an Obsidiar detonator. A broken one, but the intention was there.

JN> This is a bomb factory?

BK> I think the Estral have simply been doing whatever the hell they like on Isob-2.

Nation checked his databanks. More than a century ago, humanity had detonated a massive stabilised Obsidiar-Teronium bomb, which had produced a blast sphere with a radius of 112 billion kilometres and utterly annihilated an entire solar system. The Confederation had not attempted to build another, only on the basis that the Estral hadn't come close to working out how to set off the necessary chain reaction required to produce their own version of the weapon.

Humanity would do whatever it took to survive, but some roads you just didn't travel until it was absolutely unavoidable.

JN> Mutually assured destruction.

BK> I've had a bad thought. We know the Estral already have plain old standard Obsidiar bombs, but what if they were trying to leapfrog straight over the Obsidiar-Teronium version of the bomb in order to produce an Istoliar version?

JN> I don't want to think about that.

BK> Well there are people in the Space Corps who already have. Do you want to hear the projections?

JN> I don't think I do.

BK> Part of me wishes I hadn't looked.

JN> I thought the one thing both we and the Estral agreed upon was the futility of bombing the crap out of populated worlds. They've had enough of it and we've had enough of it.

BK> Let's hope nothing has changed. Anyway, I'm sending this all back to base. It could be really bad news.

JN> I've got to keep going. We need to learn exactly what tech they're working on.

BK> And we still don't have a clue what the hell they've been shooting at.

Nation spent a short time studying the movement of the enemy troops and trying to gauge their mood. He wasn't sure what he expected to learn from them and the anonymity of their spacesuits made the task far harder. In the end, the Estral were as impassive as ever and he found it impossible to reach a conclusion.

BK> The fleet they have above Isob-2 has just begun deploying incendiaries, in what they hope is the vicinity of the SC *Gundar*.

JN> I take it you are not in the vicinity they think you are?

BK> Of course not. Their efforts are very enthusiastic.

JN> They're not going to tolerate having the SC *Gundar* in their territory now that hostilities have begun.

BK> This attack is probably meant to drive me away so that I don't destroy their departing shuttles.

JN> Don't shoot them down. They might ground the others.

BK> Okay. There is a possibility I may have to move temporarily out of the arc of their comms antenna, depending on how accurate their battle computer predictive algorithms are.

JN> Can the *Gundar* defeat the remaining ships in orbit?

BK> It wouldn't be a good idea to try. Teal predicts a 15% chance of success.

JN> That's with Teal in control.

BK> No, that's with me in control. If I left it to the *Gundar's* own battle computer, it's down to 3%.

JN> Better not try anything, then.

BK> Not for the moment.

Nation set off warily into the room. This area was certain to be comprehensively monitored, and he didn't wish to be discovered before he had a chance to find out what the Estral were working on. Try as he might, he couldn't spot a single security sensor and he guessed they were fixed to the higher parts of the walls or the ceiling. He didn't like the peculiar quality to the air, but if it prevented him from being detected, it wasn't entirely bad.

With the Estral soldiers streaming across the centre of Sub-62, Nation kept close to the walls. He sprinted to a squat crane and paused next to its pitted, unpainted flank. He rested a hand against it, expecting to feel the thrum of its gravity motor. It was quiet – either in a state of failure or switched off. He stared up past its solid Gallenium boom, searching for security sensors. There was still nothing visible, so he ran the eighty metres to the cover of a low building, following the curve of the outer wall to get there.

This next building was a monitoring station. Its sliding metal door was wedged open by a chunk of rock and, through the gap, Nation saw room for a dozen Estral to sit in front of a bank of screens. There were no aliens inside and the screens were blank. It gave him hope that the security systems had failed or were not being closely watched.

After the monitoring station came a long sprint to reach the next building, and he was required to skirt around a crawler, with its engine as lifeless as the one in the crane. When he reached the building, he saw it was of a modular construction, no doubt brought down the main cargo lift in pieces and fitted together by the cranes. It was covered in gauges and thick, inflexible cables protruded in a line a few metres from the ground, before vanishing into an adjacent, smaller building. There was a deep, low, humming sound which was nearly as thick as the miasma in the air.

JN> The cold is more pronounced here. There are traces of Obsidiar-Teronium, as well as Istoliar.

BK> I don't recognize the function of either of those two buildings. It's not like their design gives anything away.

JN> I think this smaller building is an Obsidiar power generator. I have no idea what the larger building is for.

Nation followed the wall, the chill beating against the artificial skin of his face. There were no Estral close by and he was sure that during normal operations, this area would be swarming with technicians keeping an eye on things. He looked at a few of the gauges – the majority showed no activity, whilst others were nailed on maximum.

A little further on, he caught sight of some more airlifts, which had so far been completely obscured by the refinement buildings. There was a single cargo lift, with no door. Its platform was on a different level, leaving the shaft open. To the right, were eight personnel airlifts and on the far side of those was a dark opening over which hung the sign *Stairs*. Estral soldiers came from the stairs in a constant stream.

JN> The personnel lifts are out of action. I can't see any lights.

BK> How'd they get the artillery up?

JN> It's coming up on the cargo lift. I can hear it.

BK> The cargo lift must be powered from a different source.

JN> I'm going to have to get down one way or another.

He hurried towards the cargo lift shaft. It took him to within twenty metres of the Estral soldiers coming from the stairs, but they weren't equipped with anything which could detect his presence. Nation had no fear of heights and he stood on the perfectly-cut stone edge to peer over. The cargo lift was coming from somewhere far below. He could only make it out indistinctly – enough to see that it was filled with troops and artillery, neatly arranged.

Nation stood for a few seconds and considered his options. He didn't like the idea of attempting the stairs with all the Estral coming upwards and nor did he wish to hitch a ride on the cargo lift on its way back down.

The choice was denied him. A creaking sound came from the shaft and then changed abruptly into a screech of tortured metal. The cargo lift stopped and suddenly tilted sideways. The artillery had onboard systems to keep them level, but the soldiers did not and Nation watched them slide towards the gap created at one side. Some of the troops clung to the artillery, while others fell to their deaths.

Just as Nation was about to turn away from the sights, the entire lift platform plunged away into the depths of the facility. A few seconds later, he heard the solid thump of its impact.

BK> Must have lost power.

Nation found it hard to tear his eyes away.

JN> Unavoidable death is my greatest fear. Did I ever tell you that?

BK> No. Is that why you're always nervous in flight?

JN> Yeah. Oblivion in a metal coffin.

With a sadness he couldn't understand, Nation stepped away from the edge. The stairs were the only way down to the deepest parts of the Isob-2 facility and it would be tough to avoid the soldiers coming up.

BK> We've got what we came for. Really, we have.

JN> You know the mantra as well as I do. Good intel is worth a hundred spaceships.

BK> So don't miss out on a chance to fill your boots. Yeah, I know the doctrine.

With a mixture of caution, resignation and determination, Joe Nation headed towards the stairwell and its hundreds of Estral troops.

CHAPTER THIRTEEN

DESCENDING the stairs was as much of a ball-ache as Nation anticipated. The flights of stairs were wide, but the Estral were big and they carried lots of equipment. The only thing which made the journey at all possible was the aliens' observance of personal space. It ensured that even on the busiest sections, there were gaps for Nation to exploit and he twisted and turned his way through the enemy soldiers. Once or twice, he brushed against one, luckily without blowing his cover in the process.

It was peculiarly quiet – the Estral didn't generally communicate much and whatever words they exchanged were hidden by the spacesuit helmets they wore. The loudest sounds were their footsteps and the occasional clatter of a metal weapon against the stone walls.

The depth of the cargo lift shaft had him prepared for a lot of steps and his assumption was correct. After each flight, he came to a wide landing and then the stairs switched back. Down and down they went, while Nation's positional systems tried to add to the 3D map of the facility. Before he reached the bottom, he was confronted by two separate problems, one of which was definitely serious, the other being an unknown quantity.

JN> Something's draining my power cells. Their reserves are trickling downwards.

BK> A leak or an active drain?

JN> I've just run a system check and there's no leak. Something's actively pulling at the cells.

BK> Enough to cut the stealth modules?

JN> Not close. Not yet, anyway.

BK> You've also begun drifting more out of phase. You are now an additional tiny fraction of a second behind me.

JN> How much leeway until the comms cut out?

BK> I don't know if there'll be a problem. The *Gundar*'s comms array can cope with small variations...ah, you mean the Estral antenna?

JN> Which may not be so sophisticated.

BK> We'll have to hope the Estral fitted the good stuff to their base. After all, they must have known they were going to start pissing around with products which have been proven to alter the timestreams of anyone in close proximity.

JN> Keep me informed.

BK> Will do.

Damnit, thought Nation sourly.

The Space Corps had thousands of its best people researching the effects of altering the flow of time. That research wasn't advancing as rapidly as the top brass hoped and consequently there was only a limited quantity of useful technology which took advantage of time manipulation.

One thing which *was* known was that it was possible for pockets to exist in which time flowed faster or slower – Nation's timestop augmentation was an implementation of research in this field. An individual might pass through a fast or slow zone without ill-effects and without even realising it had happened.

However, when there was too much discrepancy between *normal* time and *altered* time, whoever was in the altered time zone would simply disappear until he or she emerged once again into normal time.

Long before he reached the entrance to Sub-63, Nation heard the bass rumbling of plasma detonations somewhere below. He wasn't in the best place to stop and figure out the details, so he kept moving, working his way in the opposite direction to the Estral. At one of the landings, he was able to make use of a gap in the flow of alien troops to pause and evaluate. The explosions made an overlapping series of booms, leaving him sure there was an artillery bombardment going on.

At last, Nation saw the entrance to level Sub-63 at the end of one of the flights of stairs. There was no door, simply a square opening in the wall, wide enough to permit six or seven Estral to walk through abreast. This was completely unknown territory and, as Nation descended the last few steps, he experienced an unexpected nervousness at what he would find.

The booming increased markedly in volume when he reached the Sub-63 landing. To his left, the steps switched back again and continued down. There were Estral coming from below and others coming from level Sub-63 itself.

BK> I just ran a predictive model on the frequency of Estral you're passing. There are fewer of them coming now than when you started down.

JN> You ran a model just for that?

BK> I'm trying to be useful, okay?

Nation smiled to himself.

JN> Their withdrawal is coming towards completion.

BK> Yep. Get a move on.

Through the doorway, Nation found himself in another large space, five hundred metres across and with a ceiling fifty metres high. The uncertain thrum of a failing Gallenium generator underlay the thunder of plasma explosions. There was a lot to take in, but the first thing Nation did was cut left from the doorway and run across the level stone floor, in order to get away from the ebbing stream of Estral leaving the area.

The source of the blasts wasn't difficult to locate – in the centre of the room, Nation saw a huge, circular shaft, with a diameter of two hundred metres. Artillery in the form of plasma launchers, and a few repeaters, surrounded the shaft, spewing rockets and projectiles into the hole. The brightness of the plasma fires was intense and constant, whilst shockwaves from the sound buffeted Nation's body. Underfoot, he felt the ground shake with the force of the blasts.

JN> I imagine this is what hell is like.

BK> All that plasma light is really screwing up your sensor feed.

Nation caught sight of an ominous shape. The planet buster bomb had been left to one side of the cargo lift shaft and it lay on its longest face, unguarded, like it had been dumped her and forgotten.

JN> They have a field generator holding this place up. I can't see where it is, but I can hear it failing.

BK> Once that goes, that entire level will fall in and possibly the levels above it.

JN> Yeah, there's no way this rock would hold against the shocks from that artillery.

BK> What the hell are the Estral doing? That was rhetorical, by the way.

JN> I'm going to have a look at this planet buster first and then I'll check what's in the central shaft.

From his current position, Nation didn't have an angle to make out the bomb's control panel, so he ran over to it to find out if the Estral had set it on a countdown.

JN> Online but inactive.

BK> Ready to be triggered remotely.

JN> I bet that's the idea. I'm going to the shaft – I can't see any Estral around the edges. They must have left the artillery to fire on auto until it runs dry of ammo.

BK> How are your power cells?

JN> 75%.

BK> Not good.

Nation turned towards the central pit, desperately curious to find out what it was that the Estral judged so dangerous they decided to bombard it with artillery. He jogged cautiously across the floor, avoiding the wide cracks in the stone. Once or twice, he saw rock dust come from the ceiling, where it created thick clouds which floated in the pockets of harsh, uneven light. Stone chips rattled off the ground nearby, followed by another, larger shower of rock fragments.

JN> The roof is going to come down.

BK> Get out of there.

JN> Soon.

The heat increased with each footstep. It caused the damaged material of his spacesuit to smoulder and waves of it beat against the lab-made skin of his face. He ignored it and kept focus on the array of artillery the Estral had brought here. By the time he was close to the lip of the shaft opening, Nation had counted as many as forty heavy weapons in a ring around it. More than half had fallen silent, their magazines empty. The others continued with their combination of rocket and projectile fire.

Nation stood at the edge, near to the still shape of a multi-barrelled repeater. Below, it was incredibly bright and his sensor augmentation cut out the glare, to allow him to see into the depths. The view was like staring into an abyssal pit.

The shaft cut through the rock for hundreds of metres, maybe thousands. The bottom was a maelstrom of churning plasma fire.

Further up, the rock was tinged with oranges and reds. He could see the movement of the molten rock as it slid deeper into the shaft. Near to the top, it was like a furnace, but not so hot that the rock had melted. The walls here were not the same grey colour as the rest of Isob-2. Instead, they were black as night.

BK> That is – or was – an Obsidiar centrifuge. You need one to complete the early stages of the refinement.

JN> It doesn't seem like there's anything down there.

BK> You've jumped even more out of phase since you got to that shaft. Maybe the Estral have left something volatile at the bottom.

Whatever unwanted by-products the centrifuge might have produced, Nation wasn't aware of anything which required artillery to suppress.

JN> Maybe they've created something really cold and only heat can keep it stable.

BK> There's nothing in the Space Corps databanks which matches that description.

JN> Is that the polite way of telling me I'm talking crap?

BK> I'm saying nothing. Anyway, you've been in Isob-2 for thirty minutes. It might be time to steal a shuttle.

Nation stared into the depths for a few moments longer. He was on the verge of breaking off, when he thought he saw *something* amongst the flames. It was like a creeping darkness was gradually asserting itself over the superheated stone. He blinked – a mannerism his eyes no longer required – and looked again. His mind cast up a thought and, in spite of the tremendous heat from the conflagration below, he felt a chill.

JN> I think there's something at the bottom of the centrifuge.

BK> What kind of something?

JN> I don't know – what do you make from my visual feed?

BK> Flames and Obsidiar walls.

JN> Yeah, that must be it.

BK> Come back, Joe.

With a backward glance, Nation turned away from the centrifuge. He was already ten paces away when he noticed a reduction in the quantity of discharges from the artillery. His feet slowed and he stopped. Seven or eight of the plasma launchers had suddenly fallen silent, as though the Estral had set them on auto at the same time and now they were all out of ammunition.

An irresistible curiosity drew Nation back to the edge of the centrifuge and once more, his eyes reached into the depths. This time it was unmistakeable. There was something doing its best to suppress the plasma light and, with the artillery running out of ammunition, the tide was turning. Blackness reached upwards. Tendrils of it intertwined with the flames, climbing ever higher up the sides of the centrifuge. There was no reduction in the intense heat and Nation was unable to determine if whatever he bore witness to was crushing the flames, or if it was simply climbing through them.

Nation stood motionless for seconds, aware it was past time to leave. This time, he did leave, and hurried away towards the exit. He was still a good distance from the doorway, when he experienced a strange sensation – it was like something pulling at the edges of his consciousness, felt and not heard. Whatever it was, no sensory input registered on his processing cores. It was unpleasant - an unavoidable invasion of his privacy and it whispered with endless, infinite hunger for something Nation couldn't comprehend. Worse, he recognized something undeniably hostile in the susurration and he shook his head angrily to try and clear it away.

BK> You're really lagging now. Three seconds behind. Why are you still there?

JN> I don't know. My power cells are at 53%. Whatever's leeching them, it's doing it a lot faster than when I first noticed.

Keller's response wasn't immediate, owing to the time gap between them. In terms of neural talk, it felt like an age.

BK> We'll run a full diagnostic and audit once you're on the *Gundar*.

Nation increased the pace, just as the ever-present vibration of the Estral gravity field generator cut out entirely. He heard a tremendous, rending crack from above and looked up in time to see a massive slab of stone detach itself from the ceiling directly overhead. His feet pounded hard, carrying him away from the area of impact. The slab crunched against the floor, sending shards in every direction. One of them struck Nation in the shoulder, like a punch from an Estral prize-fighter. He grunted in annoyance and ran on, keeping one eye on the snaking fissures spreading like a maze across the ceiling.

The field generator grumbled and fired back up. This time its note was lumpy like a misfiring combustion engine and Nation was sure it would shut down imminently. He sprinted through the doorway and onto the stairs. His legs were strong enough to carry him up two at a time and he charged away from the centrifuge room as quickly as he could manage. As soon as he was into the stairwell, he experienced an overwhelming sense of relief to be away.

Endless stairs lay ahead and Joe Nation didn't slow.

CHAPTER FOURTEEN

LIEUTENANT BECKY KELLER felt at home on the bridge of the *SC Gundar*. It was slightly too bright and slightly too cold, but the feeling of being at the centre of this perfectly-machined alloy creation with its Istoliar drive and its seemingly endless potential, fulfilled a need she couldn't put words to.

Probably one for the psych team to figure out, she thought drily.

She estimated there was a total of eleven Estral warships in the vicinity of Isob-2. Some had left to be replaced by others, and she had the suspicion one or two with advanced stealth modules lurked somewhere out there.

At the moment, the *Gundar* was a quarter of a million kilometres from Isob-2 and at the furthest extent of the wide transmission arc of the facility's secondary comms antenna. Keller wanted to keep in close contact with Nation, aware that he might need immediate advice while he made a dash for the upper level hangar bay.

The visible Estral ships threw out a continuous barrage of guided incendiaries, in the hope they'd land one of them on the

Gundar's shield. These incendiaries were little more than high-yield plasma bombs which contained fragments of unstable Obsidiar. They could produce a blast sphere anywhere from ten thousand to eighty thousand kilometres in diameter. As far as flushing out stealthed ships went, the weapons were not greatly efficient.

"Those last two incendiaries came to within twenty thousand kilometres of our shield," announced Teal. "Their predictive algorithms are becoming gradually more accurate."

Keller hardly glanced at the sensor feed of the explosions. She'd seen the incendiaries many times before – they were carried on a propulsion section capable of travelling at a fraction below the speed of light for a short time. When they exploded, they produced an irregular fire which burned with a blue flame so deep in colour it was almost black. Where the flames contacted an energy shield, they would stick and burn with a greater intensity, highlighting the hidden spaceship and allowing it to be targeted with missiles, particle beams or whatever the hell else the Estral had turned out of their weapons factories.

"I would like to remain in comms contact with Lieutenant Nation."

"It is not wise to stay so close to the planet's surface, particularly with there being a planet buster in the facility. I will withdraw to a distance of one million kilometres, ma'am."

Three of the Estral fleet remained within fifty thousand kilometres of Isob-2's surface, so it didn't strike Keller as particularly likely they'd let off the planet buster soon. The time to worry would be when they left orbit. On the other hand, this was a good time to be cautious.

"Fine, take us to a million klicks."

The *Gundar*'s acceleration was immense. The output needle on the Istoliar drive flickered and the spaceship went past thirty thousand kilometres per second. Soon, it reached a position Teal was happy with and the AI set the spaceship onto a circular course that kept the Isob-2 facility in direct sensor sight at all times. Immediately, the Estral dropped a row of incendiaries at the midway point between the old position and the new. It was likely their sensors were beginning to fix on the *Gundar*'s trail of positrons, which were almost impossible to completely hide.

Aware that time was running out, Keller ran a check on the estimated time for a response from base. *One hundred minutes.*

BK> Hey, you still there?

JN> The Estral must have hot-footed it up the stairs to Sub-62. I didn't see a single one.

BK> It gives us an idea of what's about to happen.

JN> A full withdrawal. It's no surprise.

BK> The Estral fleet haven't slackened off their attempts to find the *Gundar*. They might get lucky.

JN> It's not going to be easy to get out of here.

While she took part in the neural conversation, Keller watched another four Estral shuttles exit the hangar bay. At a million kilometres away, the sensor feed was still pretty sharp. The small craft accelerated in tight formation across the surface of the planet, staying low in the misguided hope that the *SC Gundar* wouldn't detect them amongst the storms of dust. The three warships which remained close to the surface moved in close to the shuttles, using their energy shields to minimise the firing angle and thereby guard the transports from attack.

"I believe those shuttles intend to dock with a ship the Space Corps records believe is called *Vastiol*," said Teal. "A model with which our fleet had a single engagement in the final days of the Eighth War."

Keller brought up the file on the *Vastiol*. It was one of the earlier new-design models, partially shrunk down from the old, yet far more capable. The spaceship measured two thousand metres from nose to tail and was wedge-shaped with landing skids. Details of the single engagement suggested it had an early-model Istoliar drive.

"What else do they have out there?" she asked herself.

The *Gundar's* sensors recorded the details of every Estral ship they detected and Keller had another look through the spaceships in the vicinity of Isob-2. They were made up from varying shapes and sizes, but none were known to be fitted with an Istoliar drive.

"The *Vastiol* must be Admiral Redar-Finor's ship. Teal, what do you think?"

"The known facts favour that as the most likely probability, ma'am."

"I hope he hates the fact that we're the ones in control this time."

"There is nothing in our rules of engagement which prevent us from firing upon those shuttles."

"I know."

Keller had no intention of attacking them. A single discharge of the *Gundar's* overcharge repeater would be sufficient to destroy all four – were the enemy not currently out of range or protected by the three warships - but the Estral would be able to trace the beam to a point near to its source and she didn't want to betray her position. Instead, she ordered Teal to follow the course of the shuttles whilst still remaining in sight of the Isob-2 base.

It didn't take long to confirm her beliefs. The *Vastiol* emerged from the blindside of the planet, coming at high speed to meet the shuttles, its rear bay already open. The first of the transports docked whilst the others waited. Then, the rest followed. Two minutes later, it was done and the *Vastiol* executed a tight turn, activating its stealth modules as it did so. The Estral warship vanished from sight.

"Can you lock onto that?"

"Certainly, ma'am. The *Vastiol* is leaving behind a thick trail of positrons."

The *Gundar's* AI helpfully added a label to the tactical display, in order that the *Vastiol* not be lost amongst the others of the Estral fleet.

"With the planet buster so deep underground, Admiral Redar-Finor will be required to use the facility comms array to transmit the detonation codes."

"That is correct, ma'am."

"He'll be required to keep his spaceship in the arc of the antenna."

"No hiding behind the planet for him," said Teal with a note of satisfaction.

"If it comes to hostilities."

Keller accessed the Space Corps records on previously-observed planet busters. The Estral had deployed a few in the past and their effects varied little.

"We need to be half a million klicks from Isob-2 for safety," she concluded.

"Or closer if we are prepared to perform an escape into lightspeed."

"Let's see where the good admiral orders his ship."

Keller watched the tactical display with interest. The *Vastiol* accelerated hard until it was three hundred thousand kilometres from Isob-2 and at the extreme edge of the antenna transmission arc. Four other Estral ships converged on the same location. Three of these craft were varying sizes and ages, what the Space Corps would label as Class 3s, though the last one was equipped with enough weaponry to be more like a Class 2. Whilst these craft moved into position, the remaining six continued their attempts to hit the *Gundar* with incendiaries. If there were any more in the arena, relying on distance and stealth to avoid the SC *Gundar's* sensors, they remained unseen.

She received a message from Nation through the neural link.

JN> There are a lot of Estral trying to use the airlifts. Looks like it's the stairs for me.

BK> That's a long way to run.

JN> Yeah - I'm about eight klicks beneath the surface, according to my internal map.

BK> Maybe you should wait for the Estral to clear and then get in a lift.

JN> Most of those lifts are powered off now. It won't be long until the rest of the field generators fail and I don't want to be on Sub-62 when that happens. I'm guessing most of the upper levels are self-supporting and don't require generators to prevent them collapsing.

BK> You're the one who's there. I'm not going to argue with your logic.

JN> Besides, I don't want the lifts to break down while I'm waiting like an idiot at the bottom. I'll climb a few levels and think about trying the lifts again.

BK> Do you have any idea what you saw down there?

JN> I don't know. I'm sure it wasn't a by-product of an attempt to make Istoliar bombs, or even Faor.

Nation's words triggered something in Keller. She couldn't be certain if it was an insight into the infinite model of the universe, or something as mundane as a hunch.

BK> You believe it's another species.

JN> I haven't had much chance to think about it, but yes, I think there's a good chance it was something alien to both human and Estral.

Keller sensed something more.

BK> And?

JN> Whatever it was, it was definitely hostile.

BK> You'd be hostile too if the Estral fired a few hundred plasma rockets into your face.

JN> No, that's not it. This was something else. This bastard hated *everything*.

BK> Whatever it is, it's not going to live through a planet buster.

JN> I don't like it. Where there's one, there could be more.

BK> Something for Admiral Cody to worry about.

JN> He's got a war to fight.

BK> Not much we can do about that. You're not telling me something.

JN> Don't laugh, but I can't shake the feeling I'm being followed.

BK> I'm not laughing. Keep me updated.

JN> Will do.

Minutes went by and the Estral continued launching incendiaries, whilst the three escort ships returned to their earlier positions close to the hangar bay. Any faint hopes Keller had that the aliens believed the SC *Gundar* had flown elsewhere were completely dashed by the ongoing attempts to flush her out.

She kept in contact with Nation and used their neural link to watch the feed from his sensor augmentation. There were a lot of stairs within Isob-2 and Nation kept himself away from the lifts. He didn't mention the possibility of being followed again. Nevertheless, Keller knew him well enough to be certain he was worried and a deep unease settled into her, unrelated to the efforts of the Estral fleet to knock the *Gundar* out of stealth.

After twenty minutes, another group of shuttles exited the hangar bay, leaving only four plus the cruiser behind. These ones weren't treated to an escort and they all flew towards the main transport vessel Keller had observed earlier. The Estral lacked humanity's intense loyalty towards their soldiers, but they didn't exactly treat them as expendable. Consequently, Keller was reasonably sure they wouldn't detonate the planet buster until the evacuation was complete. Or until they considered it unavoidable.

A few updates trickled into the *Gundar*'s database and she read through them. The Estral attack on Sindar's Istoliar plant was a well-planned precision assault, designed to reduce humanity's ability to expand its warfleet. The attack also revealed new information about the enemy capabilities.

The aliens had arrived in five previously-unknown spaceships, each equipped with a lightspeed catapult, which allowed them to cross from Estral territory to human territory in close to zero time. They had bombarded the facility's defensive energy shield with sub-light missiles and high-intensity particle beams until the shield fell. Afterwards, they'd simply destroyed the Istoliar plant and used their lightspeed catapults to escape.

There were numerous overcharged particle beam turrets on the surface of Sindar, which had been sufficient to destroy one of the attacking spaceships and damage another badly. It was nothing which could be classed as a victory, since the Sindar plant produced a significant proportion of the Confederation's Istoliar. It also highlighted the fact that these new Estral spaceships were significantly tougher than any known model.

If a positive could be taken from decades of conflict, it was a mutual acknowledgement that wholesale destruction of entire planets, and the people living on them, was no longer an acceptable tactic of war. As a result, the people living on Sindar were still alive, rather than being reduced to cinder by Estral incendiaries.

With Lieutenant Nation still on level Sub-15, the Isob-2 facility hangar bay doors opened once more. Keller cursed when she saw what was coming out.

BK> I've got four more shuttles waiting to depart the facility. If my count is correct, that leaves no more transports in the bay and only the cruiser yet to leave.

JN> There's no way they can have completed an evacuation in that time.

BK> It must be so serious they aren't waiting for stragglers.

JN> Shit. That means they're going to set off the planet buster as soon as the cruiser leaves.

BK> Maybe I can delay them.

JN> How?

BK> By killing the one with the detonation codes.

JN> Sounds like a plan. Mind if I listen in?

BK> Nope. How's your stalker?

JN> I've seen nothing, heard nothing.

BK> And you still think something's wrong.

JN> I'm convinced.

BK> In that case, don't slow down.

Keller ended the link and checked the sensor feeds and the tactical screen. The *Vastiol* was a little over a million kilometres away from the *Gundar* and still approximately three hundred thousand above Isob-2. Its stealth modules were active, whilst the four escort ships left theirs turned off. It was a standard, outdated tactic to try and draw fire from the most important ship in a fleet.

Closer to Isob-2, the last four shuttles raced directly away from the planet's surface. As soon as they were clear, the Estral cruiser followed, rising vertically through the shaft at high speed. It reached maximum velocity and kept on going.

The tactical computer bleeped twice, alerting Keller to a deviation in the *Vastiol*'s course. Sure enough, the spaceship was on its way, with the four escorts clustered around it.

"The time has come to act. Teal, do you mind if I take over?"

Keller always felt slightly embarrassed to ask, but in a way the spaceship was so close to sentient it would have felt like a betrayal to simply go ahead.

"No, ma'am. There is a greater chance of success with you in command."

"Thank you."

With a half-smile of anticipation, Keller closed her eyes and made a connection with the SC *Gundar*. Her consciousness expanded into every one of its thousands of control systems. Information poured in through the Faor augmentation's interface and she *felt* herself become a part of the spaceship. Whilst her biological brain remained aloof, the Faor's near-limitless processing capabilities received updates from the warship's onboard systems far faster than the *Gundar*'s own Istoliar clusters.

The end result was a human pilot, with a level of intuition beyond almost anyone else in the Confederation, tied in with the infallibility and speed of the most advanced technology the Space Corps could produce. Lieutenant Becky Keller picked her target and prepared to fight.

CHAPTER FIFTEEN

BK> PRIORITY 1 TARGET: Estral ship *Vastiol*.

Keller gave the command for the *Gundar*'s Istoliar drive to fire. It took a moment to warm up and then it threw the spaceship into high lightspeed. Keller monitored the flight and cut the engine a tiny fraction of a second later. The *Gundar* re-entered local space, this time ninety-five thousand kilometres from the *Vastiol*'s positron trail.

BK> Exit into local space complete. Locking on to *Vastiol*. Max range of overcharge repeater = 99800 klicks.

The *Gundar*'s main armament had varying capabilities, depending on the range. At anything less than one hundred thousand kilometres, it was absolutely devastating.

The particle beam turret fired three times in rapid succession, each expulsion sending an invisible beam of energy into what appeared to be an empty area of space. The repeater was stopped by an energy shield and the *Vastiol* remained undamaged, still with its stealth modules active.

BK> Damnit, they have a phase-shifting shield.

The *Vastiol*'s battle computer caught up with the sudden attack and sent the ship into lightspeed.

BK> Target ship has entered lightspeed. Running fission model to determine its destination.

Almost every spaceship left an identifiable cloud of energy behind as a result of the transit into lightspeed. Any would-be pursuers with the technological knowhow could generate a predictive model from the cloud and from this model, extract the details of where the fleeing ship would emerge. Keller's augmentation had more than enough processing brute force for the task.

BK> Model 80% complete. Inbound phase-shifting missiles from Class 2 Estral vessel. The *Gundar*'s shields have absorbed three overcharge particle beams from the enemy warships. They've picked up on my location quickly. Shield capacity: 95%. Model complete, entering lightspeed.

Keller activated the Istoliar drive in pursuit of the *Vastiol* and before the phase-shifters could crash into the *Gundar*'s energy shield. The Estral warship hadn't gone far – only a billion or so kilometres off into an area of Isob-2's solar system that wasn't close to anything in particular. The *Gundar*'s drive shut off and it entered local space.

BK> The *Vastiol* is keeping within the antenna arc. Searching...

JN> Get the bastards. I can think of better places to die than this miserable piece of rock.

The fission prediction model wasn't always one hundred percent accurate, but on this occasion, it brought the *Gundar* to within twenty thousand kilometres of the *Vastiol*.

BK> Target locked, firing.

The overcharge repeater fired again and again. After the fourth shot, the power drain on the *Vastiol*'s shield was sufficient to shut down its stealth modules and the enemy spaceship abruptly came into view. It was seemingly undamaged, but Keller was sure it didn't have much in reserve.

The *Vastiol*'s four escort ships appeared from lightspeed and started firing at once.

BK> Targeting Class 2 vessel with stasis emitters. Success.

The *Gundar*'s stasis emitters made no sound, but they did produce a noticeable spike on the Istoliar drive's power gauge. The most potent of the Estral escort vessels was shut down completely. Every single one of its onboard systems went offline and its Obsidiar-Teronium drive stopped generating power. Immediately, it began drifting.

Before Keller was able to capitalise, the *Vastiol* went to lightspeed. She ran the fission prediction model and sent the *Gundar* after it. Once again, the enemy hadn't gone far, this time jumping to the blind side of Isob-2. If Keller had been using sensors to track them, the tactic might have worked. Unfortunately for the Estral, lightspeed travel didn't care what physical objects were in the way. A spaceship simply appeared at its destination regardless.

BK> Targeting *Vastiol*. Firing. Damnit, out of antenna arc. You're probably not receiving this.

The enemy shields resisted two hits and partially absorbed a third. The energy from this third, successful repeater strike, was substantially absorbed, but it retained enough destructive energy to set much of the *Vastiol*'s right-hand flank alight. Sparks trailed from the damaged ship in a wondrous shower of orange, before they dwindled and died in the endless darkness.

BK> The next hit is a definite kill.

The *Vastiol* was granted a stay of execution. An inbound comms request from the Estral vessel made Keller pause and she opened a channel. Redar-Finor sounded pissed, as well he might in the circumstances.

"If you destroy my ship, you will allow the Antaron to escape."

"What is the Antaron?"

"We believe it seeks Istoliar. There is a planet buster bomb in the Isob-2 facility. Only I have the codes."

"How will the Antaron get away? How did it get here?"

"I don't know, human. Let me destroy the planet."

In the few seconds they'd been talking, six Estral warships appeared from their own lightspeed jumps and at varying distances from the *Gundar*. They didn't attempt diplomacy and filled the area with incendiaries in the hope of bringing the *Gundar* out of stealth. The Estral got lucky and one of the incendiary cannisters burst apart, scattering an enormous quantity of self-fuelling plasma onto the *Gundar*'s energy shield. The spaceship's Istoliar drive automatically fed more power into the shield and the reserve gauge trickled below 90%.

With the *Gundar* highlighted in an ovoid of crackling blue-white, the alien ships were able to target and fire. Keller watched a dozen missiles appear on the tactical screen briefly before they exploded. The Estral phase-shifter missiles carried a tremendous payload and, though they couldn't bypass the *Gundar*'s advanced energy shield, their detonations engulfed the spaceship in white-hot plasma fires.

It was Keller's preference to speak to Redar-Finor at greater length and find out what the hell an Antaron was. However, she couldn't allow the Estral to blow up Isob-2 while Nation was still inside the facility, and she had no intention of talking while the other alien ships shot the *Gundar* into pieces.

"Sorry, Admiral. No can do."

With a grimace at the lost opportunity to gather some solid intel, Keller activated the particle beam repeater again, before Redar-Finor could respond. The weapon fired once, heating the *Vastiol* so rapidly the entire spaceship was ripped into molten pieces. She fired the overcharge again, this time at the largest remaining section of the *Vastiol*'s wreckage. The destruction was complete and lumps of semiliquid alloy sprayed out in every direction.

With the main target destroyed, Keller set about doing as much damage as possible to the other Estral warships. The *Gundar*'s overcharge repeater connected with an Estral cruiser. This spaceship wasn't equipped with a phase-shifting shield and the beam cut straight through it. A single hit was sufficient to destroy the vessel completely, producing half a billion tonnes of molten wreckage. Keller re-targeted and hit another with the same outcome.

One of the remaining Estral warships entered lightspeed. Keller gathered the fission data but didn't waste any processing cycles producing a model from it. Another enemy ship launched a phase-shifter and dumped its remaining stocks of incendiaries.

The Estral ship jumped to lightspeed, a fraction of a second after Keller gave the same instruction to the *Gundar*'s Istoliar drive. When the *Gundar* exited lightspeed, it was back within the Isob-2 antenna arc and within three thousand kilometres of the planet's surface. The incendiaries were tenacious and they clung to the energy shield even after the lightspeed transit.

Keller ignored the steady drain on the shield and worked the sensors, searching for enemy warships. Of those she'd just engaged, one was within five thousand kilometres. Keller hit it with two rounds from the repeater, destroying it and sending it in pieces towards Isob-2's desolate surface.

BK> Unlucky for some.

JN> ?

BK> I had to kill Redar-Finor. Got to go.

Neural talk was very quick, but it did take a small amount of time, and Keller didn't have a lot of it spare at the moment. There were two other Estral vessels on this side of Isob-2 and two more jumped in from the scene of the recent engagement with the *Vastiol*.

Keller surveyed her opponents – the four enemy ships likely had an average time in service in excess of thirty years. They were the type of old, semi-obsolete craft which padded out the Estral's admittedly extensive fleet of spaceships. In sufficient numbers they could cause problems for some of the Space Corps' less capable craft, or, in mass combat situations, soak up a few hits meant for more significant targets.

Against the SC *Gundar*, they were completely outmatched. Keller caught two of them with the stasis emitters, knocking them out of the fight. The third one fired its particle beam, while the fourth entered lightspeed. Keller recorded the fission cloud, without attempting to run a model.

BK> You were correct to think that was a new species in the Isob-2 centrifuge.

She fired the particle beam repeater at the final operational enemy spaceship. It proved surprisingly resilient, no doubt having been fitted with a heat-dissipating hull, and it took a second shot to finish it off.

JN> What is this species?

BK> An Antaron. Fighting. Be right back.

Keller didn't enjoy shooting at disabled ships, but war was war. She destroyed the two affected by the stasis emitter, at the same time as she finished a sensor scan for the one she'd hit with the weapon earlier. There was no sign of this third spaceship. The stasis emitters could generally keep a smaller, older ship offline for a considerable time. They weren't quite so effective against the newer Istoliar-cored stuff, but there were no such opponents in the vicinity.

She accessed the fission cloud data from the two fleeing ships. The longer the intended lightspeed journey, the greater the effort was required to predict the destination. Keller ran both models simultaneously and cancelled the calculations after a few hundredths of a second. The fact there was no output after such an extensive modelling run meant the Estral weren't waiting anywhere close by.

BK> Finished.

JN> Already? What happened to *15% chance of success?*

BK> They were poorly trained, poorly led, or both. In addition, half of them cut and run.

JN> No Redar-Finor, means no bomb, right?

BK> Not necessarily – I'm running some checks and I'll tell you about it in a moment. Where are you?

JN> Crossing through the middle of Sub-11. It's a little more crowded than I was expecting. This place is falling apart.

Keller accessed Nation's sensor feed. He had his stealth modules active and was making his way through what looked like an office complex. She saw lots of doors, as well as an open plan area to one side. The power was off and there were plenty of Estral soldiers to avoid. Some of the aliens walked aimlessly in seemingly random directions and others were standing still, with their weapons lowered.

JN> They're aware they've been abandoned and they don't have any idea what to do about it.

BK> So they're waiting to die. Still being followed?

JN> I have no evidence one way or another, and knowing wouldn't change what I have to do. I'm just going to keep running until I get to the hangar bay.

BK> I don't like it. Something's bugging me.

JN> I don't like it either. Anyway, what about this bomb?

BK> I am certain there is no officer in the vicinity of Isob-2 with the authority to detonate a planet buster. However, I am in the process of checking known Estral command and control locations to find out where there might be someone with the seniority to make the decision and send the codes.

JN> And?

BK> Here we are – there is a suspected mobile space station thought to fly a route between Ganar-12A and Ganar-193F. If we assume one of the Estral at Isob-2 fired off a comms alert, the station commander may be able to transmit the activation codes for the planet buster.

JN> I'm not going to like the answer, but tell me how long this process might take if we assume the Estral space station is at its closest point to Isob-2.

BK> Outbound comms from here to there, eighty seconds. Another eighty seconds to return the transmission codes. If the station is midway on its route, you can add another twenty seconds to the combined total.

JN> So I'm relying on the message taking its time to reach an officer capable of making the decision.

BK> The wheels of the military.

The sensor feed showed Nation jumping and smashing his fist into the metal helmet of an Estral soldier which was blocking a narrow passage between two rows of tall storage cabinets. The alien was hurled face-first to the floor and Nation hardly even slowed.

BK> That must have hurt.

JN> I doubt he felt a thing. Are you going to send one of the *Gundar*'s shuttles to pick me up?

BK> No, I intend to land the *Gundar* in the bay. Escaping on the shuttle will take many extra seconds.

JN> What if the bomb goes off? I know it's a Retaliator class, but surely there's no way its shield can withstand the effect?

BK> Theoretically? Maybe. I promised I'd wait for you, which in my head equates to a promise that I'd get you away in one piece. So there you go. No arguments.

JN> I appreciate that, but I don't want to be responsible for you getting it in the neck from Admiral Cody.

BK> Cody looks after his troops. He'll understand. Besides, you probably cost as much to produce as a Destroyer. Maybe a repeater turret. Or a gauss pistol.

JN> Yeah, they won't tell me what the final cost came to.

BK> I'm surprised they didn't ask you to set up a payment plan.

JN> This is one bill the Space Corps can deal with. They're working me hard for it.

Keller ended the neural connection and continued to run a series of detailed sensor sweeps over the visible area of local space. It was still possible other Estral ships waited nearby, operating under the cover of their stealth modules. Each scan came back negative, suggesting she was either being overly suspicious, or the hypothetical Estral ships were equipped with newer stealth tech. If it were the latter, it was surprising the enemy hadn't taken the opportunity to join in the attack with the others.

An unwanted thought intruded upon Keller's activity and she felt her heart thump hard in her chest.

JN> You remember I said something was bugging me?

BK> Yes.

JN> Redar-Finor said this Antaron came seeking Istoliar. You are equipped with Istoliar power cells and processors.

BK> Assuming this Antaron was what I saw in the centrifuge, I don't want to meet it face-to-face.

JN> Get yourself to the hangar bay. I'll be waiting.

Keller had no proof that the Antaron had any interest in Nation. Even so, her muscles felt tight from tension. With her interface to the *Gundar* still active, Keller watched and waited.

CHAPTER SIXTEEN

LIEUTENANT JOE NATION'S escape to the hangar bay was not proceeding as well as he hoped. In an effort to locate a bank of airlifts which were not crammed with escaping soldiers, he tried to outguess the unknowable and cut straight across the centre of one of the lower levels, aiming for a place his 3D map estimated was directly below one of the hangar bay lift shafts.

The near-infallible positioning system built into his sensor augmentation didn't get the location wrong, however the airlifts he came to were disabled, out of power, or both. The cause didn't really matter, but it committed him to the stairs until level Sub-8 where the stairwell ended, forcing him to look for another way to the hangar.

There had been few Estral in the lower levels, but the higher he climbed, the more of them he found. They were listless and acted without guidance. Some of them simply sat, clutching their gauss cannons. Others he found in front of consoles as if they were trying to make contact with family members on other planets. These Estral knew they'd been abandoned and they were doubtless aware of the planet buster on Sub-63. In short, they knew they were going to die.

Nation had sympathy for the plight of the common soldier, but he had no intention of offering his condolences. Where the aliens got in his way, he killed them with surprise blows to the neck. On one occasion, he used his shockwave augmentation to kill a larger group blocking his way through one of the corridors. The shockwave took a lot out of his power cells and was something he preferred to keep in reserve.

Added to his other problems was the certainty that the Isob-2 facility was collapsing. Every so often, the floor shook violently beneath his feet, or his sensor registered a sound or a vibration from the lower levels. On more than one occasion, he noticed cracks in the floor and ceiling, along with several areas where the ground sagged.

Once or twice, he was sure he heard the whispering sound he'd first noticed in the centrifuge. It was so faint, the rational part of his mind told him it was down to jumpiness, and that he was imagining things. It was tempting to accept this easy explanation, but he'd never been good at fooling himself. Nation checked over his shoulder. Behind, he saw only stairs, walls and clouds of fine dust drifting down from above.

BK> Where are you?

JN> I found some more stairs and I'm heading up to Sub-6. The lights have been out since Sub-15.

BK> You've had your 180 seconds comms travel time. Now you're eating into the decision-making time at Estral HQ.

JN> There's only so fast I can run.

BK> Try harder.

JN> It probably wouldn't be wise, but I could try hacking into the base mainframe if I see a terminal. I doubt the monitoring team cares anymore.

BK> Here I am telling you to run faster. At the same time,

you think there's an unknown entity following you. And you ask if it's a good idea to stop? It's not worth the risk. Besides, if they flush out the code I left in the comms hub, there's no way in hell we'll be able to coordinate your escape.

JN> I just thought I'd mention it.

BK> Are you aiming for the security room on Sub-6?

JN> Not if I can help it. Anyway, I'm at the opposite side of the base.

The conversation was interrupted by a sudden, rending crack. Four steps ahead, a wide gap opened up, jagging diagonally across the stairs, passing by Nation's left side and continuing behind him. Nation felt the stair he was standing on give way and he sprang forward to the next. This one moved with the weight of his footfall and he jumped again and again, dropping his gauss cannon to free up both hands. With a rumbling sound, accompanied by the rattling of stone and dust, the entire flight of steps behind him dropped into the darkness.

Nation didn't slow and he reached the next landing at full speed. There was an Estral soldier here, a few metres away, with his pale, grey eyes visible through the visor on his helmet. The alien had his plasma repeater raised and somehow, he must have sensed that Nation was coming. The repeater gave off a sound like thunder in the confines of the landing and an arc of white-hot slugs tore through the air.

Nation's augmented brain could evaluate a situation with the luxury of time. He saw the alien's finger tighten on the trigger and he calculated where the first bullets would fly. Without hesitation, Nation threw himself below the deadly spray and rolled twice, silently. He reached up his hands and took hold of the repeater barrel. It was hot and the material of his suit blistered, but it didn't stop him wrenching the weapon out of the Estral's hands, the strength of the alien no match for a fully-augmented human.

With a twist, Nation got his legs underneath him and he surged to his feet, his weight enough to unbalance the Estral. He wanted to twist the barrel of the plasma repeater towards the armoured chest plate the alien wore, but the weapon wasn't made to be reversed. Instead, he bent the alloy tube almost double, hurled the Estral to the ground and sprinted off towards the next flight of stairs.

BK> Should have used the timestop augmentation.

JN> I had it under control.

BK> If you always keep something in reserve for emergencies, you'll never end up using it.

JN> Thanks for the advice.

BK> You're welcome!

Nation shook his head and hit the stairs at top speed. His power cells were at 40% and they dribbled downwards at a higher than expected rate. If the Antaron was responsible, it was close enough to suck out the juice and Nation desperately wanted to cling onto enough battery reserves to keep his stealth modules running.

He heard the distant sound of something unimaginably heavy crashing down and he saw more cracks on the wall and underfoot. He took the stairs two at a time, reaching the next landing in a few seconds. His map informed him he needed to climb three more flights until he reached the opening to Sub-6 and he grimaced at the realisation he might soon be buried underneath a few billion tonnes of rubble.

He found two more Estral on the next flight of steps. They walked slowly upwards and abreast, as if they didn't give a damn about the walls coming down around them. A chunk of stone dropped away silently, carrying one of the aliens into the depths and leaving an enormous gap on the left of the stairs. The other didn't even turn and trudged past the broken section.

JN> Did you see that?

BK> Bizarre behaviour. It's easy to forget how little we know about the Estral.

Nation wasn't happy to wait for the remaining alien to reach the top in order that he could get past. He ran up behind it and, with a twinge of guilt, knocked it off the edge. The Estral toppled into the hole and Nation saw it tumbling down. He swore at the sight of what lay below – the entire stairwell was in a state of collapse and he was only just ahead of it.

He made it to Sub-6, uncertain if luck or speed was the primary reason for his success. Once he exited the stairwell, Nation found himself in what might have been a storage area, with a high ceiling and distant walls. Long crates and anonymous metal boxes had been pushed haphazardly to the side walls to make room for the troops passing through. A large section of the ceiling had landed on a row of cabinets to Nation's left, crushing them and covering the floor in chunks of stone and dust. His eyes swept from corner to corner, but his sensor detected no movement.

The main exit was opposite and it headed in the direction he wanted to go. He dashed over, trying his best to make out what lay along the passage. It ended at a T-Junction and he turned right, joining a long passage with doors to either side. From his earlier experience of Sub-6, he assumed these would be offices. Everything was dead, with no lights on any of the access panels.

JN> Along here, turn right and there should be another bank of lifts and more stairs.

BK> There's no way those lifts are working, you realise that, don't you? Best-case scenario is they're still locked down from when RRT Alpha were poking around.

JN> I won't try the lifts. I'm going for the stairs.

Nation was almost to the end of the corridor when he noticed one of the doors ahead was inexplicably open. He slowed in order to look into the room beyond, and his eyes went wide. Through the door was another office, near-identical to the one he'd entered earlier. The lights were out, yet the room's console was operational and connected to the central mainframe. A timer counted down in the corner of one screen, showing how long until the console would be automatically logged out because of inactivity. Whoever had logged it in originally was gone and probably didn't care one way or another.

JN> That's about eight seconds in human time.

Nation heard another rumble and the floor lurched to one side. He glanced over his shoulder and discovered the whole passage was at an angle, as though a huge section of the Isob-2 facility had tipped whilst remaining intact.

BK> Get out of there. Now!

Nation tore himself away from the doorway, gritting his teeth at this missed opportunity.

JN> Damnit.

BK> We found what we came for.

JN> It's the stuff we didn't come for that worries me.

At the end of the corridor, he turned right and, as expected, found himself at one side of a large area with a bank of airlifts opposite and an opening for a stairwell leading up.

He paused in the opening, checking for danger. The room was similar to the other security station on Sub-6, through which he'd passed on the way down. Another one of the clear polymer screens cut the room in half, once again with three openings for personnel. Sensors peered from corner mountings, focused on two circular console stations. There were no guards.

BK> I count two problems.

JN> Three.

BK> The stairwell has collapsed and there's a repeater turret to your left which you have no hope of outrunning, assuming it's tied into those security sensors.

JN> And the lift is locked down.

BK> Hey, at least it's got power. It must run off a secondary generator.

Nation grimaced. He had to assume the security sensors were operational and that they'd detect him as soon as he entered the room. A split-second after that, the repeater would begin firing and he'd be torn to shreds before he could pass through the security screen. Afterwards, there was a collapsed stairwell to navigate.

BK> There's no alternative – you need to hit the repeater turret with your timestop augmentation and run through.

JN> That'll knock 20% off my power reserves.

BK> You should have plenty. What're you down to?

JN> 38%

BK> They're draining again?

JN> Yup.

BK> Why didn't you say?

JN> It wouldn't have changed anything. If I fall below 10% available power, the stealth modules shut off automatically to ensure the cells are able to keep my motors going. At zero percent, everything stops working until the cells recharge.

BK> What's the rate of decay on your batteries?

JN> If I use the timestop, the stealth modules will switch off somewhere close to the hangar bay.

BK> What choice is there?

JN> None.

BK> Then do it.

Nation targeted the squat, dark form of the repeater turret with his timestop augmentation and fired. The discharge knocked a big chunk off his energy reserves and the cells dropped to 17%. Across the room, a pocket of zero-time surrounded the Estral repeater. The gun remained floating on its gravity motor, but its barrels stopped rotating. In exactly twelve seconds, it would return to normal.

Nation sprinted across the room, vaulting over the edge of a console without slowing. There was no outward sign the security sensors were operational. If they were, he'd find out about it in approximately nine seconds.

The gaps through the security screen were wide and Nation got through the right-hand one. His brain took in the details of the stairwell. From the far side of the room, it looked partially blocked. Now he was closer, he realised it was completely sealed. There was a huge slab of stone at an angle behind the doorway, with more rubble on top. One thing was sure – the stairs weren't an option.

BK> That's not a natural collapse.

JN> The Estral must have blown the stairwell after they got out.

BK> They were scared in case the Antaron followed.

JN> Four seconds and that repeater is going to open up.

The dull-glow of the airlift's access panel caught his eye.

JN> You've got to hack into the base mainframe and operate those lifts for me.

BK> Okay.

Keller was quick and the lift panel turned to blue – open access – after only a few tenths of a second.

BK> There's good news and bad news. The good news: the lift is working and it's on its way.

JN> The bad?

BK> It's at the hangar bay and might take a few seconds to get here. Just in case the Estral flush out my code and the neural link drops, I'm bringing the *Gundar* inside in exactly five minutes.

JN> What about the facility energy shield?

BK> It failed a few minutes ago. Get to the hangar in five.

JN> Be there or be square?

BK> Be there or be lunch for the Antaron.

Nation turned so that he could watch the repeater turret. The edge of a metal console was in its firing line, as well as the clear security screen. He'd seen what one of these compact weapons could do, and he doubted it would take long for it to smash through both obstacles.

JN> This lift is taking its sweet time.

BK> Uh-oh. You're drifting out of phase again.

Keller's warning coincided with a noticeable drop in the temperature, which took place over the space of less than two seconds. It plummeted from minus twenty to minus sixty degrees centigrade and Nation heard the damaged material of his space-suit crinkle and tighten.

Twelve seconds elapsed. The Estral repeater turret rotated on the spot and its multiple barrels opened up with impersonal ferocity. Dense slugs crumpled the security console and continued through into the far side of the clear screen with their velocity hardly diminished. The screen was tough and it didn't break immediately. Thousands of bullets thundered against it, each one producing a piercing crack. The sounds merged into a single, horrendous drone.

The lift arrived with the muffled sound of grinding metal. The door opened and Nation hurled himself inside, taking cover against the side wall of the car. He heard the screen splinter and then crack. Repeater slugs hammered against the rear wall of the lift, most of them smashing clean through.

After what felt like a hundred years, the lift door slid unevenly across until it was closed. Still the repeater didn't stop. The doors were made of thicker material than the rear wall and they resisted the onslaught, though a series of dents appeared on the inside surface.

Under Keller's control, the lift began its ascent up the shaft with the groan of a failing Gallenium winch. The clattering of bullets died quickly away.

JN> That was fun.

BK> It was most definitely *not* fun.

JN> It'll be all plain sailing from here, eh?

He received no response.

JN> Keller?

"Damnit," he swore, striking the side of the lift car with his clenched fist. He had no idea if the Estral had detected the piggy-back code Keller left in their hub, or if something else had caused her to drop the link. He had a five-minute timer running and he checked its progress. He swore again when he saw it was still at four-minutes-thirty. When your brain moved fast, a lot could happen in thirty seconds and it was easy to assume more time had elapsed than was the case.

Lieutenant Joe Nation's day wasn't about to improve. The temperature inside the lift dropped steadily lower than minus sixty and the whispering sound returned. It was like having tinnitus inside his brain and he hated the feeling.

Even worse, his powerful sensor augmentation detected a new and entirely unexpected sound. There was a metallic tapping sound in the lift shaft beneath the car. It was impossible to get an exact fix on its distance owing to the rumblings within the Isob-2 base and the tortured sounds of the airlift's gravity motor.

Nation had visited some shitty places during his time in Covert Ops, but the Isob-2 facility was up there with the worst of them.

CHAPTER SEVENTEEN

THE TAPPING DIDN'T STOP. Instead, it increased in frequency and intensity, as though whatever made the noise was excited by something. Nation bitterly guessed what it was.

It's coming for the Istoliar I'm carrying.

The lift climbed higher, passing through Sub-4 and then Sub-3. Nation clenched and unclenched his fists, wishing he had a weapon of some sort. His power cells were at 13% and falling. Once his stealth modules failed, he'd need something other than his fists if he came across any hostile Estral.

Logic suggested any of the aliens which made it to the hangar bay would have escaped on one of the shuttles. Nation could never quite bring himself to rely on logic - especially when his life was on the line - and he fully expected there to be hostile troops waiting for him.

Something screeched against the underside of the lift and Nation felt the entire car shake from side to side. The screeching came again, like steel talons across a hollow sheet of iron.

JN> Keller?

The neural link remained dead and Nation punched the wall in frustration.

The airlift reached Sub-2 and kept going. Nation closed his eyes and hoped its power supply wouldn't fail. Whatever was in the shaft struck the car with tremendous force, buckling the floor. It happened again and the floor split, allowing Nation a view into the shaft. His sensor augmentation tried to understand what was there, but the only interpretation it could offer was one of solid, pure blackness, emanating a deep, numbing chill.

Nation stepped away from the breach. The lift passed Sub-1, just as his power cells dropped to 11%.

JN> If you're there, get into the hangar bay immediately.

Another blow shook the lift, splitting the floor open further. The overhead hatch caught Nation's eye and he wondered if he should try and get through. The ceiling of the lift was ten feet over his head – easy enough to jump, yet without anything grab onto. He crouched and sprang, hurling his fist into the centre of the grey hatch. His fist left a circular indentation in the metal and he dropped to the floor, leaving the hatch still in place.

The stealth modules will cut out at any moment. Not that the Antaron is fooled by them.

The lift shook once more and the panel indicated its arrival at the hangar bay level. The door crept open an inch or two and stopped. Nation pushed his fingers into the gap, leaned to the side and heaved. For a moment, he felt the resistance. Then, the door shot open, giving him plenty of room to escape. Without pausing to evaluate what lay beyond, Nation threw himself into the hangar bay.

3:30. *Damnit, that's too long. Unless...*

JN> Keller?

There was no reply and Nation sprinted away from the lift. His eyes scanned the hangar. It looked different from this side and it took a moment for everything to click in his head. There were no spacecraft inside, but the hangar wasn't empty. It was filled with hundreds of alloy cargo crates. They were arranged in rows and from their positions, it was possible to see where the shuttles had originally rested between them only a short time previously.

There were a lot of Estral in the hangar bay. These were the ones who'd reacted to the evacuation order too slowly and been left behind. If Keller hadn't killed Admiral Redar-Finor, Nation was sure Isob-2 would now be an expanding cloud of rubble and these soldiers reduced to atoms.

A group of five Estral milled near to the lift, looking for all the world like a squad of human soldiers killing time waiting for their shift to end. Nation was relieved to find his stealth modules remained active and he sprinted past the aliens, just as they began taking an interest in why an empty lift had arrived.

BK> Wh&:$%t

The reply left Nation confused for a split second, until he realised what it meant. The base mainframe had definitely flushed Keller's code from the comms hub, but now that he was in the hangar bay, his comms augmentation was just about able to reach Keller. The range was clearly extreme and the comms unit was receiving a corrupt version of the neural message. On top of that, he was evidently a couple of seconds out of phase.

JN> Get into the hangar bay! Now!

Nation wasn't expecting an immediate response and didn't get one. He ran hard, trying to put as much distance as possible between himself and the airlift. A row of crates ran from left to right in front of him and he cut to one side. From a distance and in the enormity of the hangar bay, the cargo crates seemed small. It was only up close that their true size became apparent – they were three metres high and deep, with many of them several metres long. They had codes stamped into the metal to indicate the contents. Nation lacked the necessary software to read the codes and he also lacked the time to go looking inside the crates for something useful.

BK> Co&/#es q1%///

On the far side of the crates and three hundred metres directly ahead, lay an abandoned, twenty-metre crawler with a huge, circular console cluster on the back of it. The crawler's gravity engine was offline and the vehicle rested on the hard ground.

The middle of the console was as good a place to hide as any and Nation made for it. Behind, he heard the distinctive, pulsing roar of a plasma repeater. He thought for a moment his stealth modules had failed and anticipated the feeling of hot metal ripping into him. Death didn't come and his stealth unit stayed operational.

He looked over his shoulder, in time to see the squad of Estral firing their weapons towards the lift. Whatever had followed Nation up the shaft, it hadn't stayed there. An undulating carpet of darkness flowed outwards onto the floor, spreading rapidly like a spillage of crude oil, except this was guided by a consciousness. The whispering in his brain resumed, as powerful as ever, and any doubts he'd possessed were swept away. This *thing* was coming for him.

The Estral evidently accepted their fates and they didn't move. The dark energy flowed around them and Nation saw with disgust how the material of their suits withered and crumbled, as though it had aged a hundred thousand years in only a moment. The Estral toppled as a group, falling to the ground.

Other Estral came running at the sound of gunfire, but Nation didn't stay to watch. His feet took him onwards until one of the crates blocked his sight.

The Estral were fully mobilised, their doomed lives given new purpose. They came from all corners of the hangar bay and Nation dodged his way between them. The sound of gunfire reached a crescendo and was joined by a series of thumping detonations. Nation recognized the sound as that of a mobile plasma launcher, which he guessed had been too late into the bay for removal into orbit.

With his power cells at 10%, he reached the flatbed crawler and sprang two metres onto its loading surface. The console looked brand new and cutting-edge and he had no idea if it was so valuable the Estral had attempted to remove it during the evacuation, or even if they were in the process of bringing it here before everyone started dying.

Nation's power cell reading changed to 9%, just as he tumbled across the top of the console and into the central space where the operators would sit. His stealth modules cut out, leaving him crouched, weaponless and vulnerable, in the Isob-2 facility hangar bay.

JN> Where are you hotshot? I'm going to die in approximately two minutes.

JN> That's assuming they don't blow the whole damned planet to pieces beforehand. I need a beer.

His original five-minute timer was still ticking dutifully and the reading showed two minutes ten seconds remaining. Nation did his best to ignore it and tipped his head back, feeling his hair rub against the ice-cold surface of the console. The equipment was utterly dead, with not even a buzz from its inbuilt backup power supply.

BK> &^dd!—Kj

JN> Yeah, whatever. Don't you ever run a spell check?

The sounds of gunfire continued, no greater and no less than before. Nation didn't know much about the Antaron, but he was sure the Estral weren't going to hold it for long. Their far more extensive efforts had failed, so a couple of hundred soldiers with launchers and repeaters weren't going to do the business.

BK> %^&qqzon't stand beneath the hangar doors.

BK> hn$$low intensity beam ^&& but yeah you don't $*&& drop it on your foot.

The corruptions in the link weren't enough to prevent Nation from understanding the gist of the message. He didn't need to move his head far to realise that he was offset to the overhead hangar doors. That didn't mean he wouldn't be crushed or reduced to carbon if Keller misjudged the particle beam.

A new sound joined with the others. This one was far deeper and much more resonant, and Nation felt it within the alloys of his bones. It was the groaning of an incredibly heavy slab of reinforced metal expanding and warping with the heat of an attenuated particle beam. There was an enormous bang, so loud it drowned out every other sound. Nation tried to guess what produced such a noise, and the best he could come up with was the upper door landing on the lower. Something told him it was about to get messy within the hangar bay.

Suddenly, the inner bay door turned from dull grey to a bright orange which bordered on white. Nation hunkered down, ready for the draught of blistering heat to wash over him.

BK> Coming in!

Keller was evidently aware that a second shot from the particle beam might produce enough heat to incinerate everyone in the bay. Rather than risk it, she dropped the SC *Gundar* straight down on top of the softened hangar doors. The Retaliator was incredibly dense and its weight pushed the spaceship clean through, punching a vast hole into the metal. To Nation's immense relief, one of the Space Corps' most advanced spaceships arrived in the centre of the Isob-2 facility.

With superheated air howling around him, Nation struggled

to his feet, only to be sent staggering by the colossal soundwave produced by the *Gundar*'s impact with the doors. He clutched the edge of the console and dragged himself upright. Keller must have been concerned that the *Gundar*'s energy shield might crush anyone in the bay, so she'd switched it off for this trick. Lumps of burning metal clung to the *Gundar*'s underside and part of the armour plating was flattened by the impact.

With a muted howl from its Istoliar drive, the *Gundar* dropped to the ground and landed with such force that Nation saw visible flex in its landing legs. He vaulted over the console and off the end of the crawler. The nose of the *Gundar* was aimed directly at him and its front ramp was partway down, with Keller holding it in that position until she was certain it was Nation coming onboard.

JN> On my way.

BK> What the hell is *that*?

There were several things Nation could imagine Keller referring to and he didn't ask her to elaborate. After everything so far, he wanted nothing more than to get away from Isob-2. His eyes fixed on the part-open front boarding ramp a hundred metres away and he ran for it.

Movement in his periphery made him look up, just in time to see a five-hundred-tonne chunk of red-hot hangar door detach itself from the edge of the hole made by the *Gundar*. It dropped quickly, landing between him and the spaceship. He swore and changed direction, passing as close as he dared to the smouldering metal. The smell of charring hair and cloth reached his nostrils.

There was something else to his left. His eyes caught sight of a spreading carpet of darkness. It seemed to rise from the floor, warping it and lifting the stone upwards in mounds, from which tumbled crates and gravity cars. The Estral were all dead, or at least he couldn't see any who were still alive.

JN> Shoot at the damned Antaron!

As soon as he sent the words, Nation knew Keller couldn't do what he asked.

BK> I can't! It'll kill you or bring the roof down!

Repeater turrets didn't have a physical recoil as such. Instead, when they fired, they expelled a separate wave of force to disperse the build-up of energy in the turret. A single, low-intensity shot in the vicinity of anything breakable could do plenty of damage. The expulsion after a full-blown overcharge round was enough to flatten a town.

JN> Lower the ramp!

The boarding ramp clunked against the ground and Nation covered the lower eight steps with a single jump.

JN> Raise it!

Nation felt the ramp lifting behind, bringing him up into the airlock space even as he continued to climb. A surge of acceleration pushed against his body, whilst through the narrowing gap he could see the floor of the hangar bay rapidly recede. Hot air was sucked inside just as the boarding ramp closed, sealing him inside.

It was tempting to spend a few seconds enjoying the elation he felt at the close escape. However, he had no idea if it was time to celebrate yet. Weariness wasn't something Joe Nation felt anymore, but a check on his Istoliar cells told him how close to failure he'd come.

JN> 5%

BK> Get up here. You want to see this.

Nation clambered through the airlock and into the *Gundar*'s nose section. A spaceship's Istoliar drive produced an easily-recognized high-pitched whine when its stealth modules were activated and he heard the sound through the walls. He braced for the transition to lightspeed, but it didn't come.

On his way to the bridge, Nation stopped in the tiny medical bay and waited patiently while a purple light swept over him a few times. There was no visible effect, but the bay computer announced he was now free from contaminants. Nation double-checked and his sensor located no traces of Granol-42, Poly-sempe or Istilin.

When he reached the bridge, he found Keller sitting in the pilot's chair with her head twisted to look at him. She gave him an enormous grin.

"You look like absolute crap."

Nation checked out what remained of his spacesuit. The material was blackened, split and torn. He pushed a finger into one of the gaps and saw that his artificial skin was mostly unmarked. There was no such thing as a vanity mirror on a fleet spaceship, so Nation was unable to check his face for damage. Keller helped out.

"Nothing that won't wipe clean," she said.

"Thanks."

"Sit down and look at this."

Nation dropped into the second chair, his eyes resting on the *Gundar*'s main sensor screen.

"And you stink," said Keller, wrinkling her nose.

"What she means is *welcome aboard,* Lieutenant Nation," said Teal.

Nation grunted a response.

The *Gundar* was already a million kilometres from Isob-2 and the planet looked exactly the same as before. Nation had seen hundreds like it during his years in service. The first few, you tended to notice the details, the striking bleakness of which most of the universe was comprised. After a while, they all looked the same. One grey sphere after another, with a trillion trillion others out there in the universe, so many that even the longest-served man or woman couldn't hope to see more than a fraction of them.

Isob-2 was dying.

"How long ago?" asked Nation.

"The ship's sensors detected the first stages of the reaction twelve seconds after I took us out through the hangar bay door."

"It might take hours to finish."

"I feel obliged to watch."

"I hate the place, but I don't want to see it fall apart."

In spite of their name, the Estral planet busters were subtle in their effect. Rather than shattering a planet with explosive force, the bombs undid the bindings of gravity, allowing a planet to simply fall apart. Sometimes the reaction happened quickly, other times it could take a day or more. The Estral word for the weapons translated roughly as *Disintegrator*.

The sensor image focused on the area around the Isob-2 facility began to shimmer, as though the array was imperfectly calibrated. The storms of dust whipping across the surface appeared to thicken, until they completely obscured the ruined hangar bay.

Over the course of the next few minutes, the dust became a progressively heavier cloak, until the entire visible surface of Isob-2 was covered. As the planet continued orbiting its distant, uncaring sun, it left behind a thick trail of tiny stones and grit. Keller piloted the *Gundar* afterwards, matching the speed of Isob-2's orbital track. The dust trail expanded and spread across thousands and thousands of kilometres as the planet shed trillions of tonnes of its existence every second.

"There's got to be something better to do than this," said Nation. "Why are we waiting here?"

"For a man who deals in death, you don't enjoy it."

"As soon as I start enjoying it, that's the time I quit."

"We're waiting to see if anything survives."

"You think the Antaron can live through that?"

Keller gave a shrug. "I didn't like what I saw on your feed."

"Maybe we should get back to base."

"Another few minutes."

"Thanks for getting me out of there."

"No problem. I promised, didn't I?"

"You did. To a lot of people that doesn't mean much when the going gets tough."

"How do you think that Antaron got there?"

"Beats me."

"Spaceship?" Keller pressed.

"There's was no sign of anything that wasn't Estral."

"It didn't just appear on Isob-2."

Nation sighed. "Look, it's dead and we can't keep a Retaliator out here watching a planet fall apart."

"This could be really significant, you know?"

"There's a chance it could be significant. On the other hand, a ninth war with the Estral is *definitely* significant. The facility is gone and we found what we were sent to find."

"I'll get the lightspeed catapult ready and take us back to Eriol."

"Still not happy?"

"You're right – we can't wait here any longer."

Nation opened his mouth to respond, when he caught sight of Keller's changing expression.

"What?" he asked.

"Something just came away from Isob-2."

"A sensor ghost?"

"No, not a ghost. It appeared on the edges of the array's detection range. Oh shit!"

Keller tried to activate a lightspeed transit. The speed of her Faor augmentation was such that her reaction time was as close to zero as could be measured by the Space Corps' existing technology. She was too late. The Antaron appeared with an immense speed that defied the ability of the sensor arrays to track it perfectly. It bypassed the *Gundar*'s energy shield and engulfed the ship, wrapping the rear two-thirds of the hull in darkness. Keller sent the spaceship into lightspeed and the SC *Gundar* tore away from the slowly disintegrating planet Isob-2.

On the bridge, an automated siren wailed.

CHAPTER EIGHTEEN

"ALERT, ALERT," said Teal in soothing tones which suggested everything was fine.

"I know there's an alert. Stop saying it."

"Can you turn off this bridge siren?" asked Nation. His hands roved, as if he were on the brink of pressing something at random.

Keller turned off the bridge siren, without interrupting her diagnostic checks over the warship's onboard systems.

"We've lost the Antaron, right?" asked Nation. "Nothing can hold onto our hull at lightspeed."

Before today, Keller would have agreed with Nation's tentative assertion. Not now. She tapped a finger on one of the monitoring screens. Nation looked.

"Istoliar core, 85%."

"And falling."

Nation sometimes pretended he didn't know how a spaceship worked. In reality, he knew a lot more than most, even if the bridge siren had him stumped. "A standard lightspeed jump only knocks off a couple of percent."

"We have an unwanted guest," said Keller grimly.

"I told you the Antaron was significant."

Keller ignored the comment. "It got through our shields – our *phase shifting* shields – like they weren't there. It covered a million klicks faster than anything this side of a lightspeed cata-pult and now it's latched onto us."

"It wants Istoliar."

"Just like the Estral told us."

"How long until it sucks the core dry?"

"Ten minutes at this rate." Keller's diagnostic check finished. "Crap. It's not simply draining the core. It's killing it entirely."

"You mean the Istoliar drive won't recharge?"

"Not the part the Antaron has already damaged. The rest will. Should. Might."

Nation cast his eyes around the bridge. The *Gundar*'s sensors didn't function properly at lightspeed, so there was no way to get a visual on whatever was happening externally. There were errors across every one of the *Gundar*'s main and sub-systems.

"It drained my cells, but they recharged."

"Maybe you weren't close enough. Maybe your cells are small fry and it wasn't hungry enough for them."

Nation cast his eyes up to the ceiling. "Metal coffin," he muttered. "I feel like I'm back on Isob-2."

"We're not dead yet. I'm trying to figure out what to do." She tapped the side of her head with a fingertip. "This is one thing a Faor implant can't deal with."

"Humanity still has a use, huh?"

"Yes it does, so please give me your ideas."

"The Antaron is cold. The Estral were keeping it in place with heat. Maybe we should hit it with the stasis emitters, followed by a couple of shots from the overcharge and see what it thinks of that. Or fly in close to a star."

"They are both excellent suggestions."

"Except...?"

"The overcharge isn't designed to be fired at point-blank range, nor are the stasis emitters. If I activate the emitters at such close range, we'll be shut down ourselves. I don't know what'll happen with the particle beam. I can't imagine it'll be anything good."

"So we'll fly near to a sun."

"Our energy shield will prevent the heat getting through. I could switch off the shield, but then we might burn up. A plasma rocket explosion is a hell of a lot hotter than the melting point of our hull, and those are what the Estral were firing at the Antaron."

"The lightspeed catapult takes fifty percent off a fully-charged Istoliar core. We're at 81%. Why not drop out of light-speed and see if our friend can hold on during a catapult run?"

"The catapult takes a long time to warm up. We're already past the point of being able to try it."

Nation threw up his hands. "This feels like one of those question-and-answer sessions I keep getting invited to, where there's always a senior officer with a counter-argument to every suggestion. It pisses me off!"

The words hit home and Keller's face fell. "You're right." She tapped her head again. "Too much reliance on this." She pressed her palm over her heart. "Not enough reliance on this. Let's do something to fix this crap."

Without any more talk, Keller cut the *Gundar*'s Istoliar drive to bring the spaceship into local space. A small node of her Faor core examined the sensor data and registered the lack of any input whatsoever. Not only had the Antaron held on during the transition to lightspeed, it had also spread itself completely around the hull, blocking the *Gundar*'s extensive array of external monitoring instrumentation.

Deep inside the *Gundar*'s battle computer, Keller's mind

spent a few processing cycles studying the activation commands for the stasis emitters. Her earlier words to Nation held true – they would knock the *Gundar*'s Istoliar drive offline for a short time and render the spaceship vulnerable.

BK> Maybe that's it! If the Istoliar core is prevented from generating power, the Antaron might leave us.

JN> We stasis-emit ourselves?

BK> I don't think that's the correct terminology, but in a nutshell, yes.

JN> Go for it.

Keller gave the command and the two wing-mounted stasis emitters fired. The effect was instantaneous. The *Gundar*'s Istoliar drive went offline, Teal lost power and Lieutenant Joe Nation slumped into his seat, his eyes open, but seeing nothing. The lights remained on and the bridge screens didn't even flicker, since they were designed to switch to a secondary backup system. Everything else ran off the main drive.

Keller flashed a look of sympathy in Nation's direction.

"Sorry, Joe. Maybe I should have mentioned that part."

Nation was fitted with a few plain old Obsidiar-Teronium backup cells which were there purely to kick-start his Istoliar main system. Keller had no idea how long it would take them to work. It was probable no one had thought to test this specific scenario and come up with an answer.

"He'll definitely be okay," she said to herself, with a sudden, crashing wave of guilt. "Definitely."

A few seconds went by and Keller drummed her fingers against the arm of her seat. Deep within the SC *Gundar*, its own series of Obsidiar-Teronium power cells and processing cores were doing their best to fire up the warship's main drive again. She monitored the process, unable to tell how long it would take. If it wasn't for the fact that she wasn't in a hurry – yet – Keller would have used her own Faor implant to speed things along.

The Space Corps had extensive documentation on the effects of a stasis emitter on a fleet warship, including a simulated scenario in which its craft were forced into combat with rebel-held or stolen spaceships. The estimated time for a Class 1 Retaliator to remain locked down by a stasis emitter attack from another Class 1 Retaliator was between nine and three hundred seconds. It was one of those occasions where the minimum and maximum where so far spread that the prediction was meaningless.

Twenty seconds so far.

The seconds ticked away and Keller did her best to accept her helplessness. She could monitor the *SC Gundar's* internal systems and maybe give them a push in the right direction if it became necessary, but she couldn't do much other than watch, wait and hope.

There were two scenarios.

Either the Gundar's drive comes back online and the Antaron is gone. In which case, yippee. Otherwise, the drive comes back and the Antaron is still here. In which case, boo.

At exactly twenty-seven seconds, the *SC Gundar's* Istoliar drive kicked into life, producing a noticeable shudder through the walls and floor. Having been offline, it would require a few seconds before it reached its full potential again. The Istoliar processing cluster which housed Teal came to life and she felt the AI checking the time stamps on the main data array as it investigated what was going on.

Keller accessed the sensor feeds and breathed a loud sigh of relief. Every one of the arrays was clear and receiving external data. She reached across and gave Nation a pat on the arm.

"I knew it would work."

Nation remained unresponsive and Keller wondered if she should connect and take a look at what was going on with his backup systems. He would never know.

"I made a promise," she said to herself.

The Antaron was no longer attached to the spaceship's hull, but it didn't seem wise to stick around any longer than necessary. She checked the Istoliar drive to see how much of its potential had been drained in the attack. It was at eighty percent and showed no sign of recharging beyond that. It would cost a lot to refit the *Gundar*, but until the Space Corps decided it was time for it to return to the yard, the *Gundar* was still an exceptionally capable weapon of war.

It was standard procedure to perform a random lightspeed jump away from the combat arena in situations like this one and Keller did exactly that. She chose a location and activated the Istoliar drive for ten seconds, before switching it off. The *Gundar* emerged once again into a place occupied by nothing more notable than dust. It was good to put the extra distance between the spaceship and the encounter with the Antaron and Keller felt as though she had a bit more room in which to think.

"The comms response from Fortress-3 is overdue, so if they won't come to us, we'll go to them."

Keller sent the command to warm up the lightspeed catapult. Its Obsidiar detonators rumbled and before the sound could die away, it was joined by a muted howl which cut through the dense structure of the spaceship.

The lightspeed catapult technology was proven reliable and failure rates were exceptionally low. However, the fact that not one of the Space Corps' scientists could honestly claim to know *exactly* how the devices worked, ensured the catapults had the power to engender a degree of fear in even the most battle-hardened officers. In Keller's mind, it was akin to riding a wild animal and hoping that when the beast ran out of steam, you'd be able to hop off right where you wanted.

The upsides were obvious. The catapult could open a wormhole from one place to pretty much anywhere in known space. If you targeted too far out, say into the complete unknown, the device simply wouldn't open the wormhole. Many questions remained unanswered and each question had a dozen associated theories – many of them officially classified as crackpot – about the reasons for this failure.

"Teal, we're going to Eriol."

"Yes, ma'am. My sensors indicate Lieutenant Nation is in a state of hibernation."

Keller rubbed her chin. She'd made a promise that she wouldn't invade Nation's privacy again. Teal had made no such promise.

"Wake him, please."

"Certainly. Commencing interface."

It was done quickly. Nation blinked once and looked around him. He lifted a hand and studied it for a moment, as if it were a stranger to him.

"We made it?"

"The Antaron is gone. The lightspeed catapult is warming up and we're going to Eriol."

Nation raised his voice to be heard over the howl of the catapult. "Great. How much damage did we take?"

"Just what happened to the Istoliar drive. Everything else is fully operational," Keller replied, equally loudly.

The muted howl of the lightspeed catapult reached a crescendo, indicating it would shortly fire. With a single second left before the lightspeed catapult threw the *Gundar* into the partially-unknown, Keller performed one final sensor sweep of the area, simply to occupy a few trillion cycles of her Faor augmentation.

She saw movement way out in the distance, several million kilometres away. It was a fleeting hint of a hint on one of the super-far lenses, exactly the same kind of disturbance that she'd seen coming from Isob-2. The Antaron was back and it was coming towards the *Gundar* at tremendous speed. There was something about it which made the sensor feed difficult to interpret, like the alien was hidden behind a frosted window. The only impression she got of its shape was that it was tapered like an arrowhead.

One thing was certain. The Antaron was *huge* – far, far larger than she previously imagined. It was thousands of metres in length and it must have weighed twenty billion tonnes or more. In comparison, the SC *Gundar* was tiny. Keller had no time to feel shock and no time to even forge a neural connection with Nation.

Now she knew what it was, Keller didn't hesitate. She targeted the Antaron with the particle beam, cursing the slowness of the Istoliar-cored battle computer, which seemed to take forever to accept the instruction.

In those few processing cycles, the Antaron crossed two million kilometres.

The particle beam turret could hit a target from as far out as five million kilometres – at such a range, the weapon might destroy a single vehicle on the surface of a planet. At thirty thousand kilometres - the range at which the Antaron was struck - the effects were usually far more devastating. In this instance, there were no fireworks – the Antaron simply veered off and passed a few thousand kilometres to the *Gundar*'s starboard.

JN> What's wrong?

Keller didn't respond immediately. She desperately tried to locate the Antaron, to find out where the hell it was and if it was damaged or simply distracted. There was no sign of it on any of the sensor arrays, but she wasn't at all convinced it was gone. Keller monitored each array simultaneously, watching out for anything which might indicate the Antaron was coming for another attack.

She did see movement. At the precise moment the lightspeed catapult fired, the Antaron showed up on one of the rear super-fars. Then, a wormhole appeared around the *Gundar* and the spaceship was carried across several galaxies towards its destination world, Eriol.

CHAPTER NINETEEN

THE LIGHTSPEED CATAPULT was a fairly accurate tool, something which had not been true of the earliest generation versions of the devices. The SC *Gundar* completed its journey through the wormhole and entered local space, eighty million kilometres from Eriol. In terms of the distance travelled, it was an acceptable result.

"You might have missed that, but the Antaron came back just before the catapult fired," said Keller, in case Nation hadn't realised.

"I wasn't tied in to any of the *Gundar*'s critical systems," he confirmed. "I did have time to wonder what you were doing."

"The overcharge particle beam scored a direct hit."

"Did you kill it?"

"No. We got away from it and I hope I never see another one. Not without a fleet of spaceships to shoot it to pieces."

In truth, Keller had a lot to think about. The Antaron had followed the *Gundar* though lightspeed and, while such a capability wasn't unusual, it did mean the alien was technologically advanced. Not that she had any doubt, simply based on its speed of travel.

Keller put the matter aside. It was entirely unheard of for pursuit to take place through a lightspeed catapult wormhole and it was easiest to believe the Antaron was several years' lightspeed travel behind them and with no way of following. She noticed Nation studying her. He nodded and she knew he understood exactly what she was thinking.

"It's in Estral territory. Let the Estral deal with it," he said. "We're back home, for the moment at least."

"Yeah." Keller paused, wondering whether to say what was on her mind. "There's something else. You said you heard it in your head, didn't you?"

"I did. It wasn't a good feeling."

"I sensed something similar, only I got more than hatred from it. I think it noticed the presence of Faor on the *Gundar* and it was...interested."

"Like a dog sniffing a crap?"

"I wouldn't have used those precise words."

"We've got to forget about it for now. We can provide all the details over the course of what I assume will be a thorough debriefing. I'm interested to discover how the early exchanges in the war have proceeded."

Keller wasn't to be distracted. "The Antaron has me worried."

"Yeah, me too."

With the *Gundar* at maximum sublight speed and heading towards Eriol, Keller checked in with Fortress-3. The base mainframe acknowledged the arrival of the spaceship and arranged a landing slot for them to set down. Keller handed control over to Teal and made herself comfortable with a cup of adequate coffee from the replicator. The *Gundar*'s sensors focused directly on

Eriol and the pair of them watched the planet, with its drab greens, blues and large polar ice caps.

"Not the most hospitable world in the Confederation," said Nation.

"I like it. It's good to be back." Keller took a sip of her coffee and suppressed a grimace. "Even if it's just for the length of a debriefing."

"Now we're in Confederation Space, the databanks should be fully updated with details of the war."

"I haven't checked," admitted Keller.

"Nor me. Sometimes it's better to hear a potted summary straight from the horse's mouth."

The words were prophetic.

"Admiral Scott Cody requires a comms channel," announced Teal. "I will open one immediately."

BK> Ever get the feeling we're not going to get our feet on the ground?

JN> Yup.

"Admiral Cody, sir," said Keller loudly.

"Sir," said Nation.

Cody did have fleeting moments during which his mood could be tenuously linked with the word *good*. Now wasn't one of those times.

"I've read through the outline reports you sent from Estral Territory," he said. "I'm not happy."

"What aren't you happy about, sir?" asked Keller.

"There's a damn war going on and you ask why I'm not happy?"

"I thought there might be something more specific."

Cody drew in a deep, shuddering breath, clearly audible across the comms. The sound of cogs turning in his brain was almost as loud and Keller imagined Cody trying hard to rein in his temper.

"My apologies, Lieutenants. I imagine you have only sketchy reports about what has happened so far and I'm sure you are desperate to hear what's going on."

"The *Gundar*'s databanks don't populate quickly out in Estral space, sir," said Nation.

"Quite right." Cody drew in another breath. "I don't have a lot of time, so here's a quick recap. The Estral attacked our Istoliar processing plant on Sindar, using a fleet of hitherto unknown warships equipped with lightspeed catapults. In addition, they staged two more attacks on other deep space facilities."

Nation caught the note of relief in Cody's voice.

"Dummy facilities?"

"Yes, Lieutenant. The Estral attacked and destroyed two of our dummy plants. In order to accomplish this feat, they used a total of nineteen warships with lightspeed catapults."

"The numbers are adding up," said Keller.

"My intel team have had something of a wake-up call. Every few minutes I receive a revised estimate on the number of warships in the Estral fleet which are equipped with lightspeed catapults." The sound of papers rustling came through the *Gundar*'s bridge speaker. "The estimate is now as high as seventy."

"Putting the Estral two behind the Space Corps fleet," said Nation.

"Assuming the next estimate isn't twenty higher. Or fifty. A hundred."

"Numbers aren't everything, sir," said Keller. "What are their capabilities?"

"We are busy analysing data from the reports. Our first impressions are that the newest Estral ships are similar in capability to one of our Retaliators."

"It's not like we've ever been a generation ahead of the

Estral," said Nation. "We get our noses in front and then they pull it back."

"That may be true, Lieutenant Nation, but it doesn't help us at the moment. The Estral have made a successful attack on one of our primary Obsidiar-Teronium refinement plants. We can increase output from our other plants, though it will not be sufficient to cover the losses from Sindar. In addition, it is certain the enemy have their deep space monitoring stations trained in our direction in the hope of locating our real processing facilities. That is not all."

"What else?" asked Keller.

"The Estral fleet – those of their warships without lightspeed catapults – are coming through the Primol wormholes in great numbers. They are pressing us hard."

BK> It sounds like we're losing already.

JN> He certainly isn't telling us the whole story.

BK> I bet most of it's classified. Maybe he doesn't even know himself.

JN> I don't like any of this.

BK> Me either.

"What retaliatory action have we taken?" asked Nation.

"As yet, little - we've been taken by surprise, so we are on the back foot. Neither I, nor my colleagues, wish to offer a piecemeal response which might see members of our fleet picked off. Therefore, we are in the process of regrouping."

"How many of the Estral refinement facilities do we know about?" asked Keller.

"According to the peace treaty, we know them all." Cody gave a dismissive laugh. "However, I'm certain our *friends* have rather more facilities than those we are aware of. A rough guess suggests these new warships in their fleet would require two or three times the total output of the known Estral refinement plants to produce."

"Why did we let it get so far, sir?" asked Nation.

"A question for another time, Lieutenant. And probably a question to ask another person. Anyway, I'm running out of time. You're no doubt wondering why I chose to speak to you in mid-flight, rather than bringing you in for a full debrief."

"Yes, sir, I think we were both wondering exactly that."

"We've been caught on the hop, but the Confederation is not exactly helpless. As it happens, only three days ago, one of our own deep space monitoring stations caught sight of an anomaly on the extremes of Estral Space, out in the middle of nowhere. After some intense analysis, we concluded that what we have located is an Obsidiar-Teronium refinement facility."

Nation raised an eyebrow. "It's not on a planet and we managed to spot it?"

"Far from anywhere, Lieutenant. Where the Estral assumed we would never find it."

"The crew on the monitoring station deserve a medal for that one."

"It's what we pay them for. We are going to launch a strike on this facility, and hope that it isn't a dummy," said Cody.

"Sounds like a plan. Does this place have a name?"

"In the mission documentation, we refer to it as *Zantil*. This is too good an opportunity to pass up and we have gathered an attack fleet. I am sending further details to the *Gundar*'s data-banks. You will rendezvous with Attack Fleet Z..."

BK> Attack Fleet Z? Who thinks these up?

JN> Beats me.

"...and you will execute the details of the plan."

"I have received coordinates for our destination," said Teal.

Deep within the *Gundar*'s hull, the Obsidiar detonators grumbled. The entire vessel shook and the sound of the light-speed catapult came to the fore. Keller interfaced with the space-ship and discovered it had been issued with a remote command from the Fortress-3 mainframe to activate the catapult immediately.

"Sir, we are being sent into this mission without adequate briefing," said Keller.

"While we were talking, I received an order that there should be no further delays," said Cody. "I ordered the *Gundar* to be sent on its way. You were here and now, and in one of our Class 1 warships. If the Zantil facility is well-defended, the *Gundar*'s firepower may well be the deciding factor."

Keller was experienced enough to know when a decision had been made. She went with the flow. "How important is Zantil, sir?"

"It could be very important, Lieutenant. The distance is extreme, but our monitoring station picked up emissions which suggest it could produce enormous quantities of Istoliar. We believe this to be a genuine refinement operation. If the mission is successful, we can even things up in the war. Remember – the side which controls the Istoliar controls the outcome."

"Yes, sir."

The whine of the catapult increased in volume and it would launch in a short time.

"What about the Antaron, sir?" asked Keller.

"It's a low-priority, Lieutenant. A single entity that is far, far from here. Once this war is over, I will dedicate a team to study your findings."

"Sir, this thing is dangerous. It's not like we found an amoeba frozen in a pool of ice. The Estral were unable to defeat it and then it attacked the *Gundar*."

"Another time," warned Cody. "I told you I'd get people onto it." He gave another short laugh and then repeated word-for-word what Nation had said only a few minutes ago. "It's in Estral territory. Let the Estral deal with it."

The lightspeed catapult hit full volume, held for a second and then discharged, taking the SC *Gundar* an enormous distance back towards the hostile territory of Estral Space.

CHAPTER TWENTY

UPON THE *GUNDAR'S* ARRIVAL, Keller checked the sensors for signs of hostile activity. The mission briefing files Admiral Cody sent to the ship were sparse to say the least and, though Keller had used the speed of her augmentation to read them, she wasn't left much wiser about whether or not the light-speed catapult was meant to drop the *Gundar* right on top of the Zantil facility, or a distance away.

As it happened, the arrival coordinates placed the *Gundar* within a few million kilometres of Attack Fleet Z and a short lightspeed jump from Zantil.

"This fleet is unmanned," said Keller. "I thought Cody was holding back on a few details."

"It's not unusual for AIs to run the show, is it?"

"No, I mean it's completely unmanned. No human oversight at all."

Nation raised an eyebrow. "That *is* unusual."

"Welcome to the future. They also have an armoured lifter with them."

"Cody made no mention of that."

"Like I said, he was holding back."

"He must have received a message from the fleet admiral midway through our comms talk, or something. Anyway, show me this lifter."

Keller focused one of the sensor arrays on the Military Heavy Lifter *Argonaut* and brought up the image for Nation to look at. The *Argonaut* was one of largest ships in the fleet and it dwarfed the warships around it. The lifters were the only thing left which bore any resemblance – size-wise – to the warships in Eriol's Graveyard. At twelve-thousand metres long, the *Argonaut* was shaped like a flattened cylinder, which tapered at the front end. It had cargo bay doors running the full length of its underside and it was equipped with Istoliar engines, as well as an Istoliar winch which could haul a small moon out of orbit.

The days where an MHL was a floating target were long gone. The *Argonaut* wasn't meant for fighting, but it was fitted with a Class 1 phase-shifting energy shield, as well as being covered in massive armour plates. In addition, it could defend itself with its overcharge particle beam turret and a single stasis emitter.

"There is an inbound communication from Retaliator class SC *Atlantis*," announced Teal.

An unmanned attack fleet didn't need direct, spoken communication. The AI of each ship would coordinate their attacks using lines of code, transmitted near-instantly from one to the other. Where humans were involved, it was common courtesy to speak, as long as it didn't interfere with the mission.

Keller accepted the comms. The moment she did so, the rest of the warships joined the channel.

"I am AI Gane-Q12 from the SC *Atlantis*." The voice had a hard-edged, distinctly male voice.

"I'm Lieutenant Becky Keller. With me is Lieutenant Joe Nation."

"I know. I assume you are aware of the mission outline. It would be a failure on your parts if you did not."

Keller exchanged a look with Nation and rolled her eyes.

"Why don't you fill us in? Zantil, wasn't it?" she asked.

"You are aware that one of our deep space monitoring stations detected the Zantil mobile processing facility very recently," said Gane-Q12. "We are certain the Estral scum have been using it to produce quantities of Istoliar, far beyond that which they are permitted."

Keller's eyes opened wide at the AI's use of the word *scum*. AI Gane-Q12 was balancing on a knife edge and it would be shut down if it spoke like that during one of its psyche evaluations. The beginning of each new war was the time when a susceptible AI tended to go off the rails.

"I am aware of what the Estral are doing at Zantil."

"We are going to strike," said Gane-Q12. "We will deliver punishment for what they did to our people on Sindar."

"What's the plan?" asked Nation. "I assume there's a plan underneath the rhetoric?"

"We will disable the Zantil station with the force of our weapons."

"And I will carry it back," spoke another voice, this time from the *Argonaut*. This voice was deeper and manly. Keller winced when she realised the lifter's AI had given itself the name Jason.

"I thought this was a simple in-destroy-out kind of mission," she said.

"Admiral Jacks wishes to stick it to the Estral," said AI Nox from the Invoke class SC *Piledriver*. "To insult them by stealing that which they hold most dear."

Keller frowned. "I thought Admiral Cody was in charge?"

"Our orders come from Admiral Jacks," replied Gane-Q12.

Nation tapped Keller on the arm and shrugged, to indicate it didn't matter who gave the orders.

BK> Capturing Zantil will quadruple the risks.

JN> More than quadruple. It'll increase them tenfold.

BK> This must be a real high-priority target.

JN> It's nothing to do with sticking it to the Estral. We want their tech and we want to see how efficient their refinement process is.

BK> And, if we're lucky, find a few million tonnes of Istoliar in the facility hangar bay.

JN> That would be a bonus.

The spoken conversation resumed.

"We are not the only mission," said Klister, the AI from the second Retaliator class, SC *Granite*. "As the Estral attack us, so we shall attack them."

BK> This is like attending a sermon.

JN> At least they're up for the fight.

BK> I wonder if this is going to be a short war.

JN> The Eighth War was settled by lightspeed catapults. There's no reason to think the Ninth won't be.

"What are the projections for an Estral response during this mission?" asked Keller, switching to normal speech.

"We will destroy whatever they send," said Gane-Q12.

"That does not answer my question."

"The projection is for a minimal response," said AI Rune, speaking from the SC *Sunder*. "If the enemy have no lightspeed catapult-enabled warships available, we may be able to capture Zantil station before they can offer any response at all."

"It is anticipated that comms travel time from Zantil to the closest Estral command and control station, in combination with the delay associated with decision making, will allow us more than twenty minutes to overcome the processing facility," said Klister. "Twenty minutes is more than sufficient for a mission with such simple aims."

"Death to the enemy," said Flex.

"Victory for the Confederation," added AI Sol.

Warship AIs were permitted a certain amount of patriotism, without it being actively encouraged. To Keller's ear, Flex and Sol were just about within acceptable levels. It was Gane-Q12's expression of hatred in calling the Estral scum which overstepped the boundaries.

BK> Let's hope they're just excited.

JN> That makes them sound like children. Children in control of life and death. It's worrying.

BK> And it's nothing new.

JN> I suppose. I'm sure the AI programming guys have it under control.

There was no choice other than to get on with it. Warship AIs had been replaced on a few occasions in the past, but there was no record of one actually going rogue. The consequences of that happening were unthinkable and the Space Corps had all sorts of contingency planning in case the worst ever come to the worst. A few officers even had the temerity to suggest that a return to the *good old days* where men and women were in charge would be a positive change. Keller smiled at the thought and cleared her throat.

"We're ten minutes' high lightspeed from Zantil. I will remain in control of the SC *Gundar* for the duration of the mission."

"That is contrary to orders," said Gane-Q12. "You will relinquish control of the *Gundar* to its AI, to maximise our chances of success."

"Negative. The orders we received gave no mention of who would pilot the *Gundar*. Until I hear to the contrary, I am in charge of this ship."

There was a pause, too short to be recognized by a normal human, but which registered as significant on Keller and Nation's internal clocks.

"Very well," said Gane-Q12. "A transcript of this conversation will appear in my report. You will join our battle network to ensure you are able to synchronise with the rest of Attack Fleet Z."

"Agreed," said Keller. "Now let's get going."

The comms channel went silent. Gane-Q12 offered a series of synchronisation codes to the *Gundar*'s navigational computer, which Keller accepted.

BK> We're departing at once.

JN> Like you said, no point in hanging around.

Gane-Q12 triggered the launch and, as one, the ten warships in Attack Fleet Z entered high lightspeed. The *Gundar* was hampered by the damage to its Istoliar core, but it was still considerably faster than the Class 2 Invokes. This was the purpose of the synchronisation codes – to ensure every ship arrived in the same place and at the same time.

"So, this is how the Ninth War proceeds," said Nation gloomily. "We slug it out with the Estral until we've destroyed each other's Obsidiar-Teronium refinement plants, shoot down a few warships and then come to another settlement."

"Except this this time the Estral will be looking for a more favourable outcome. One which permits them to rebuild their refinement facilities bigger and better than last time."

"Then, in a few years we say hello to the Tenth War, except this time we lose."

"If not the tenth, then the eleventh or the twelfth. Until the Estral gain the upper hand."

Nation growled. "I thought we'd learned from our mistakes."

"The Confederation has always been peaceful, ever since its inception. We know how to fight, but up here," Keller tapped her head, "we've never been ruthless enough. Every time we win, we leave the door open for a rematch."

"Except when it came to the Ghasts. Our success with them proves the method is viable."

"The Ghasts keep themselves to themselves."

"Tell me the Lieutenant Becky Keller solution. How do we keep humanity alive without making our enemies extinct?"

"Maybe that's the only way," she said sadly. "Maybe we're just not strong enough to take that extra step to ensure our own survival."

"I don't know what I think."

They lapsed into silence and the seconds to the *Gundar*'s arrival at Zantil counted down.

CHAPTER TWENTY-ONE

THE ZANTIL PROCESSING facility was an immense construction, which floated stationary in an area of space far from anything else. It was clad in sheets of black warship-grade alloy and its main platform was eight thousand metres in length and three thousand in depth. Along the middle two-thirds, five huge cylinders made from the same dark metal jutted upwards for two thousand metres, each one representing its own single-fingered salute to the terms of the Human-Estral peace treaty.

JN> Centrifuges.

BK> The intel guys got it right.

JN> I still can't believe we spotted this place from so far out.

BK> The sensors are pickup up emissions consistent with the presence of significant quantities of Istoliar, somewhere in that central section and in front of the middle three centrifuges.

JN> How significant?

BK> Somewhere between twenty and sixty million tonnes.

JN> That *is* significant.

BK> Enough to fit out plenty of new warships.

JN> Now all we have to do is take it.

The Zantil station was not quite so defenceless. At each end of the upper platform, wide-bore gauss cannons protruded from enormous turrets. At the base of these turrets was a row of square launch hatches.

JN> Missiles, gauss turrets. Maybe incendiaries.

BK> And I count eight generators slung underneath the main platform. The *Gundar*'s sensors confirm they contain Obsidiar-Teronium.

JN> Shield generators.

BK> I think we can safely say this is going to be a tough one to break open.

JN> And that huge dome in the centre of the underside? It's too big to be a particle beam, surely?

BK> It's definitely a beam weapon of some kind and from the signature, it's running off Obsidiar. I reckon it doubles as backup power for the main facility.

JN> And we have twenty minutes to neutralise this thing?

BK> Yes. Tap into the battle network and see how it unfolds.

JN> Will do.

BK> On the plus side, we get a surprise attack from stealth. Looking at the facility, I don't think it'll take long before it's shooting back.

JN> Let's get on with it, then.

"Twenty minutes is more than sufficient for a mission with such simple aims," said Keller, imitating the voice of AI Klister.

Normal speech was painfully slow in comparison to the speed of the neural link and during the course of this single sentence, the fighting began.

The *Atlantis* and *Granite* executed short-range lightspeed transits, bringing them within two thousand kilometres of the processing facility.

AI Gane-Q12 (*Atlantis*):: Deploying Tactical Devastator.

AI Klister (*Granite*):: Deploying Tactical Devastator.

The Retaliators were each equipped with a single Obsidiar-accelerated plasma incendiary cannister. The cannisters were huge and the technology old. Once the weapons were deployed, they tumbled onwards, using the momentum imparted by the parent spaceship to carry them to their target.

AI Spindle (*Foolhardy*):: Launching Sublight Lambdas.

AI Sol (*Rust*):: Overcharging particle beam. Neutralised by phase-shifting energy shield.

AI Rune (*Sunder*):: Overcharging particle beam. Neutralised by phase-shifting energy shield.

The list of updates rolled up the *Gundar*'s tactical screen, too quickly for the human eye or brain to comprehend the details. Nation was tapped directly into the feed and his augmented brain had plenty of time to study and digest. He sensed Keller nearby, except she wasn't interfaced with a single system – she was everywhere at once.

Keller (*Gundar*):: SRT complete. Target: Zantil Obsidiar-Teronium generator one. Stasis emitters one and two fired.

BK> Here comes the response.

Keller's earlier prediction that the Zantil base wouldn't take long to see through the Attack Fleet Z stealth modules was accurate. The processing facility's guns opened up so quickly Keller was certain it must be packing thousands of dedicated sensor arrays tuned specifically to the task of locating cloaked warships. Zantil's many gauss cannons fired, their recoil visible on the *Gundar*'s sensor feed. At the same time, a dozen or more hatches protecting the missile launch tubes opened up and high-yield phase-shifter missiles raced out into space.

JN> They are focusing fire on the SC *Revelation*.

In the age of fast-regenerating shields, a common tactic was to focus attack a single target until it was destroyed. Past strategies involved dividing firepower between two or three targets in order to keep the enemy guessing, or simply to hope for a lucky kill.

The *SC Revelation*'s shield was lit up in the centre of a plasma explosion a hundred kilometres across.

AI Flex (*Revelation*):: Damn they're fast. Shield at 78%. Executing SRT.

The *Revelation* jumped away to a distance of five million kilometres and launched a wave of eight Lambda sublights. The Zantil facility defences had an impressive range, backed up by an equally impressive targeting computer. Its guns retargeted and fired. The *Revelation* executed a second SRT, this time emerging at ten million kilometres. The Zantil tactical computer switched targets, this time aiming at the *SC Rust*.

The Tactical Devastators were the first weapons launched, but not the first to impact. They struck the Zantil facility's energy shield, a few hundred metres apart. Nation watched the sensor feed, his eyes narrowed in anticipation.

The twin detonations were incredible to behold. White fires, tinged with blue and specks of darkness, swept around the Zantil facility's energy shield in a split second. They expanded, further and further, until the Estral station was at the centre of an inferno thirty thousand kilometres across. The fires were wild and they burned in a turmoil of chaos, hotter than the corona of the hottest star.

JN> We're looking to salvage this facility, right?

BK> Don't be too worried. The *Gundar*'s sensors can read the output from their generators and believe me, they're coping.

Enemy missiles and gauss slugs continued pouring from the centre of conflagration, striking the *SC Rust*'s shield time and again. The spaceship retaliated with stasis emitters, missiles and an expulsion of its overcharge particle beam. Another volley struck the *Rust*.

AI Sol (*Rust*):: Shield at 70%. Executing SRT.

The warship entered lightspeed for a short moment,

emerging close to the *SC Revelation*. Gauss slugs and missiles pursued it across the void. The *Rust* vanished again.

The exchange continued. The Zantil station's defences switched target time and again, whilst the focused Space Corps vessel took the punishment and then jumped away. The Tactical Devastator incendiaries showed no sign of burning out and they continued to chew away at the facility's energy shield.

JN> Any sign of give?

BK> Not yet. Those are big generators. This place was designed to soak and that's exactly what it's doing.

JN> Have we got the firepower for this?

BK> We can knock out their shield. It's just a question of whether or not we can do it before the Estral cavalry shows up.

Each attack against one of the Space Corps vessels whittled away some of its Istoliar core's reserves. Once a spaceship's power core ran out of juice, its shield would fail and the craft would become vulnerable. The core would regenerate over a period of between twenty and thirty minutes, so these hit-and-run tactics would eventually be successful, as long as the Estral fleet didn't get here in time to intervene.

AI Gane-Q12 (*Atlantis*):: Order: Target Zantil generators with stasis emitters.

With three of the Attack Fleet Z spaceships – including the *MHL Argonaut* - keeping their distance, the remaining six, including the *Gundar*, swooped beneath the space station. The large turret Keller had seen earlier was indeed a beam weapon with a short range and a repeating capability. It opened up on the *SC Gundar*, and a series of concealed missile clusters launched dozens of smaller warheads at the ship.

Keller (*Gundar*):: Firing stasis emitters. Firing overcharge particle beam.

She kept the warship in close for a harsh exchange of blows. The *Gundar*'s overcharge repeater thumped five times in quick succession. The Zantil station's shield showed no sign of collapse and Keller swore under her breath.

BK> This place packs a serious punch.

JN> And half of the *Gundar*'s weaponry is sitting on the landing strip at Fortress-3.

BK> They should have recalled us for a proper fitting out.

JN> Since we're here and in the line of fire, why aren't our stasis emitters shutting down their power cores?

BK> I don't know. They've either got another huge core somewhere in the upper section, that's able to keep the shield going, or they've developed a way to deflect the effects of the weapon.

Keller (*Gundar*):: Shields at 68%. Executing SRT.

Under Keller's control, the *Gundar* jumped out of range, before it could sustain a significant draining of its shield. The accepted strategy was to take a modest amount of damage before jumping away, rather than pushing it to the edge.

AI Nox (*Piledriver*):: Deploying plasma incendiaries.

AI Feds (*Boxer*):: Deploying plasma incendiaries.

AI Klister (*Granite*):: Deploying plasma incendiaries.

AI Gane-Q12 (*Atlantis*):: Deploying plasma incendiaries.

BK> Here we go. Subtlety out of the window.

JN> You class the Tactical Devastators as *subtle*??

BK> There's no need for a double question mark. Gane-Q12 has decided it's time to push things along. Anyway, the TDs are burning out.

Keller was right. The fires from the main incendiaries were fading. Once their fuel was spent, they receded fast and the sphere of flames surrounding Zantil shrank like they were being sucked into a giant hole.

The standard incendiaries exploded before the Tactical Devastator fires could vanish. They detonated in pure white and with a far smaller blast radius. Still, they clung to the station's energy shield, pulling at its reserves. A second deployment of incendiaries followed, feeding the flames.

Through it all, missiles from both sides flew back and forth, along with heavy slugs of hardened Gallenium. Modern weaponry could travel close to the speed of light and often a missile launched and detonated with only a tiny interval between each event. The SC *Granite* suffered a sustained bombardment and broke away, whereupon the SC *Revelation* rejoined.

BK> There's a flicker.

JN> Their shield is coming down?

BK> No. They've switched it from one power source to another.

JN> It's a start.

AI Gane-Q12 (*Atlantis*):: Lambda SL full launch. The Estral bastards will succumb.

AI Nox (*Piledriver*):: Deploying plasma incendiaries. Executing SRT.

AI Feds (*Boxer*):: Victory for the Space Corps!

JN> Are they meant to be this happy?

BK> Unfortunately. It's all business until their battle sim tells them victory is a certainty. Then they celebrate. It's in the programming.

JN> What's your battle sim telling you?

BK> I don't have one running. There's something depressing about having a processing cluster telling you if you're going to live or die.

JN> This time we win, huh?

AI Gane-Q12 (*Atlantis*):: Die, Estral filth!

Nation shook his head, wondering what was more depressing – Keller's feelings about the battle sim dictating her future, or the relish expressed by Gane-Q12 about the death of its enemies. There was no wonder the Confederation had laws to prevent computers becoming fully sentient. This glimpse into the world of the Space Corps' most powerful warships left him completely bemused.

JN> This is what we used to do to our soldiers. Train out their personality to make them better killers. Now we do it to our spaceships.

BK> The underbelly of war. The price of winning we don't ask too many questions about.

JN> Yeah. I'm no revolutionary, but it leaves a strange taste.

BK> Odd words from a covert op. And not the time to explore them further.

JN> I'll shut up until this is over.

Nine minutes and fifteen seconds after Attack Fleet Z arrived in proximity of the Zantil station, the facility's energy shield collapsed in the heat of incendiary fires and a sustained bombardment of Lambda sublights and particle beam repeaters.

Whilst the *MHL Argonaut* remained at a distance, the other warships circled around, directing precision strikes of reduced-intensity particle beams at the facility's missile launchers, gauss cannons, sensor arrays, and the underside repeater turret. Keller joined in and she flew the *Gundar* in a tight arc, firing its particle beam again and again, each hit enough to melt shut one of the missile launch hatches or disable a gauss gun.

In less than two minutes, the Zantil weaponry was completely disabled. At the end of the process, both end sections of the facility were a mess of burning, misshapen metal in a range of colours from sullen red to bright orange. Lumps of molten alloy occasionally fell into space, leaving trails in their wake.

The five main centrifuges hadn't completely escaped. When the facility's energy shield failed, burning plasma had fallen upon them in places. Here and there, sporadic fires burned, one or two looking serious to Nation's eye and he wondered what would happen if they opened a breach into one of the centrifuges.

AI Gane-Q12 (*Atlantis*):: That's game over for the Estral

dirt. Commence mission phase two. Time is passing, let's move it people.

Nation felt his head swimming at the words. Keller offered him a sympathetic smile and a shrug. She was far less a stranger to this than he was.

"We got the prize," she said.

"A good result."

AI Jason (*MHL Argonaut*):: Mission phase two commencing.

Keller and Nation prepared themselves for the second stage of the attack on Zantil. With the facility's defences out of action, it was time to capture it and take it back to the Confederation.

CHAPTER TWENTY-TWO

THE HEAVY LIFTER, *Argonaut*, was only a few million kilometres away from Zantil and it didn't take it a moment to lightspeed jump close enough to commence its pickup operation.

"Is it safe for the *Argonaut* to attach its winch with the station still alight?" asked Nation.

"Safer to get it into the *Argonaut*'s hold and get away from here than it is to wait for those fires to burn out."

"I knew that already. My mouth is just talking while my eyes watch."

"You do that as well?"

"Don't tell anyone."

The *Argonaut* was huge, but it wasn't ponderous. It turned parallel to the Estral facility, climbed a few thousand metres vertically and then flew sideways, until it was directly above. At the same time, the heavy lifter's main cargo bay doors opened smoothly and steadily, until they disappeared into their recesses in its double hull.

Nation and Keller watched in fascination. It wasn't that neither of them had seen an operation like this before, it was simply the fact humanity had spaceships which could lift ninety billion tonnes without breaking a sweat, that made it impossible to look away from the spectacle.

AI Jason (*MHL Argonaut*):: Targeting main winch. Targeting forward chains. Targeting aft chains.

AI Sol (*Rust*):: This is one hot potato.

"Here we go," said Keller. "It shouldn't take long to pull it into the hold."

They watched and nothing happened.

"What's taking so long?" asked Nation.

"I don't know."

AI Jason (*MHL Argonaut*):: Main Istoliar winch has failed to couple. Forward and aft gravity chains connected.

"What does that mean?" Nation performed a quick search through the *Argonaut*'s design documents, but found nothing to explain the reason for this failure.

"I'm not sure. The gravity chains are powered by plain old Gallenium and they're just used to stabilise loads, rather than do the heavy lifting. The Istoliar winch does the hard work."

AI Jason (*MHL Argonaut*):: Second attempt to connect Istoliar winch. Failure.

Part of Nation's processing cluster continued to pore over the design plans for the *Argonaut*, before moving onto the technical specifications of the main Istoliar winch.

"I've checked the plans. The Gallenium chains have a maximum lift of fifteen billion tonnes. This is a vacuum – there should be no trouble, right? The *Argonaut* could drop right down over the space station, close its doors and then we leave this place."

"It can't go to lightspeed with an unsecured load. A lifter's life support modules don't cover what's in the hold. It relies on its lifting gear to keep everything stable."

AI Jason (*MHL Argonaut*):: Third attempt to connect Istoliar winch. Failure. Aborting.

AI Gane-Q12 (*Atlantis*):: You will not abort. Resume.

AI Jason (*MHL Argonaut*):: The winch will not attach.

AI Gane-Q12 (*Atlantis*):: Then there is a technical problem.

AI Jason (*MHL Argonaut*):: There is no technical problem with the module. The winch is being repelled.

AI Gane-Q12 (*Atlantis*):: Connect at a different location.

AI Jason (*MHL Argonaut*):: The load would be unbalanced and I would be destroyed entering lightspeed.

AI Gane-Q12 (*Atlantis*):: If the Istoliar winch will not attach, we must destroy the target.

AI Feds (*Boxer*):: If we do so, the mission will be a failure.

AI Klister (*Granite*):: Partial success is not the same as failure.

AI Feds (*Boxer*):: Success is an absolute.

AI Spindle (*Foolhardy*):: No. There are degrees of success. What you are referring to is perfection.

AI Feds (*Boxer*):: I hold myself to higher standards.

AI Spindle (*Foolhardy*):: I see the bigger picture. The outcome of this war depends on more than one success.

AI Feds (*Boxer*):: That is apparent, and also irrelevant to our discussion.

"This is unbelievable," said Nation, speaking just to get away from the bombardment of information into his brain cluster.

"They'll acknowledge the existence of an impasse eventually."

"The trouble is, they're acting like each of their voices carries equal weight. That simply doesn't work in the military."

Keller performed a high-speed search through the mission briefing data carried on the shared battle network. There was something missing.

"The protocol document for this mission is incomplete."

"You're shitting me?"

"Nope."

"That's why they're arguing over the details?"

"Yes, they have nothing from high command which explains what they are expected to do in the event of a partial mission success. That's their point of reference in the event of uncertainty or disagreement. Without one, they're left trying to figure it out for themselves."

"So the Space Corps cobbled this mission together so quickly, they let the basic stuff fall through the net?"

"Looks like."

"Someone needs to lose their job over this!" Nation said in anger. "What a pile of crap."

"I'm sure Admiral Cody, Jacks or whoever's in charge of this mission will be delighted to read that in your report."

"This is serious. What are we going to do?"

Keller's eyes twinkled. "I keep telling you they'll never replace humans entirely."

"I thought that was my line." He narrowed his eyes. "What do you have planned?"

"How about you take one of the *Gundar*'s shuttles over to the Zantil station and see if they've got all of that Istoliar nicely packaged up in a cargo ship and ready to go?"

The question didn't exactly catch Nation by surprise, since he was already thinking along similar lines. He rubbed his chin in thought. "I thought we were up against the clock?"

"We are. An estimated clock based on guesswork and supposition, which has slightly less than seven minutes left on it."

"At least twenty million tonnes of Istoliar," Nation mused. "Enough to turn the tide of war."

"If we destroy Zantil, we deny the Estral access to it, so in that respect we're poised to give the enemy a kick in their collective balls."

"In the hands of the Space Corps, it's the chance to double up."

"I reckon."

"What happens when the Estral fleet shows up and I'm onboard Zantil?"

"I'm sure I can persuade Attack Fleet Z to remain here in order to repel the enemy. There's a good chance the Estral will have their catapult ships tied up elsewhere. We can deal with whatever they send." She looked him in the eye. "This was my idea, so I'll stay regardless of what comes."

"I trust you, you know that."

"I wouldn't suggest something if I were sure it would get you killed."

"How do I get inside?"

Keller traced a finger over an area of the sensor image which showed a nearly-imperceptible seam in the front of the Estral facility's main platform.

"You can't burn them open," said Nation. "You might destroy the Istoliar."

"I wasn't suggesting I burn them open. Look here next to the doors – there are shuttle docking bays."

Nation zoomed in the sensor feed and saw a vertical row of square openings to one side of the main bay doors. The openings were unlit, making them hard to distinguish from the surrounding metal.

"Universal docking facilities," he said.

"It means they don't need to open the main hangar every time a shuttle comes in to dock. A rather more sensible arrangement than how they managed it on Isob-2."

"And they're blind, so they won't see me coming?"

"There are no functioning sensor or comms arrays on Zantil. The crew won't see you."

Nation rose from his seat and tore off the remains of his

damaged spacesuit which he hadn't bothered to remove after his escape from Isob-2. He dropped the pieces on the floor and grabbed a second suit from the bridge locker, as well as a visor to go with it.

"Don't want to risk your pretty face getting burned up, huh?"

Nation's artificial skin was tougher and more resilient than the spacesuit polymers. The Space Corps churned out hundreds of thousands of spacesuits, but not many like Joe Nation. They could afford to fit him with the good stuff.

"I don't want to spend three days in a medical block getting patched up," he said. "I'll get dressed in the shuttle. Why don't you spend the time getting your Attack Fleet Z buddies onside?"

Nation exited through the main bridge door and hurried towards the closest of the *Gundar*'s two shuttles. Back on the bridge, Keller tuned herself into the ongoing conversation between the AIs. Unbelievably, it was still in progress, with the majority of the warships trying to figure out how to get the *Argonaut*'s winch attached, whilst the remainder argued over the definition of success.

Keller (*Gundar*):: BE QUIET!

She allowed several processing cycles to elapse before she was assured the AIs had stopped arguing.

Keller (*Gundar*):: Command Override Code: KEL2199Q995.

AI Gane-Q12 (*Atlantis*):: Command code acknowledged.

Each of the other warships returned an acknowledgement of Keller's override. There weren't many in the Space Corps trusted with such a top-level override and Keller was one of them. With the code issued, she was now in charge.

Keller (*Gundar*):: Lieutenant Nation has agreed to fly a shuttle onto the Zantil facility in order to investigate whether the Estral have already loaded their Istoliar onto a transport vessel. If they have, he plans to steal that vessel and fly it into the hold of the *MHL Argonaut*.

AI Klister (*Granite*):: There is not much time.

Keller (*Gundar*):: There is a lot of Istoliar inside Zantil. We cannot leave without attempting to recover it.

AI Nox (*Piledriver*):: This is an opportunity to destroy many more Estral spaceships.

AI Klister (*Granite*):: Or to be destroyed ourselves.

AI Nox (*Piledriver*):: We defend the Confederation.

Keller was beginning to wonder if the AIs in Attack Fleet Z were all on the Space Corps' list of semi-sentient entities which required urgent psychological attention. Maybe the normal ones were being prepared for a strike against other targets.

Keller (*Gundar*):: Enough talk. Lieutenant Nation will shortly depart and we will keep the Estral at bay while he searches the processing facility. He is the only one who can bring the mission success rating to one hundred percent.

She wasn't expecting an argument and she didn't get one. Out here, too far away for a quick comms exchange with base, the AIs were eager for guidance. While Keller was only a lieutenant, her position in Psi made her importance to the Space Corps significantly higher than her rank suggested.

The AIs knew weapons, flight and enemy attack patterns. Most of all, they were programmed to understand that their mission was the most important thing of all. As a consequence, they were eager to listen to what Keller had to say.

AI Spindle (*Foolhardy*):: We will defend this officer of the Space Corps against our foes. Come what may.

Keller (*Gundar*):: My report will include details of your excellent service.

With the decision made, the warships flew off to position themselves at varying distances from the Zantil station, so as not to be caught out by a surprise incendiary attack. The *MHL*

Argonaut remained exactly where it was and Keller brought the *Gundar* to within two thousand metres of the facility, to ensure Nation wouldn't have far to travel.

Against the slab sides of the main Zantil platform, the *Gundar* looked small. Keller studied the sensor feeds – the spaceship was so close to the facility the images didn't require magnification. The darkness of Zantil's metals made it appear cold and foreboding. One-by-one, the fires burned out and the patches of orange and red faded.

JN> I'm ready to go.

BK> Good luck.

JN> I won't need it, right?

Keller couldn't bring herself to smile. She watched the *Gundar*'s shuttle fly away, heading rapidly towards the Zantil facility. Soon, it was little more than a glinting speck and she increased the zoom in order to follow its path. There was something she didn't like about this mission and she already regretted mentioning it to Nation. He'd been eager enough, but maybe if she'd kept her mouth closed, he wouldn't have suggested it himself.

The shuttle slowed as it reached the docking facility. Becky Keller shivered and struggled with the urge to contact Nation and ask him to come back.

CHAPTER TWENTY-THREE

LIEUTENANT JOE NATION sat impassively in his seat and waited for the shuttle's autopilot to guide the vessel into the confined space of the Zantil docking facility. The *Gundar's* shuttle wasn't exactly huge, but there wasn't much room left on either side as it flew into the square opening. It was utterly dark and he used the image intensifiers on the forward sensor array to check what lay ahead.

The docking facility wasn't unusual. The opening continued for two hundred metres, through the impressively thick outer armour of the Zantil station. Near the end was a universal latching mechanism, this being little more than a movable cylinder which could attach to the hull of an incoming craft. Humans and Estral didn't share a lot of technology, but at least the transport vessels from one side could dock in a facility owned by the other.

The shuttle came to a halt and Nation listened out for the tell-tale thump which would indicate the vessel was securely fastened. The thump came and he felt the shuttle shake gently with the soft impact.

JN> I'm docked.

BK> Any lifeforms showing up on the sensor?

JN> Negative. Looks like I made it without being detected.

He stood and flexed his shoulders to get them comfortable within the spacesuit. The reflective visor lay nearby and he picked it up. After a moment's thought, he put it over his head. There was a HUD, meant to display pertinent information about his wellbeing, as well as maps and other useful data. None of it was done better than his augmentations could manage and he switched off the HUD, so the visor would operate as protection only.

The gauss pistol clipped beneath the shuttle's console caught his eye and he considered taking it. His stealth modules ensured he was rarely required to engage at a distance and he didn't want the gauss coils making him visible every time he pulled the trigger. He left the weapon where it was.

A last-minute diagnostic check told him his Istoliar power cells were at maximum and that his onboard systems were functioning properly. He activated the stealth modules and the familiar feeling of comfort descended upon him.

A red light glowed next to the release button for the door. After a few seconds, it changed to green and he pressed the button. The door opened to reveal a narrow airlock tunnel, with a ceiling high enough for an Estral to stand upright. The floor was covered with plates of roughly-finished metal grating. Orbs in the ceiling cast out a dim blue light, and green-glowing symbols betrayed the presence of access panels at each end of the corridor.

JN> It's cold. Minus two.

BK> You're in outer space and there're a few million tonnes of Istoliar nearby. It'll take more than a portable heater to keep it warm.

JN> Will we lose the neural link once I get deeper inside?

BK> I've scanned the exterior and there'll definitely be areas where the link will drop. As long as the Estral fleet doesn't show up I should be able to fly the *Gundar* into the best position to maintain a stable connection with you.

JN> What if I found a comms hub? Could you send me some piggyback code like you used on Isob-2, for me to inject into their mainframe?

BK> That would be a great idea if we hadn't already destroyed their antennae. Zantil routes its comms through its sensor arrays in the same way a spaceship does. Their sensors are gone and so are their comms.

JN> Okay. I'll deal with it. How long until the Estral get here?

BK> I've told you, it's not exact. The twenty-minute timer is down to two minutes. Don't think about it. Me and my good buddies in Z will take care of the heat.

With a quiet laugh, Nation stepped out of the shuttle onto the grating. The metal plate wasn't perfectly-fitted and he felt it shift slightly beneath his weight, the noise suppressed by his stealth augmentation. Behind him, the shuttle door whispered shut. With quick steps, he advanced along the corridor towards the far door.

BK> Take care.

JN> Will do.

Nation was half-expecting the entire facility to be locked down as a result of Attack Fleet Z's arrival. He was relieved to discover the panel at the far end of the airlock was open access. He had the number cruncher, but it was going to be far easier if he didn't need to rely on it.

The door whooshed to the side, revealing another, wider, corridor running perpendicular. His sensor informed him the light was slightly dimmer and the temperature was slightly colder. He paused, listening. The only things he could hear were the indistinct sounds which possessed every vast metal construction. There were creaks and groans of flexing walls and far away he could hear something heavy banging against something equally solid.

JN> How many people do you think it takes to run an Istoliar processing facility?

BK> According to the databanks, the Sindar plant required three thousand operators, a few thousand guards, several Colossus tanks and various ground-to-air defences.

JN> Zantil is bigger than what we had on Sindar.

BK> We can't draw comparisons between an Estral facility and one of ours. You could argue our technology is superior, therefore we require fewer personnel to operate our refineries.

JN> I get the message. It's time for me to stop guessing.

BK> Why do you ask?

JN> Because I can't hear anyone.

BK> I doubt they're following their usual routines. Besides, you only just got there.

JN> Point taken. I'll start looking.

Nation guessed the new corridor ran alongside the main hangar bay and probably led to it. He turned right out of the airlock and hurried towards a T-junction at the end. He trailed his fingertips along one of the solid metal walls, trying to get a sense of the place. He detected a vibration so faint he couldn't be sure if he were imagining it.

At the T-junction, he looked both ways. To the right, a passage headed away to another junction, whilst to the left, the corridor ended at a room. He went left and found himself in what he guessed was a breakout area. A dozen or more angular chairs were scattered around the floor, along with a table. To the left, Nation saw a flat blue panel above a horizontal slot, which he knew to be an Estral replicator. A tray waited, forgotten on the table, and Nation blinked when he spotted something dark on top of a pile of semi-edible nourishment paste.

JN> You need to see this. Connect to my sensor feed.

BK> Have you found the Istoliar?

JN> No. Come on! Quickly!

Keller made the link.

BK> An insect?

JN> Looks like.

BK> You got me down here to look at a dead bug?

JN> It's the first time I've seen one in a deep space facility. You don't see many insects out here.

BK> Hmmm. It's an ugly-looking thing. I wouldn't want to find it in my sock drawer.

Nation didn't pursue this minor diversion any further and turned his attention away from the frozen insect. There were three exits and he chose the one he thought would bring him closer to the Zantil main hangar bay. He passed two closed doors, before succumbing to temptation and opening the third.

The room inside was unlit, as if the power had been cut. Nation's sensor adjusted and he saw the longest two walls were covered in screens. There was a central console, along with three chairs, each of which was designed to rotate in order that the occupant could see every one of the monitors without having to twist around.

JN> Internal monitoring station.

BK> Where's the power?

JN> I don't know.

BK> Did I mention that I have a bad feeling about this?

JN> No.

BK> Well I do. A really bad feeling.

JN> Psi premonition?

BK> Sometimes it's hard to work out if what I feel is a hunch or a glimpse into the infinite model.

JN> And you feel guilty if it's only a hunch and you get it wrong?

BK> Pretty much. If it's a *real* premonition, I can blame the universe if it turns out to be inaccurate.

Nation entered the room, more out of curiosity than necessity. He located the main power switch on the central console and flicked it upwards. The unit remained powered off.

JN> Attack Fleet Z shot up all the underside generators. Maybe some of this internal stuff was linked into those.

BK> Could be.

JN> How come you manage to fit so much doubt into two words?

BK> Practise. You should get out of there.

JN> What threat do you think there might be?

BK> I don't know.

JN> I think I'm close to the main hangar. I'll give it a couple more minutes and then come back. How does that sound?

BK> Are you ready to face the righteous anger and disappointment of Attack Fleet Z?

JN> I think I can cope.

Nation exited the room and jogged along the corridor, still heading away from the shuttle. He crossed over two more intersecting passages, each time listening carefully for signs of life. Whatever was making the banging sound earlier, it was now quiet, however the creaking of the hull was louder than ever. The exterior of the facility had taken a beating and Nation thought it probable the place was terminally damaged.

There was a flight of steps ahead and he descended. Afterwards, the passage turned and turned again, whilst his internal computers tried their best to build a map and also to predict the internal layout of Zantil.

BK> AI Jason is certain the facility has been fitted with a device specifically to prevent it from being towed away.

JN> Is this device vulnerable to external attack?

BK> We don't know and I'm not about to recommend we attempt it. Not with you onboard.

JN> Is that an unsubtle hint to let me know I'm holding up the show?

BK> Got it in one.

In spite of Keller's words, Nation found himself torn between the options of exploring for another couple of minutes, or simply turning around and running for the shuttle. His feet carried him on to the next intersection, where he promised himself he would stop and go back.

Nation reached the T-junction and looked both ways. A short distance to the left, the passage ended at a room and, on the opposite side of the room, was a viewing window.

BK> You can't resist that window.

JN> No, I can't.

BK> Looks like a flight monitoring station from here.

Nation hurried into the room and took in the details. It was a large space, with no further exits. Monitoring screens covered the left and right walls, and two circular consoles squatted in the middle of the floor. A sign overhead informed him that this was indeed a flight monitoring station.

JN> The power's off again.

The viewing window was seven or eight metres wide and about a metre thick. Nation tapped it with his knuckles as he looked through.

JN> There's the main hangar bay.

BK> It's got to be.

The hangar stretched away into the distance and Nation got a ping off the far wall, three thousand metres away. The bay was long, but comparatively narrow, being less than a thousand metres wide. There were a few lights - sporadic spheres of blue amongst the immensity of the bay, and far from sufficient to dispel the darkness. Nation didn't require illumination to make out the vessel which was docked. Its bulky shape was clamped to the inner wall and its hull filled a third of the available space.

JN> A cargo vessel.

BK> A big, armoured cargo vessel. Any emissions that might indicate it's carrying Istoliar?

JN> I'm getting a garbled response from my sensor. The one I'm fitted with isn't as powerful as that in the *Gundar*. Can you attempt a focused scan on this area of Zantil's hull?

BK> I just did and I can't pinpoint the precise location of the Istoliar. It's either on that cargo vessel or it's behind the hangar bay bulkhead wall and waiting to be loaded. Oh crap, I'm getting something else as well.

JN> What?

BK> Granol-42.

JN> Was it there before?

BK> No. The reading is faint. Oh crap.

JN> That's a second *oh crap.*

BK> There's an inbound fission signature – a big one. I'll have to deal with this.

The neural link went quiet, leaving Joe Nation alone on the Zantil station.

CHAPTER TWENTY-FOUR

FOUR SECONDS after Lieutenant Becky Keller detected the fission cloud, eight Estral warships emerged from lightspeed. They spread across half a million kilometres of space, and the closest was a hundred thousand kilometres from Zantil. Their synchronised arrival made it likely they had departed from the same place, which implied the enemy were organised instead of this being a random collection of ships ordered to attend the scene of an attack.

Keller's Faor augmentation ran the shapes of the enemy warships through the databanks of known Estral vessels. Two of them were known to the Space Corps – the battleships *Gulazan* and *Tirinax* had served as far back as the Sixth, Seventh and Eighth wars. Each vessel was a thousand metres long and shaped like a wedge, with landing skids and angular metal plates designed to deflect sublight gauss rounds aimed at the bridge. Their hulls were old and scarred, but they'd been extensively refitted, to the point where the databanks categorised both as a Class 1 threat.

The remaining six were between four and five hundred

metres long and with more recent designs. A sweeping scan across their hulls indicated only one was fitted with an Istoliar core. The databanks had no record of an engagement with any of these vessels and listed them as a mixture of Class 2 and Class 3 threats, with advisories of caution.

Keller (*Gundar*):: Focus on the *Gulazan*. Let's shut that one down and then switch to the *Tirinax*.

AI Gane-Q12 (*Atlantis*):: Do not hold back!

AI Jason (*MHL Argonaut*):: I will remain in place at Zantil and will not attack.

Keller's practised eye sized up the opposing fleets and she reckoned the Space Corps had the edge over the Estral. She found herself smiling in anticipation – the chaos of multi-vessel combat was a craving she pretended didn't exist. This was the time when a skilled pilot or an experienced battle computer could fall to the vagaries of luck. It was also the time when the very best could decide what they wanted their future to be and impose their will upon the whims of fortune.

The warships of Attack Fleet Z were running with their stealth modules active. There was a tiny window after a space-ship's emergence from lightspeed, during which it couldn't power up its shield or stealth units. This was the time during which a battle could be decided.

AI Rune (*Sunder*):: Firing stasis emitter. Target: *Gulazan*. Failure.

AI Klister (*Granite*):: Firing stasis emitter. Target: *Gulazan*. Success. *Gulazan* main Istoliar drive offline.

AI Feds (*Boxer*):: Firing stasis emitter. Target: *Tirinax*. Failure. Range extreme.

The other ships of Attack Fleet Z were out of range and unable to use their stasis emitters. The SC *Revelation* and *Piledriver* were able to fire their particle beams from outside the overcharge range. They scored hits, but not enough to put their targets out of action.

Keller (*Gundar*):: Firing overcharge repeater. Target *Gulazan*.

She activated the particle beam and its turret thumped violently, eagerly. Keller allowed it to fire four times, when twice would likely have been enough. The *Gulazan* was heated so rapidly it was torn into molten pieces, some of which burst away at enormous speeds.

The remainder of the Estral fleet activated their stealth modules. Two kills would have been preferable, but one was better than none. Now came the fun and games. Each warship of Attack Fleet Z sent out broad, sweeping wave from its sensors, in the hope of picking up the location of one of the enemy space-ships. Details from each sweep were tallied across the local battle network and analysed for anomalies which could indicate the location of a hidden craft.

Soon, the area of space surrounding the Zantil station was filled with the detonations of speculatively-launched plasma incendiaries as the game of cat-and-mouse progressed.

Keller (*Gundar*):: The sooner we get this over with, the better. These won't be the only Estral warships inbound.

AI Gane-Q12 (*Atlantis*):: Your two statements were self-evident and required no waste of processing cycles.

Keller (*Gundar*):: I have plenty to spare.

A wide-area sweep flickered across the *Gundar*'s hull and Keller detected an incendiary launch a quarter of a million kilo-metres to starboard. She activated the particle beam, which stabbed through space at the exact location of the launch. The attack missed and Keller activated a short-range transit to escape the incoming incendiary.

When the *Gundar* reappeared, Keller's augmentation fed her the coordinates of three converging anomalies nearby and she fired the particle beam again. The truncation of the beam informed her of a successful hit and she followed it up by firing both of the *Gundar*'s stasis emitters. One of the Estral Class 2 vessels appeared. Anticipating an immediate response from the other Estral warships, Keller entered another SRT.

AI Nox (*Piledriver*):: Firing overcharge repeater.

AI Sol (*Rust*):: Firing overcharge repeater.

AI Nox (*Piledriver*):: Enemy neutralised.

The discharge of weaponry was sufficient for the Estral to get a lock on the SC *Piledriver* and it was suddenly caught in the centre of an immense blast from three incendiary warheads. A moment later, the *Piledriver* dropped off the battle network.

Keller (*Gundar*):: Successful enemy stasis emitter strike against the *Piledriver*.

A dozen missiles, launched from three different places, plunged through the sphere of hot plasma. A series of new, hotter, explosives added their fury to that of the incendiaries.

Keller (*Gundar*):: SC *Piledriver* destroyed. Damnit!

The only positive to be taken from the loss of the *Piledriver* was the fact Keller believed she might have just got a lock on the second Estral battleship, *Tirinax*, and it wasn't too far away. She went for broke and created a strafing pattern with the overcharge repeater. It took a chunk out of the *Gundar*'s Istoliar power core, but it had the required effect. The beam connected with the phase-shifting energy shield of an enemy vessel, producing a huge spike in power output which the Space Corps sensors could read easily. The *Gundar*'s stasis emitters hadn't yet recharged and were unavailable. Keller activated an SRT to reduce the chance the enemy would lock on.

AI Flex (*Revelation*):: Firing stasis emitter. Target: *Tirinax*. Failure.

AI Sol (*Rust*):: Firing stasis emitter. Target: *Tirinax*. Failure.

AI Gane-Q12 (*Atlantis*):: Firing stasis emitter. Target: *Tirinax*. Success.

With its Istoliar core shut down, the Estral battleship was dumped out of stealth and it drifted without power. Lambda sublight missiles launched from the *Granite* and the *Boxer* homed in on the enemy ship. The warheads didn't have a chance to explode. The *Atlantis* and *Sunder* were close enough to overcharge their particle beams and a third enemy warship was destroyed.

AI Klister (*Granite*):: The failure rate of our stasis emitters is unacceptably high.

Keller (*Gundar*):: Agreed. The Estral must have developed a deflector.

AI Feds (*Boxer*):: It will not save them here. We have the upper hand.

The words came too soon. The *Gundar*'s sensors detected the formation of another inbound fission signature. Keller cursed the fact that her warship didn't have a full loadout and waited to see how much the odds would shift once the additional Estral vessels emerged from lightspeed.

———

WITH KELLER ENGAGED ELSEWHERE, Joe Nation decided he'd do whatever he could to prepare for the aftermath of the conflict outside the Zantil station. In his mind, he'd been granted a few extra minutes in which to act and the best use for that time would be to come up with a plan that allowed Attack Fleet Z to make off with the Estral's precious Istoliar reserves.

Nation stepped away from the viewing window and approached the nearest of the two consoles in the room. If this was the flight control room, the operators would be aware of exactly when the cargo ship was due to leave, and also what it would be carrying in its hold.

He reached beneath the console and snapped the power switch downwards and then up. The console remained dead. Nation crossed over to the second station and located the power switch. It was already in the *on* position, so he didn't hold out much hope. He pressed the switch down and pulled it up.

"Yes!" he said under his breath.

Lights came on and the console started loading up and connecting to the Zantil network. It took a few seconds before the logon screen appeared and a cursor blinked softly in green as it awaited a password.

Nation looked over his shoulder to make sure nobody was coming. The coast was clear and he couldn't hear an alarm. He activated his number cruncher and the augmentation began the process of breaking through the security on the console. Nation crouched low and kept an eye out.

The number cruncher finished and the logon screen vanished, to be replaced by a long menu of different options. Nation read through them until he discovered one which looked interesting. He opened up the menu.

Cargo ship: Nisprol. Loading Commencing.

Cargo ship: Nisprol. Loading Aborted.

Cargo ship: Nisprol. Loading Status Unknown.

Nation had no idea what the cause of the delay was and this screen gave no indication whether or not the loading had completed, or the nature of the cargo. He looked through another two menus and discovered the docking time of the *Nisprol*, as well as its intended time of departure.

"Overdue," he muttered. His internal clock helpfully compared the time of Attack Fleet Z's arrival with the *Nisprol*'s intended departure time. It turned out the cargo ship was due to leave Zantil thirty minutes prior to the arrival of the Space Corps fleet. Delays weren't entirely unheard of, but thirty minutes was significant considering it was likely the *Nisprol* was here to collect a vast quantity of Istoliar. He attempted to connect with Keller across the neural link.

JN> Are you there?

Nation waited a couple of seconds before he accepted the walls of Zantil were blocking the signal, or that Keller was out of range.

Working in isolation was nothing new to Joe Nation, so he put the matter out of his mind. There were a few more unexplored options on the console, and he went through them in turn, seeking anything which might provide a clue about the status of the *Nisprol* cargo vessel. If the craft was loaded, and, if it was in his capabilities to do so, he intended to get onboard the Estral spaceship and fly it into the hold of the *MHL Argonaut* once the coast was clear.

It didn't take him long to decide this room wasn't the place to move things forward. The consoles were heavily locked-down and were here to allow monitoring only, rather than perform any useful task such as opening the external hangar bay doors. He switched the console off, left the room and followed the exit passageway past the intersection which would return him to his shuttle.

Now he'd seen where the hangar bay was located, the computers in his head were able to make a much better prediction of Zantil's internal layout. The specifics weren't important to Nation. As long as he knew he was heading in the right general direction, he was certain he could find the airlock leading onto the cargo vessel.

JN> Hello?

There was still no response and Nation descended more stairs. There were numbers painted onto the walls, presumably to denote the level within the Zantil facility. At the bottom, he reached a passage heading to the left and right, with more stairs leading downwards. Doors lined the corridor, each of them closed but not locked down. Nation stepped across to one of the control panels and swiped his fingers over it. The door wouldn't open.

Everything on this facility must tap into a separate power source, he thought. *And we disabled the external generators during the attack.*

The realisation didn't offer any reassurance that his job was about to get any easier. Even the hangar bay doors might run off one of the power cores which were fixed beneath the facility. He ignored the insidious thoughts about failure. If Attack Fleet Z could make off with the Istoliar, rather than being required to destroy it, it would be a victory which would sap the morale of the Estral high command, as well as offering compensation for the loss of the Confederation plant on Sindar.

Without much hope, he tried the door opposite and it opened at once. He leaned carefully into the room, in case Estral hid within. What he found was living quarters intended for two of the aliens. There was a steel-framed bunk bed bolted to the far wall, along with a table and a metal locker fixed to the wall. An Estral space suit dangled from a hanger which was hooked over one of the partially-open locker doors. There was an uneaten meal on the table – a few of the Estral's bland pastes were piled up on a tray and a spoon lay on the floor. A red light cycled silently through a range of shades from blood-red to near-pink.

The alarm must have sounded as soon as Attack Fleet Z appeared and the facility personnel went to their muster points, he told himself.

Nation withdrew from the room, feeling inexplicably relieved at having found proof of why no Estral patrolled the interior.

His internal map calculated he was still several levels above the hangar bay floor, so he descended once again. The interior of

Zantil felt strangely cramped, with its criss-crossing corridors and rooms which were much smaller than the Estral usual. Nation guessed the refinement operation took up more than eighty percent of the internal space, with the rest given over to the hangar bay and the places where the Estral lived.

At the bottom of the steps, he paused in a compact room and listened. A distant alarm wailed somewhere deeper in the facility and the thickness of the walls made it difficult for him to get a fix on the location. Something else caught his attention – his sensor registered trace particles of Granol-42 and Istilin in the air. The quantities weren't anything like as concentrated as on Isob-2, but still sufficient to cause death for anyone who didn't have a protective suit on. Nation recalled Keller saying that she'd only detected Granol-42 recently and he guessed the attack on Zantil had ruptured some of the processing equipment. It would be another reason for the Estral to keep their heads down.

With a shrug, he moved on.

JN> Hello, hello, hello?

Keller gave no response on the neural link and Nation admitted to himself he was beginning to get worried. Zantil was clearly vitally important to the Estral and it was sure the enemy would respond forcefully to this attack. The best hope was that the bulk of their warships were deployed elsewhere and unable to assist. Nation told himself it wasn't so far-fetched an idea, especially since the discovery of Zantil wasn't something either side could have predicted.

He came across more stairs and climbed down them. This flight was much longer than the others and with each step the air became colder, until the temperature fell to minus twenty Centigrade.

At the bottom, Nation found himself in a red-lit open space, which stretched hundreds of metres into the distance. The room was comparatively narrow at three hundred metres, and his internal map informed him it ran parallel to the hangar bay. He tipped his head back and sent a ping off the ceiling. It was two hundred metres away.

The floor space was covered in a haphazard collection of huge alloy crates, flatbed crawlers, gravity cranes, pre-fabricated piping and objects which Nation recognized as modular components for an Istoliar processing operation. One especially large construction of black metal looked like an exact copy of something from Sub-62 on Isob-2.

Here we go. The operational support area.

A thick layer of hoar frost had formed everywhere and Nation felt like he'd stumbled up on a place abandoned long ago and forgotten. Elsewhere, the alarm continued and from its volume it was no closer than when he first heard it.

Two of the fifty-metre crates were stacked near to the stair exit. Estral symbols were just about visible through the frost at the base of the lower crate and Nation stepped closer in order to wipe clear some of the ice. The sweep of his hand made the ice bloom in the air and the light refracting through the crystals reminded him of spraying blood.

Crates full of Obsidiar and stabilised Obsidiar-Teronium, he thought. *A king's ransom worth of each.*

Istoliar was the way forward, but it required ever-increasing quantities of these lesser substances to create it. The Zantil station was packed with enough of both to keep the Confederation's Istoliar refinement plants running for months.

He turned away from the crate and advanced into the room, convinced he wasn't too far from the main loading bay. Once he found the bay, he was sure he could find a way onto the *Nisprol,* which he hoped was already fully-loaded with Istoliar.

At that moment, he saw the grey eyes of an Estral looking at him through the windowless opening in the cabin of a gravity crawler fifty metres away. Nation jerked around towards it, convinced the alien had somehow managed to see through his stealth modules. It only took him a moment to realise it was dead.

Nation jogged carefully over to the crawler. It was a compact model, only large enough to carry a single crate at a time. Three steps led up to the cabin and Nation climbed to the top one so that he could see inside.

The Estral wore a grey cloth uniform, which didn't betray anything about his function within the Zantil facility. There were traces of ice on the alien's lips and more in its hair. It didn't take long to find the cause of death – Nation's sensor identified large quantities of Granol-42 on the Estral's exposed skin, along with a few particles of Istilin and Polysempe.

Joe Nation swore under his breath. It was beginning to seem like there'd been an accident on the facility and he wondered if the other operators were in a safe zone somewhere deeper inside the Zantil station. If so, it was unlikely to make his job easier.

He swore again and headed once more across the storage area.

CHAPTER TWENTY-FIVE

EXTERNAL TO THE ZANTIL FACILITY, the spaceships of Attack Fleet Z were under constant pressure. The bravado the AIs had displayed after the destruction of the Estral battleships *Gulazan* and *Tirinax* was no longer on display and Keller found herself admiring the effectiveness of the Space Corps' battle computers, as well as the AIs which oversaw them.

The Space Corps vessels were some of the more capable members of the fleet, but this was Estral territory and the aliens were fully woken up to the fact that one of their primary refinement plants was at great risk. As a consequence, new enemy warships emerged from lightspeed quicker than Attack Fleet Z's stasis emitters could recharge and it was a constant struggle to destroy the newcomers before they could activate their stealth modules.

There were other problems. Each new enemy warship made it harder to predict the pattern of their incendiaries. The members of Attack Fleet Z were steadily reduced to a position where each short-range transit required another immediately after, followed by another and another. There were progressively fewer opportunities to fire back without risking exposure and a loss of stealth.

In addition, each SRT reduced the reserves of a warship's Istoliar core and with no let-up, the cores had no opportunity to recharge. It was death by a thousand cuts.

Lieutenant Becky Keller was also acutely aware that, other than the ageing ships *Gulazan* and *Tirinax*, the Estral had yet to introduce any of their more capable warships. It should have been a relief, except Keller was left with a certainty the most powerful Estral craft were involved in higher-priority missions elsewhere. It didn't take a big leap of the imagination to guess at what such missions might be. Out here in the fringes the comms took too long for a quick response, meaning Keller felt blind to the bigger picture.

A series of incendiary blasts a few thousand kilometres away reminded her that several of the Estral ships had decided to focus specifically on the task of bringing the *Gundar* out of stealth. Keller activated a short-range jump, only to find the aliens had predicted the place of her arrival. The *Gundar*'s sensors detected inbound sublight incendiaries and Keller was only just in time to activate a second jump. A couple of processing cycles later and the *Gundar* would have been lit up for the Estral to target it with stasis emitters.

Keller checked the *Gundar*'s Istoliar core. It was down to forty percent. She tried again to reach Nation with the neural link and once again failed to make a connection.

"Damnit," she said under her breath.

AI Klister (*Granite*):: This is not a fight we can win.

AI Feds (*Boxer*):: I agree. It is inevitable we will lose.

AI Gane-Q12 (*Atlantis*):: We should destroy the Zantil station. It will not be a total victory, but it will be preferable to no victory at all.

Keller (*Gundar*):: Lieutenant Nation remains on the facility.

AI Gane-Q12 (*Atlantis*):: We must not permit him to influence our decision. There is too much at stake.

Keller (*Gundar*):: A life is at stake. That is enough.

AI Gane-Q12 (*Atlantis*):: I will not debate philosophy in the midst of an engagement, Lieutenant Keller. One man's life is not significant when weighed against so much Istoliar.

Keller (*Gundar*):: It's damned well significant to me! The Space Corps does NOT abandon its personnel.

AI Flex (*Revelation*):: Lieutenant Keller is correct. We should pull together. Fight together.

AI Rune (*Sunder*):: Only through this will we achieve victory.

AI Gane-Q12 (*Atlantis*):: I do not agree with your assertion. Sending Lieutenant Nation to the Zantil facility was a bad decision.

Keller waited to see if Gane-Q12 would say anything further. It did not, and showed no sign it was about to break ranks. Keller took a breath, wondering what the hell she was going to put in her report if she got out of here alive. Deep down inside, she agreed with Gane-Q12's opinion about sending Nation to the Estral facility and she regretted ever mentioning it.

BK> It's getting crazy up here in more ways than one. I hope you can hear me.

JN> Good to have you back. It's no better down here, I can assure you.

BK> There's a potentially rogue AI in the fleet, along with more Estral warships than you can shake a stick at.

JN> There's been an accident on Zantil. I'm sure of it.

BK> An accident? We hit the place with about fifty particle beams. If there's anything going to knock a refinement process off course, I imagine that would do it.

JN> Whatever it was, I already found one dead Estral and I get the feeling there are plenty more. I'm trying to get onto the cargo ship. After that, I'll see what I can do to fly it out of here. You might need to burn the hangar bay doors open for me.

BK> It would be my pleasure. How long?

JN> I don't know. I doubt it'll be straightforward to get onto the cargo ship. I haven't come across much security so far, but I expect that to change once I reach the critical production and Istoliar storage areas.

BK> We're balanced on a knife-edge out here. Don't hang about.

JN> Never have done, never will.

The link broke and Keller fired the *Gundar's* overcharge particle beam into a smaller Estral vessel which had ventured into the arena without stealth modules or an effective shield. The enemy spaceship was destroyed at once, though Keller took no satisfaction from the kill.

Keller (*Gundar*):: I see another big inbound fission signature. Get ready.

The tactical computer was awash with data. Missiles and incendiaries flew, detonating in never-ending bursts across thousands of kilometres of space. The nine remaining ships of Attack Fleet Z were matched against fifteen Estral craft of varying sizes and capabilities. The battle would have been finely poised except for the fact that the *MHL Argonaut* was keeping itself hidden and the remaining Space Corps warships had heavily-depleted shields.

Another six Estral spaceships exited lightspeed. The SC *Rust* was close enough to obliterate one of the newcomers with a burst from its repeater. The *Boxer* got a long-range strike on another. The heat would make it easier to detect the vessel when it activated its stealth modules.

The five surviving enemy warships disappeared from the tactical computer. A new wave of incendiaries detonated and

Keller allowed herself a moment to close her eyes, wondering what she could do to fix the situation.

———

WITH GREATLY INCREASED CAUTION, Nation prowled across the floor of the storage room. Having been set on edge by the discovery of the dead body, he kept a close watch out for anything unexpected.

The storage area was full and it was difficult to be certain exactly where the exits lay. Had this been a human warehouse, everything would have been laid out in a logical fashion. Either the Zantil station was poorly organized, or the Estral themselves just didn't care. The oversized crates loomed above and Nation felt like a mouse creeping around an ice-bound maze.

The 3D map in his head predicted the closest exit passage would be on the left-hand wall and he cut across the room. The temperature fell to minus twenty-five degrees and Nation used his sensor to get a reading off one of the crates. Obsidiar and all of its derivatives were very cold. However, the crates themselves were insulated and their outer surfaces were only minus ten, so wherever the chill came from, the crates were not completely responsible.

An oversized storage area required an oversized entrance, and so it was. Nation came to a square opening in the wall, which was sixty metres high and wide, clearly designed to allow the transit of a single one of the enormous crates, with a small margin for error. In front of the opening he saw a gravity crawler. It wasn't floating, so its engine was offline. On its load bed was a crate, going nowhere fast.

Nation jogged across to the crawler, taking care on the icy floor. He half-expected to see another Estral in the vehicle's cabin, but it was empty.

The left-hand exit headed in exactly the direction he wanted to go. The wide passage was a hundred metres long and according to Nation's map, it would bring him out into the loading bay directly behind the main hangar. He stared along the passage. There was no door at either end and he could see shapes piled up in a space lit red by the alarm beacons. The sound of the siren was louder.

For the first time since his shuttle docked at the facility, Nation felt a surge of excitement, and he entered the passage.

JN> I think I'm close to the main loading area.

BK> I can't spare the time to check out your feed. Attack Fleet Z is under pressure.

JN> The temperature keeps dropping. It's at minus thirty degrees now. I can see what I believe to be loading equipment.

BK> I think I made a tactical boo-boo suggesting you go to the facility. We've bitten off more than we can chew and it's like the entire Estral fleet are coming to take shots at us.

JN> Can you hold them?

BK> Maybe.

Nation didn't need the alternatives spelling out.

JN> We can't abandon this mission without destroying the Istoliar.

BK> You have to get away from there. If another two or three significant Estral ships arrive, that's going to tip the scales too far.

JN> You have to do what you have to do.

BK> You know I'm not going to blow Zantil up with you inside.

JN> Don't say anything more. I'm going to get onto that damn cargo vessel and fly it out of here.

BK> You won't be able to simply fly it away. Go to the shuttle.

JN> It's too far. I'm taking my chances this way.

BK> Victory or bust.

JN> Not always. This time.

Nation ran flat-out through the connecting passage and found himself exactly where he wanted, which was the main loading and unloading area for the Zantil facility.

It was a high-ceilinged, square room, about five hundred metres along each side. In the centre of the left-hand wall was a huge, sealed door of solid alloy, through which the cargo came. A series of smaller airlock doors cut through the bulkhead to either side of this door, with the closest being only a couple of hundred metres away.

The room itself was filled with everything required to keep an armed Obsidiar-Teronium refinement plant running. Crates and boxes were piled around the room, in rows so deep the furthest items were impossible to easily discern.

JN> I can see magazines for the Zantil gauss guns, crates of spare replicators, a couple of boxed-up consoles, small arms, heavy arms, a rack of missiles, six medical bots. And the jackpot.

BK> The Istoliar is there?

JN> It's here.

The centre of the loading bay floor was clear, except for a lone flatbed crawler. This vehicle was no different in size to those in the previous room. The difference in this case was the cargo. The crawler's bed was piled with smaller crates, each a three-metre cube made from hardened Gallenium. Nation recognized the type – they were the Estral's standard containers for transporting Istoliar. Each crate had a tiny status panel fitted to one side and Nation saw rows and rows of green lights, indicating the containers were full.

JN> I make it approximately two thousand containers on a crawler here, waiting to be loaded.

BK> Forty million tonnes.

JN> Our friends have been busy.

BK> I don't want you to die for it.

JN> I'm here and I'm going to see what I can do. I think the crawler's offline.

BK> Get onto the cargo vessel first and see if there's any way to remote activate the loading sequence.

JN> Good plan.

BK> In other news, do you remember me saying how if two or three big Estral ships decided to show up, we'd be in a bit of trouble?

JN> Yes.

BK> Well, they've just arrived, only there are four of them. Take the cargo vessel into the bay of the *Argonaut* and then we'll hit lightspeed.

Having seen the prize, Nation was extremely reluctant to watch it slip through his fingers. On the other hand, he had no intention of putting Keller into a position where she had to choose between destroying the Zantil facility – and Nation with it – or escaping into lightspeed with the mission a complete failure.

The nearest airlock beckoned and Nation ran for it.

CHAPTER TWENTY-SIX

THERE WAS NOT a single ship in Attack Fleet Z with an Isto-liar core above twenty-five percent, and most of them were significantly lower. The four Estral warships which had just arrived were new and equipped with lightspeed catapults, leading Keller to believe they'd finished a mission elsewhere.

One of the four was unlucky enough to exit lightspeed at the precise moment the *Gundar's* stasis emitters finished their cooldown. Keller held her breath and fired both emitters. She was ecstatic when the Estral battleship was forced offline. Particle beams converged on the vessel and it was destroyed. The other three entered stealth mode.

AI Klister (*Granite*):: We must act soon, else this opportunity will be lost.

Keller (*Gundar*):: Lieutenant Nation is on the verge of recovering the Istoliar cargo. There is a greater quantity than we anticipated.

AI Flex (*Revelation*):: My battle simulation predicts a one hundred percent chance of our failure within six minutes.

AI Klister (*Granite*):: I have a similar prediction. This climbs to seven minutes if the *MHL Argonaut* enters combat.

AI Jason (*MHL Argonaut*):: If I were shut down by a stasis emitter, I would not be able to close my bay doors, nor enter light-speed, assuming Lieutenant Nation is able to pilot the cargo ship into my bay.

Keller (*Gundar*):: The *Argonaut* is too large to be completely disabled by a single shot.

AI Jason (*MHL Argonaut*):: You are correct - I have three separate power generators, spread throughout my hull.

Keller grimaced. The *Argonaut* packed a punch, but the vessel was the only way to get the Istoliar safely back to base. There was also something about the heavy lifters which drew in enemy ships like flies to honey. As soon as the Estral discovered the *Argonaut*, it was likely they'd focus fire on it, and the lifter wasn't able to execute a long chain of short-range transits in the same way a warship could.

Before Keller could decide on the best plan to maximise their chances, an incendiary exploded a million kilometres away. Using her Faor augmentation and the *Gundar*'s sensors, she watched the blast sphere expanding in slow motion. She could immediately tell this was going to be a colossal explosion and the blue flames roiled away from the centre, growing ever-bigger, yet without losing their intensity. The explosion achieved a diameter just shy of two million kilometres and its outer edge came within a few thousand metres of the *Gundar*'s energy shield.

The SC *Rust* and the SC *Boxer* were caught somewhere in the centre of the blast. Their shields were gripped by the blue flames, revealing their locations as well as draining their Istoliar cores.

AI Sol (*Rust*):: Istoliar core at five percent and falling fast. I guess this is it.

AI Feds (*Boxer*):: Core failure, switching to Obsidiar backup. That's game over.

A dozen smaller incendiaries detonated in the vicinity of the *SC Rust*, with a further five centred on the *Boxer*. Estral phase-shifter missiles streaked through the storms of plasma, one of them failing in the heat of the fires. The *Rust* and *Boxer* were destroyed, blown apart by Estral high-explosives.

Keller (*Gundar*):: See you on the other side.

In their eagerness to finish off the two Space Corps warships, several of the Estral had revealed their locations. Keller hit the closest with an overcharge beam, entered a short-range transit and hit a second enemy a fraction of a second later. She ordered the *Gundar* into another SRT, leaving the burning wreckage of two Estral ships in her wake. The combination brought the *Gundar*'s core below fifteen percent.

Keller (*Gundar*):: Two for two.

More particle beams flickered from place to place and another Estral ship was destroyed.

AI Gane-Q12:: Three for two.

Keller found herself gripped with a sudden feeling of cama-raderie with the AIs, a feeling she couldn't ever recall experi-encing with such intensity as this time. Gane-Q12 had stopped announcing itself as a subsystem of the *Atlantis* warship, as though it had made the decision to become an entity in its own right.

Keller (*Gundar*):: Let's give these bastards hell!

AI Gane-Q12:: Victory from the jaws of defeat.

The *Sunder* and *Foolhardy* landed a wave of their incendi-aries accurately enough to bring one more Estral ship out of stealth. The *Sunder* hit it with two shots from its overcharge repeater.

AI Rune (*Sunder*):: Four for two. The price is not yet acceptable.

An Estral particle beam struck the *Sunder* on its upper section from extreme range, heating the warship's armour plating too far for its stealth modules to disguise the emissions. A second particle beam from the same source followed and Keller registered six phase-shifters in flight.

The SC *Sunder* was destroyed, and, through the *Gundar* and *Atlantis* took out one of the enemy a moment later, Keller was unable to ignore the realisation that the cause was now lost.

AI Jason (*MHL Argonaut*):: I should enter the fray.

The battle network communications took hardly any time to formulate and relay, but the gap was sufficient for Keller's response to be interrupted by an unexpected event.

A volley of five sublight phase-shifters appeared, launched by a cloaked enemy ship. These missiles weren't aimed at a Space Corps vessel. Instead, they plunged into the centrifuges of the Zantil station, each warhead producing an explosion with sufficient magnitude to rip the target cylinder into unrecognizable chunks of white-hot metal.

What the hell?

ONBOARD THE ZANTIL FACILITY, Nation entered the airlock leading from the cargo loading bay bulkhead wall. There was no security lockdown on the outer door, and he was able to pass simply by making the usual gesture with his hand over the access panel. The airlock tunnel continued for twenty metres and ended at a second door, again without any additional security. With a swipe of his fingertips, the door opened, allowing him access to the *Nisprol* cargo vessel's outer airlock.

Easy as that, he thought.

The *Nisprol*'s airlock was a basic, square room, with solid metal walls. A pipe running across the ceiling betrayed the vessel's age and Nation got a sense of the ancient simply by walking onboard. He paused and listened for the tell-tale sound of a gravity engine, and was encouraged by the low hum coming from somewhere towards the front of the vessel.

Nation was half-expecting the next airlock door to be properly sealed against intruders. Once again, he was able to pass without a problem. He couldn't figure out why it was so easy – either the Zantil security procedures were completely lax, or the Estral simply didn't expect anyone to try boarding one of their cargo vessels.

Inside the *Nisprol*, it was cold and near-dark. There were lights, but only one in three was switched on, and their illumination was turned all the way down. A corridor led away from the airlock, towards the front of the ship. This passage was only just large enough to accommodate a single Estral at a time, a design feature which did nothing to dispel the feeling of age. A cargo vessel like this probably had a crew of anywhere between two and ten, so it wasn't important for there to be lots of space.

Had there been any Estral in the corridor, Nation would have been forced to kill them. However, the alien crew were elsewhere, which allowed him to proceed rapidly. A quick check of his internal databanks brought up the design plans for a similar cargo vessel. The Space Corps was careful to catalogue every feature of every known enemy spaceship, so a similar vessel to the *Nisprol* had evidently been captured at some point during a previous war.

The bridge lay a short distance ahead and he hurried towards it. With each step, he expected to come across some kind of resistance – a guard, a crewmember, anything to indicate the presence of life on the Zantil facility.

Damn but if this isn't starting to get to me.

The passage turned left and continued for a short distance, where it joined with another passage coming from the portside airlocks. To the right, a short flight of steps climbed upwards to a compact landing and a door. There were symbols painted on the door, partly eroded, but not so badly that Nation was unable to read the words. *No Entry*.

He reached the landing and found the access panel for the bridge. Unsurprisingly, this one was locked down. Nation had his number cruncher ready and he aimed it at the access panel. Time was short and he allowed the device to access ninety percent of his processing cycles. The symbols on the panel became a blur as they alternated between *No Access* and *Access Denied*. He checked behind, simply out of habit. There was nobody there.

The number cruncher never failed. Some locks took longer to open than others, but if you gave it the time, the ISOP would come up with the goods. The bridge door opened and Nation pressed himself to the side wall, anticipating the presence of a hostile crew. Like everywhere else on Zantil, the *Nisprol* was deserted.

With an increasing sense of trepidation, Nation entered the bridge. It was a standard affair, trapezoidal and with a single, wide console running along the six-metre length of the front bulkhead. There were four fixed chairs in front of the console, none of them occupied. The ceiling lights were off, but the ever-changing light from the command station filled the space with a sickly green glow.

Nation crossed the room and got himself into the pilot's seat, hoping the *Nisprol* would be ready to fly. What he saw brought a smile to his face.

The smile didn't last. Before he could get to grips with the opportunity before him, Nation heard a deep rumbling sound, accompanied by a noticeable shaking underfoot. He turned his head in order to get a fix on the noise. It was an explosion, he was sure of it.

JN> Something just blew up on the station.

He held his breath while he waited for a response. Had this been a warship, the neural signal would never get through the hull. The *Nisprol* was clad in plenty of armour, but as a cargo vessel, it might lack the density required to block the connection. Keller came back to him.

BK> The Estral took a shot at the centrifuges.

JN> What are they playing at?

BK> I have no idea. They've just about got us beaten out here, so there's no reason for them to destroy their own Istoliar.

JN> Maybe they think you've got twenty ships. Maybe the Space Corps is sending reinforcements and the Estral got wind of it.

BK> I can't bring myself to believe it. Either way, you're up to your neck in crap.

JN> Damnit, I'm so close!

A second explosion shook the walls of the *Nisprol* and this time it sounded a lot closer than last time.

BK> That was another salvo into the centrifuges.

Nation was stumped. He couldn't think of a single reason to explain the Estral's behaviour. The aliens didn't always act with motivations recognizable to a human, but there was usually *something*, a connection that could be understood.

BK> There goes a particle beam into the Zantil main section. AI Klister just lit up the culprit. Another one down.

JN> Look, I'm on the bridge of the *Nisprol* cargo vessel. The whole place is deserted, but it looks like they abandoned ship partway through the loading procedure. The *Nisprol* is online and ready to depart. Anyone could fly it.

BK> We're missing something. Maybe it's because I'm not

there, I don't know. The feeling I had earlier is stronger than before.

JN> There are consistencies with a botched evacuation procedure. Like the alarms went off, everyone panicked and dropped whatever they were in the middle of.

BK> The Estral don't panic.

JN> No, they don't.

BK> Can you get the bay doors open?

A round button, set near to the *Nisprol*'s control bars, glowed with a green light. A little further away Nation spotted another, similar button. This one was labelled with the word *Loading Sequence* and it glowed orange

JN> One press of a button and I could be on my way, assuming the Estral don't shoot me to pieces. And I just found the button to bring the Istoliar into the cargo bay.

He pressed the orange button.

BK> There isn't time. I've just thought of a way to get you out of there alive. If you hang around for the loading to complete, you're going to die and the rest of us with you.

JN> I just pressed the button to start the loading.

BK> Please. Leave it.

JN> I hear what you say – I'll abort the loading and come out through the hangar bays. I trust there won't be too warm a welcome.

BK> I'll put things in motion.

The neural link went dead and Nation gritted his teeth at having the Istoliar snatched out from under him. A good officer knew when to take a chance. Only the best knew when the hand of fate was dealing from the bottom of the pack.

In the main loading bay, the gravity crawler's engine fired up in preparation to bring forty million tonnes of priceless Istoliar into the *Nisprol*'s cargo bay. Watching it happen was galling and Nation stabbed angrily at the green button. As soon as the

Nisprol received the command to depart from the Zantil station, the loading procedure aborted automatically. The crawler remained powered up, but didn't move.

On the bridge of the cargo vessel, Joe Nation watched one of the sensor feeds showing the outer bay doors slowly opening. From Keller's words, he knew it was hell out there and he hoped her plan would be good enough.

CHAPTER TWENTY-SEVEN

ON THE BRIDGE of the almost-spent Retaliator, *Gundar*, Becky Keller hoped her plan would be good enough. The Estral hadn't been reinforced during the last few minutes and there were fewer and fewer incendiary blasts to watch out for. The aliens had deployed their explosives continuously and she was certain their ammunition reserves were running dry.

Keller (*Gundar*):: Lieutenant Nation has initiated the departure routine for the *Nisprol*. To ensure he escapes, the *MHL Argonaut* will descend over the Zantil station. AI Jason, your energy shield will protect both the facility and the *Nisprol* until Lieutenant Nation is clear. He will position the cargo vessel in your hold.

AI Jason (*MHL Argonaut*):: My gravity chains will be sufficient to restrain such a small vessel.

Keller (*Gundar*):: Once your chains have fixed on the *Nisprol*, dump the Zantil facility into space. The rest of us will assist the Estral in destroying it, in case they change their mind after we're gone. Afterwards, our fleet will enter synchronised lightspeed for one hour, which is long enough to slow down their fission modelling.

AI Klister (*Granite*):: Then, we use our lightspeed catapults and return to base for debriefing and re-arming.

Keller (*Gundar*):: Exactly.

AI Jason (*MHL Argonaut*):: I am pleased at this chance to assist. However, by my calculations, we still face ten Estral vessels, four of which are equipped with undischarged stasis emitters.

Keller (*Gundar*):: They will become vulnerable as soon as they fire. I believe I have an approximate location for two. I will attack pre-emptively, and those of us with incendiaries will deploy them.

Gane-Q12:: I have a better way. See you on the other side.

Keller remembered using those same words herself and realised she'd touched the AI in a way she hadn't intended. It was clear to her exactly what Gane-Q12 intended and the AI put its plan in motion. The *Atlantis* shut down its stealth modules, becoming instantly visible to every enemy ship. At once, missiles and incendiaries converged on the Retaliator's location and Keller counted off the discharge of stasis emitters.

One, two, three.

The *Atlantis* went completely dead and Gane-Q12 fell silent. A fraction of a second later, the spaceship was destroyed in a thundering series of explosions, a result which left Keller shaken.

There was no time for reflection. With reactions driven by immensely powerful processing clusters, the last few vessels in Attack Fleet Z acted. The *MHL Argonaut* dropped like a stone towards the Zantil station a few thousand metres below.

Meanwhile, the *SC Sunder* and *SC Granite* took out one of the Estral ships which had discharged a stasis emitter. Keller fired at the place where she believed a second such vessel was cloaked.

The *Gundar*'s beam lanced through space without hitting anything.

The *MHL Argonaut*'s enormous propulsion systems brought it straight over the Zantil station and the Estral facility was engulfed in the lifter's bay. Given the speeds involved, the margins were tight.

AI Jason (*MHL Argonaut*):: I have suffered minor damage resulting from an internal collision.

It was as good a result as Keller was expecting. The effect of the *Argonaut*'s manoeuvre was to hide the Zantil station completely from sensor and visual sight. The apparent disappearance of the facility immediately gave the game away that another cloaked vessel existed in the arena and the Estral fired their weapons at the location.

AI Jason (*MHL Argonaut*):: My forward propulsion and calculation modules have been disabled by a stasis emitter.

Incendiaries followed, engulfing the huge lifter in their fires. The Estral unloaded everything towards this new target and the *Argonaut*'s energy shield sustained impact after impact.

AI Jason (*MHL Argonaut*):: Energy shield at 73%.

BK> Advise your progress.

JN> The *Nisprol* won't detach from its clamp until the bay doors are open, and the bay doors aren't opening quickly.

BK> The entire Zantil facility is now in the *Argonaut*'s cargo bay. We can't get out of here until the *Nisprol* departs.

JN> I'm aware of the urgency. This damn hangar door isn't in a hurry.

BK> How long?

JN> I don't know. It doesn't give a countdown. I'm looking at the sensor feed and the bay doors are about halfway open.

Keller broke the link and swore loudly. Her augmentation tallied up a series of coordinates and slotted in a target. She fired the *Gundar*'s particle beam and scored a direct hit on an Estral cruiser. Keller's anger and frustration didn't go away.

AI Jason (*MHL Argonaut*):: My tactical system is awash with inbound explosives.

A second wave of phase-shifter missiles and incendiaries rained down on the heavy lifter's shield and the immense craft was lost in the midst of the explosions. The *Gundar*'s sensors struggled to pierce through the turbulent heat and Keller thought for a moment the lifter was gone.

AI Jason (*MHL Argonaut*):: Energy shield at 52%.

AI Klister (*Granite*):: Where is Lieutenant Nation?

BK> Come on Joe, what's going on?

JN> Don't blame me, blame this shitty, damaged lump of a processing facility.

BK> I'll blame whoever I like!

JN> Be right back.

Keller waited impatiently to find out what Nation was playing at. The delay wasn't a long one.

JN> The hangar doors aren't moving.

BK> Don't tell me that.

JN> I guess the last power generator is shutting down. The hangar bay lights are failing as well.

BK> Damnit, the *Argonaut* isn't going to last long. You need to get away.

JN> You'll have to leave the station behind. Destroy the Isto-liar and return to Eriol.

BK> There's got to be a way. Is there an override for the docking clamps?

JN> Not from here. I'm sure the facility mainframe could do it, or whoever is in charge of flight control. Even if I knew where the flight control room was, I don't think I could reach it in time.

BK> I should have come with you. If I were there, I could

link from the *Nisprol* to the central mainframe and detach the clamps.

JN> There's no point in beating yourself up over it. What's done is done. We saw the prize and we went for it.

BK> Just like the good old days.

JN> Yeah, just like the good old days.

BK> We should have stayed in touch.

JN> But we didn't. Anyway, you're talking like I'm already dead. Get back there and start shooting at stuff.

BK> There's another inbound fission signature forming on the *Gundar*'s sensors.

JN> A lost cause, huh?

BK> It is now.

JN> I'm going to sit tight here. Don't give up.

BK> I won't.

Keller ended the link. The part of her which was melded with the *Gundar* didn't stop hunting for an opening that might tip the scales of this engagement in favour of the Confederation. Keller was the best pilot in the Corps, but that didn't mean she could perform miracles at will. Sometimes you just ran out of options and when that moment came, all you had left was hope and luck.

And I'll take an ounce of luck over a billion tonnes of hope any day of the week, she thought grimly.

A third wave hit the *Argonaut*, long before the flames of the first and second had died away.

AI Jason (*MHL Argonaut*):: Energy shield at 29%. Lieutenant Keller, what are your orders?

A thought formed in Keller's head. It was something Nation had said about the last power generator on Zantil shutting down. If there was no power generation...

Keller (*Gundar*):: The power supply on Zantil has failed.

Whatever tech it's equipped with to deflect the Istoliar winch might fail with it! Try attaching the Istoliar winch again.

AI Jason (*MHL Argonaut*):: An excellent plan. Targeting main winch.

Keller closed her eyes for what seemed like the longest moment. A new wave of six Estral warships arrived, which was easily enough to mop up the last of Attack Fleet Z. The *SC Revelation* and *SC Granite* launched a coordinated attack on the same target and destroyed it. The other enemy vessels activated their stealth modules.

AI Jason (*MHL Argonaut*):: Main Istoliar winch successfully attached.

Keller (*Gundar*):: Please confirm, the cargo is secure.

AI Jason (*MHL Argonaut*):: I confirm the cargo is secure.

Keller (*Gundar*):: Let's get out of here. Initiate synchronised lightspeed transit for one hour.

The six spaceships which remained of the original ten entered high lightspeed. A tenth of a second later, a series of vast incendiary explosions filled the space vacated by the *Argonaut* and the *Gundar*. The Estral were too late and the Space Corps had made off with enough Istoliar to fit out a small fleet of warships, and at the same time, snatched an important processing facility from the Estral's grasp.

The comms didn't work at lightspeed, so Keller was left alone with her thoughts on the bridge of the *Gundar*. This was a significant victory, no doubt about it, and she was sure the Space Corps high command would be more than pleased at the outcome. However, the debriefing was in the future and for now, Keller was more concerned for Nation, stuck aboard the Zantil facility.

She shook away the doubts – the *Argonaut*'s winch had its cargo held in place, so Nation would be fine. Even with the generators failing on the processing plant, he could survive quite happily in a vacuum, and besides, the *Nisprol* had its engines to power the cargo vessel's life support.

Knowing these things didn't leave her feeling calm. In fact, she felt a greater concern with each passing minute and didn't know why. She checked the countdown timer for the hundredth time. This was going to be a long hour.

CHAPTER TWENTY-EIGHT

JOE NATION WASN'T the kind of man to sit twiddling his thumbs when he could be doing something. In this instance, he managed twenty minutes of contemplation before the boredom was too much to handle.

He wasn't dead and Keller wasn't responding to the neural link, therefore he knew Attack Fleet Z had escaped from the Estral. Procedure dictated a minimum of one hour at high light-speed was required in order to ensure there was enough time for a lightspeed catapult to warm up and fire before any pursuing enemies arrived. Therefore, it made sense that he had no less than forty remaining minutes in which to do something useful.

I should see if there's any power to the central mainframe and try to get the Nisprol's gravity clamps detached.

The *Nisprol's* sensor feed informed him the Zantil hangar bay was in complete darkness, so he was fairly sure the entire facility was out of power. The realisation wasn't enough to stop him.

Just face it. You're too damned curious, he berated himself.

It didn't take long to retrace his path through the cargo vessel and out into the loading bay. To Nation's surprise, the loading area was still lit, albeit so faintly that he was required to use the image intensifiers on his sensor array.

He checked around. The crawler was exactly where he left it, piled high with crates of appropriated Istoliar. He stopped to admire the neatly-arranged crates. The Istoliar was so dense it took up surprisingly little space, given its boundless potential.

The bay was a couple of degrees colder than last time and he felt the waves of cold coming from the storage crates. He jogged around the crawler, aiming for one of the exits he'd seen earlier. A single metal door beckoned on the opposite wall, adjacent to the one of the main cargo exit passages. High above this smaller door, Nation could see another window. Although this window had no view into the hangar bay, it was likely to be a control room for the cargo loading area, and the consoles inside would likely be tied into the same network. Nation was no Becky Keller, so he kept his fingers crossed the Estral had left everything powered up and ready.

Crossing the open space of the loading area left Nation feeling exposed. His stealth modules were fine, so he put it down to the size of the place. The door was in a section of the wall free from the piles of supplies which were stacked in the bay. A rack of phase-shifters was the closest thing he recognized and the missiles towered more than halfway towards the ceiling. They should have been loaded straight into their magazine or stored in a secure location. The sight of them here reinforced Nation's belief that the Estral on Zantil weren't well-led.

The access panel on the door was active, but only just. The *No Entry* script was so faint it was difficult to see, even in the near-darkness.

There's no way this door is going to open.

He activated his number cruncher and shifted from foot to foot as the augmentation burned through the panel security. A few seconds later, the door tried to open. With a scrape, it shifted two feet into its recess and then stopped. Nation peered into a short passage which turned left onto what he hoped were steps leading to the control room above. He didn't want to be trapped, so he waited a moment to see what the door would do. It rumbled once and didn't move. With a mental shrug, Nation slipped sideways through the gap and into the corridor.

Once inside, he was relieved to find a flight of steep steps heading upwards. Aware that he didn't have unlimited time, Nation climbed them quickly. His positioning system informed him he'd ascended two hundred metres when the steps ended at a landing.

Past the landing, Nation found himself in a corridor. He believed himself to be on the level beneath the room with the viewing window. The route to his destination wasn't as straightforward as he imagined and it took several minutes before he located another set of steps. He was conscious that the seconds were ticking and he was obliged to ignore several closed doors. These ones had bright-glowing access panels, which made him think the Zantil facility had several layers of redundancy when it came to its internal power supply.

These new steps only climbed one level and they deposited Nation a small distance from the viewing room he'd identified from below. What he found was mixed news, most of it bad. There was sporadic lighting and a sign hung from the ceiling. Nation muttered the words.

"Loading Bay and Personnel Monitoring Area C. Shit."

According to the sign, this wasn't the place where the Estral controlled the cargo loading, nor the departure of docked spaceships. Instead, it was one of the monitoring stations for the Zantil facility.

Nation cast his eyes around the room. There was a bank of gauges on one wall, which he made no attempt to study closer.

Most of the floorspace was filled by wide, straight-edged consoles, each of which was equipped with six screens. Nation counted twelve such consoles, all of them turned off apart from one of the four arrayed directly in front of the viewing window. The screens of this console were blank, but a tiny, blinking cursor in the corner of one gave the game away.

In a few minutes, Attack Fleet Z would drop out of light-speed and Nation was sure Keller would be pretty mad if she found he'd left the bridge of the *Nisprol*. Nation reasoned that if he managed to figure out how the Zantil station worked, it might save time in the long run, so he didn't abandon the room.

He crossed over to the console and pondered if it was worth spending any time on it. There was a remote chance the monitoring room consoles would have access to other critical systems.

I'm out of options. It's either this or spend thirty minutes wandering around Zantil looking for somewhere else.

Nation leaned over and pressed the reset switch underneath the front metal lip. The cursor vanished and then reappeared, along with a series of dots to indicate it was booting. It took longer than expected, so Nation took a look through the wide viewing window. The loading bay seemed darker somehow, and filled with menace. Nation shook off the feeling and stood at the window for a while longer, wondering where the feeling had come from.

A beep informed him that the console was finished booting and when he came to see, Nation found himself presented with a logon screen. He set the number cruncher away and waited. After a few seconds, he gave the ISOP access to eighty percent of his processing cycles and drummed his fingers against the cold metal surface of the console.

"Got you," he said.

The login screen vanished and a menu appeared. It didn't

take a second for Nation to discover this wasn't what he hoped to find.

"Balls," he muttered sourly. "Internal monitoring crap and nothing else."

Nation wasn't much of a gambler and he recognized this was the end of the road. It would be irresponsible for him to keep going and he should make himself available on the *Nisprol* as soon as possible.

"I've got a couple of spare minutes."

Only half-interested, Nation pushed at one of the menu options. Instantly, the other five displays on the console lit up. Two of them showed views into open areas elsewhere in Zantil, while the other three monitors registered a blank feed, which meant they were currently linked to offline sensors.

Another menu option brought up a huge list of the different areas within Zantil. This particular console wasn't approved to access them all. According to the labels, most of the off-limits areas were operational zones.

"Let's see what we have."

Nation cycled through a number of different plant areas, wondering if he could locate the personnel. If the Space Corps knew where to look, it would make clearing the Zantil wreck a lot quicker, easier and safer for the teams assigned to the task.

Wherever the personnel had gone to, it wasn't immediately apparent. Most of the sensor feeds were offline, in addition to those which were off-limits to this console. Everywhere he looked, it was cold, down to minus ninety in a few of the corridors.

Nation was on the verge of giving up, when he located the first bodies. On Access Corridor 1211-F, the monitor showed him six dead Estral. They wore operator uniforms, which left their faces uncovered. Nation blinked twice and zoomed in the sensor towards the only corpse which was lying on its back. The grey skin of the alien was completely blackened and split. The only unaffected part was its eyes, which remained the palest of greys.

With a growing sense of horror, Nation switched from camera to camera. He found more dead – dozens of them. From the way they'd fallen, it was obvious they were heading in the same direction, perhaps towards an evacuation point or a refuge area.

An internal alarm chimed, drawing Nation's attention away from the console. The power levels in his Istoliar cells were trickling away slowly, in the same way they'd done on the lowest levels of Isob-2. Without conscious direction from his brain, Nation's forefinger accessed the next monitoring sensor on the list. An image of an area labelled Centrifuges 1-3 Refuge and Containment came up on screen and Nation found out where the Zantil personnel had gone.

The refuge was a large room, filled with rows of forward-facing seats. In the background, protective suits hung from a rack on the wall. The place was filled with bodies. There were thousands upon thousands of them, piled up or strewn over chairs or on the floor. The skin of each Estral was withered, cracked and turned black. The corpses seemed diminished somehow, as though they'd been drained of their essences.

The damned Antaron is here.

Nation had absolutely no idea how this alien entity could have made it onto Zantil and he found himself asking if the Antaron was one of many. The thought was not welcome.

The viewing window dared him to return and Nation's feet carried him over. He stared outside and into the cargo loading bay. This time he was certain of the difference. The air was thick like on Isob-2 and there was *something* colossal inside the bay. The entire floor was cloaked in darkness, and it seethed and undulated. Nation's eyes tried to locate the crawler loaded with Istoliar, but he could not see it. The huge mass of the Antaron had rolled over the Confederation's war spoils and Nation could only watch helplessly, while his brain reminded him of what this creature had done to the Istoliar core on the *Gundar*.

Another thought struck him like a hammer blow to the temple. According to his timer, only a few seconds remained until Attack Fleet Z exited lightspeed. Afterwards, they'd warm up their lightspeed catapults and their next destination would be Confederation Space.

The timer reached zero.

JN> Do not activate the lightspeed catapults. The Antaron is on the Zantil facility.

There was no response. He tried again, in case the fleet had stayed at lightspeed for a few seconds longer.

JN> Answer, damnit!

Again, he received no response from Keller's neural augmentation. Nation turned left and right, hating the thickness of the alloy walls. The link worked fine in the loading area, but he didn't intend going that way with the Antaron inside.

I've got to get back to the Nisprol. The neural augmentation worked from there.

He knew there was no chance he could make it back to the cargo vessel. His first and only encounter with the Antaron was enough to make him certain he wouldn't be able to avoid it, and his stealth modules wouldn't fool it.

JN> Do not fire the lightspeed catapults!

It was no use – Keller was unable to receive his comms. Nation ran from the room to see if he could find a place from where his neural signal would get through to Keller. All the while, he wondered if the Antaron would come for him in the same way as it came for the Estral.

CHAPTER TWENTY-NINE

THE SHIPS of Attack Fleet Z arrived at a place somewhere in the middle of Estral Space, far from any known enemy planets or installations. Keller checked the sensors and found exactly what she wanted – several billion kilometres of absolutely nothing.

Keller (*Gundar*):: Great work guys. We're an hour ahead of the enemy. Warm up the lightspeed catapults.

AI Klister (*Granite*):: Acknowledged.

The rest of the fleet commenced the warmup procedures for their catapults. In a little over one minute, they would be back in Confederation Space, leaving a whole lot of mightily pissed Estral shaking their fists at thin air. The fanciful thought made Keller smile inwardly.

BK> Hey, Joe, looks like we made it. Which shoulder do you want them to pin your medal onto?

Nation was still not responding and Keller guessed he'd gone exploring. He was never a man to sit still.

The boom of the Obsidiar detonators faded away and the comforting whine of the catapult took over.

BK> I forget, they don't give out medals anymore, do they?

The whining became a stabilised howl. The catapult would fire soon.

BK> Maybe when we get back, they'll send us out together on another mission. What do you reckon?

JN> DON'T FIRE THE DAMNED CATAPULT!

Keller didn't waste time on pointless questions and she shut down the *Gundar*'s lightspeed catapult. The other warships were synchronised and they, too, aborted.

BK> I assume you have a good reason for this interruption?

JN> There's an Antaron on the Zantil station. It's in the process of destroying the Istoliar.

BK> Don't say that.

JN> We can't take it back to Confederation Space.

BK> Where is it now?

JN> I don't know – the only place where the neural link works is in the middle of a corridor. I can't see the cargo bay.

BK> I'll have the *Argonaut* drop its cargo. We need to think of a way to get you off there. Have you found a way to disable the gravity clamps holding the *Nisprol*?

JN> Not yet. Damnit, we've got to destroy this thing.

Keller was at a loss. The Antaron was on the Zantil facility along with Lieutenant Nation. There was no way to kill one without killing the other.

The decision was taken from her hands.

AI Jason (*MHL Argonaut*):: I have detected an anomaly within my cargo hold. Analysing...

Keller (*Gundar*):: It's the Antaron.

AI Jason (*MHL Argonaut*):: An object weighing approximately twenty-five billion tonnes has emerged from the Zantil facility.

Keller (*Gundar*):: Open your bay doors! Expel the cargo!

It was too late. One of the *Gundar*'s portside sensor arrays was aimed directly at the *Argonaut* and through it, Keller watched something burst free of the heavy lifter's thickly-armoured side wall. One moment, the *Argonaut* was intact, the next, its flank was dominated by a jagged-edged rupture with a diameter of almost two thousand metres. It happened so quickly, the *Gundar*'s sensors only captured a partial, indistinct image.

With the Antaron free of the *Argonaut*, Keller frantically tried to get an idea of where the entity had gone once it emerged from the flank of the lifter. She couldn't find it on any of the sensors. Keller tipped her head back and rubbed her face with her hands.

Keller (*Gundar*):: We're going to try the catapults again. If the Antaron comes back, shoot the crap out of it.

The Antaron didn't return and, one minute later, six light-speed catapults activated simultaneously across the fleet. The warships were dragged into temporary wormholes and transported across several galaxies in the blinking of an eye.

Keller (*Gundar*):: Welcome home. We are two hundred million klicks from Eriol. Not the best landing and not the worst.

AI Flex (*Revelation*):: A job well done. We performed at our best.

Keller (*Gundar*):: That we did.

She aimed the forward sensors towards their destination. The planet was too far away for the *Gundar*'s front array to provide anything like a clear image and Eriol appeared to be nothing more than a grainy sphere of mixed colours.

Keller (*Gundar*):: I have checked in with Fortress-3 for our orders. We are to land at once for maintenance and repairs.

JN> We made it back and we left the Antaron in Estral Space. It could have been worse.

BK> Why don't I feel happy? Let me see...we're at war, we've discovered a new and hostile species of alien and if you're right, we just lost forty million tonnes of Istoliar.

JN> On the plus side, I located a cargo manifest in one of the offices here. The Estral already managed to load twenty million tonnes of their Istoliar onto the *Nisprol*. The stuff in the cargo area was due to be loaded right afterwards. It probably got interrupted when the alarms went off.

BK> So we lost forty million tonnes and gained twenty million, plus a bonus Antaron?

JN> If you want to look on not-so-bright side of it. Me? I see it as a win.

Keller couldn't help but smile at Nation's positive swing on the situation.

BK> We'd have sixty million tonnes of Istoliar and no Antaron if you'd done your job properly and killed the thing. What's the point in having a shockwave augmentation if you aren't going to use it?

JN> It was a bit too big for me to take on. Next time, I'll throw a few punches and see what happens.

BK> At least you're alive.

JN> Admiral Cody is going to be pissed.

BK> We can worry about that later. For now, I'm going to tell him to put the fleet on full alert.

JN> Even fuller alert.

BK> Maximum fullness alert. As for us? We're going to Eriol.

JN> See you when we land.

Keller kept the *Gundar* aimed towards the Fortress-3 base and the spaceship raced towards the planet. Before the fleet were able to land, Keller received notification of an inbound comms message, which she accepted.

"Admiral Cody," she greeted him.

"I think we've got some catching up to do, Lieutenant Keller."

"That we have."

"Before you land, I think I ought to tell you the news."

Keller's heart fell at the words and she was gripped by a certainty something terrible had occurred.

ANTHONY JAMES

"What is it, sir?"

On this occasion, her psi insight let her down.

"Less than thirty minutes ago, we received a message from the Estral high command, requesting an immediate cessation of hostilities," said Cody, the tone of his voice betraying nothing about his feelings.

"What the hell? Have the Confederation Council accepted?"

"They have convened an emergency meeting to discuss the matter."

"Which way is the wind blowing, sir?"

"There'll be peace. Mark my words, there'll be peace."

"I don't know what to say."

Cody barked out a short laugh. "Welcome to the end of the Ninth War, Lieutenant Keller. It was by far the shortest war in the history of humans and Estral."

"What now?"

"Bring in the *Gundar*. I might not have time to give you an immediate debriefing. The details can wait."

"I won't get too comfortable."

"That would be wise. Where is Lieutenant Nation?"

"He's kind of incommunicado, sir."

Cody didn't pursue specifics. "When you see him, let him know he's due for some upgrades."

"Will do."

With that, Cody was gone, leaving Keller stunned at this turn of events.

BK> Looks like the war is over. The Estral have asked for peace. Why would they bother starting a war and then call it off after only a few hours? I mean, what's the point?

JN> The Antaron. It's got to be.

Nation's words sank in and Keller felt her head swim. She groaned with the force of an insight.

JN> Are you there?

BK> I think you hit the nail on the head. The Estral have realised they're in trouble and they don't want to fight the Confederation at the same time.

JN> Sucks for them.

BK> This is our problem too. I can feel it. I *know* it.

JN> If that's what you say, then that's what I believe too.

BK> We've been ordered to Fortress-3. Let's see what the future brings.

JN> The future is always war.

Keller nodded her head sadly. Humanity was about to be thrown into the grinder again, and she had no idea how the Confederation would get out of this one.

———

Follow Anthony James on Facebook at
facebook.com/AnthonyJamesAuthor

ALSO BY ANTHONY JAMES

The Survival Wars series

1. Crimson Tempest
2. Bane of Worlds
3. Chains of Duty
4. Fires of Oblivion
5. Terminus Gate
6. Guns of the Valpian
7. Mission: Nemesis

The Obsidiar Fleet series

1. Negation Force
2. Inferno Sphere
3. God Ship
4. Earth's Fury
5. Suns of the Aranol
6. Mission: Eradicate

The Transcended series

1. Augmented

Printed in Great Britain
by Amazon